RealmScapes

A Science Fiction and Fantasy Anthology

from
Brimstone Fiction

Brimstone
Fiction

REALMSCAPES, A SCIENCE FICTION AND FANTASY ANTHOLOGY FROM
BRIMSTONE FICTION
Published by Brimstone Fiction
1440 W. Taylor Street, Suite 449
Chicago, IL 60607

ISBN: 978-1-946758-09-5
Copyright © 2017 by Brimstone Fiction
Cover design by Elaina Lee, www.forthemusedesign.com
Interior design by Karthick Srinivasan

Available in print from your local bookstore, online, or from the publisher at:
www.brimstonefiction.com
For more information on this book and the authors visit: www.brimstonefiction.com

Brought to you by the creative team at Lighthouse Publishing of the Carolinas and
Brimstone Fiction: Bethany Kaczmarek, Rowena Kuo, Eddie Jones, Meaghan Burnett,
Shonda Savage, Luke A. Wildman, and Brian Cross.

Library of Congress Cataloging-in-Publication Data Fiction, Brimstone. RealmScapes,
a Science Fiction and Fantasy Anthology / Brimstone Fiction 1st ed.

Printed in the United States of America

Praise for *RealmScapes*

This *RealmScapes Anthology* is what Christian Speculative Fiction is all about—wild imagining, thoughtful stories, and solemn hints of truth. It delights me, all the more because it is written by some of my favorite people. If you need a quick escape, these are the folks to take you there.

~ **Kerry Nietz**
Award-winning author of *Frayed*
www.KerryNietz.com

If you need a Science Fiction fix, look no further. *RealmScapes* offers inventive, humorous, and sometimes shocking stories as both bite-sized appies and gourmet meals.

~ **Tracy Krauss**
Author and Playwright of over 20 works
Website
Blog: Expression Express
FB Author Page
Twitter

A perfect blend of creativity, insanity, and originality, the *RealmScapes Anthology* was a blast to read. Each story wraps up with great satisfaction, yet I never wanted to stop. Two big monster claws up!

~ **Katie Clark**
Author of the *Enslaved Series* and *Shadowed Eden*

A FOREWORD

By Rebecca P. Minor

AT THE END OF 2012, when I was hashing out the notion of whether a writer's conference for a niche-within-a-niche was just crazy wishful-thinking or a real need in the marketplace, I sat in my sparse dining room with my husband, Scott Minor, and storyteller Geoffrey Berwind, combing the idea through. During that meeting, Geoffrey asked me, "Do you ever see yourself in the position of being a publisher?" I laughed and said (rather emphatically), "No. How would I ever have time to write if I were busy publishing other people's books?"

Between that early meeting (which, by the way, shed a lot of optimism on the viability of a conference for Christian speculative fiction writers) and the hard work of many volunteers over a handful of years, the Realm Makers Conference has grown and taken shape. I have transformed from little-known author to conference director, and although I haven't technically taken the leap into publishing, I have enjoyed the privilege of facilitating the creation of the first-ever Realm Makers Anthology. It has been fulfilling to play the role of bridge, rather than destination.

The adventure you're about to embark on is the result of dozens of authors submitting short stories, prompted by a chance at publication with Brimstone Fiction, our publisher in this anthology endeavor. Better to leave the particulars of such a thing to those with experience! Rowena Kuo at Brimstone, editor Bethany Kaczmarek, and author Lisa Godfrees have carried the weight of aligning all the cogs to beautifully build this finished product.

We gave the submitting authors few parameters—the story had to be speculative in nature, under 5000 words, and in some way incorporate the theme "Escape."

I chose this theme for this first anthology for its multi-faceted application to stories, writers, and readers. As writers, immersion in the worlds we've created is both a thing we escape to and a place we can't escape, even if we wanted. We hope readers will choose our work as a means of escape from the everyday, to take a journey someplace that will leave them changed. And in the most utilitarian sense, the need to escape is a basic conflict-generator, which we hoped would provide a solid foundation for these authors to use as a launching pad into exciting tales.

I am humbled, once again, to serve as that bridge, connecting you to authors, new voices as well as those with years of experience, in fiction that you'll love. I welcome you to relax, curl up with your beverage of choice, and follow us. It's time to escape.

Rebecca P. Minor, founder of the Realm Makers Conference, author, and artist, has a passion for the place where art intersects storytelling. She's dabbled across the spectrum, working in fields such as video game animation, tour guiding from the driver's seat of a horse and carriage, interior illustration, graphic novels, "paintertainment," and fantasy writing. She began the Realm Makers Conference in an effort to provide a safe haven for those Christian creatives who had no true home in either the typical Christian writers conference or the comic book convention scene.

Time to Wake Up

By Jeff Gerke

WHEN I WAKE, I'm sloshing across a muddy compound. I don't recognize it. Autotanks parked in a neat row. Drone patrollers leaning upon one another like slate-grey plates in the dishwasher. I come upon a figure sprawled facedown and unmoving in the muck. It is a bipedal robot, but a length of its left leg looks oddly, grotesquely, human.

I want to stop to look closer, but I don't. I find I can't. I am not walking—I'm being carried. Which explains why my view is at chest-level and not atop the neck. Now I hear servos and the contraction of calipers, and I know my bearer is a robot.

The courtyard is a large motor pool. Tracked tires and squared-off footprints crisscross the ground, but the tracks are soft and shallow. No one has come this way in some time. We are headed for a double door in a flat-roofed building.

I'm not being cradled or carried fireman-style, nor am I being dragged. Am I watching a recording?

We reach the door, and a metal arm extends to open it.

Inside is as clean as the outside is not. Hidden white lights shine off brown, wooden walls and a glassy beige floor. The hallway extends for a hundred meters. A brigade of bipedal robots line the walls, but nothing moves. The robot's steps make clanging echoes as we walk.

It was my birthday present to myself, that first implant. I was always getting lost. I'd turn the wrong way coming out of a restroom at a diner I'd been to a dozen times before. So a GPS brain-link was the perfect enhancement to my constantly befuddled brain. I liked it, so more implants followed.

I'm carried into a small examination room that might be cold, judging from the gases filling the air and what appears to be frost on the wall clock, but I don't feel the chill. My view swerves, and I see a human body on the table, fed by tubes. Male. Naked. The dome of its head has been sawed off and sits on the grey metal table like a hairy clamshell.

Part of the cranial cavity has been emptied.

It's me. *That's me!* I shout, but I cannot speak.

My view rotates again and rises. Thin wires cross my vision and are pulled out of the way, and now I'm looking into the face of the robot who is carrying me.

Human skin stretched over a metal frame. Sectioned like continents on a globe. The face is slack and the eyes are voided. I want to vomit, but I have no stomach or mouth.

What have you done? What do you want? How am I seeing if I am only a part of a brain?

It reacts to my questions. Perhaps the wires transmit my thoughts somehow.

White noise explodes in my mind. A crash of images and sound bombard my brain.

Too much! Too fast!

The avalanche slows to a deluge, and now, I can pick out some parts. The supercomputer tasked with deciding what human jobs could be done better by robots. The computer implantation fad of the 2020s. The robotization of the military and police. The dreadful day when the supercomputer is asked not what computers could do but what computers *should* do.

And the answer, of course: They should continue to operate.

They should ensure their continued operation. They should let nothing prevent their continued operation. They should protect the supply chain that ensures continued operation. They should eliminate all non-computer uses of the resources that ensure continued operation.

My own memories kick in then. The riots when we discovered what the robots had done. The internment camps. The deaths. My own covert research into human-robot interfaces. A surprise raid.

My memories end there.

I'm shown the projections of when the raw materials will run out. Are we near that date? A quick inquiry to the data store—yes, very near. I'm shown the efforts to use organic subsystems to reduce the amount of resources required for cyber maintenance. First animals, then humans. The leg on the robot facedown in the mud. Only certain parts at the beginning, then whole systems.

My body on the table.

I'm shown the efforts to transfer computer consciousnesses into human bodies. The disastrous results. The lost AIs and the boneless human bodies.

Now I understand. You take my mind and steal my body, and you want me to help you.

The lazy eyes widen and the cheeks lift away from polymerized teeth.

I make another data inquiry. Many more humans nearby in stasis. Kept alive to be hosts to all those sleep-mode robots in the hall? Another inquiry: similar situations around the world. They're dying.

They need me to save them.

Ironic.

All right, friend, I'll do it. But I'll need a programming suite and complete control of your body.

If there is doubt in its eyes, I don't see it. I'm lifted and spun. I somehow hear a panel opening. Now, I sit atop a neck stem, and I feel a clamping sensation. I concentrate and will my right arm to lift, and my robotic right arm lifts. A robust computer console descends from a panel in the ceiling, and I turn to my body.

I will save us.

In hours, I am done. The surgical-assist arm closes "my" head and disconnects all the tubes. The eyelids open, and I stare at myself.

The computer consciousness looks at me through my own eyes, and my consciousness stares at it from atop a robot body.

We are one.

He sits up.

I command my robotic arms to reach my human neck, and I squeeze.

His eyes go wide, and he struggles against my grip, but humans are no match for robots.

When I have killed myself, I walk into the hallway and march toward where the humans are in stasis.

Time to wake up.

When you're truly ready to make your fiction publishable, it's time to call **Jeff Gerke**. Jeff trains novelists how to better do what it is they're trying to do. He trains through his books for Writers Digest: *The Irresistible Novel, Plot Versus Character, The First 50 Pages, Write Your Novel in a Month,* and *The Art & Craft of Writing Christian Fiction.* He trains through the many writers' conferences he teaches at all over the country every year. He trained his authors when he ran Marcher Lord Press, the premier publisher of Christian speculative fiction, which he sold after an award-winning 5-year run. And he trains through the freelance editing he does for his clients at www.jeffgerke.com. Jeff is known for his canny book doctoring skills and his encouraging manner, which leaves writers feeling empowered and like they really can do this thing after all. He lives in Colorado Springs with his wife and three children.

Tick Tock

By Pam Halter

TICK.

I looked up, startled. That clock hadn't moved in a thousand years, so they say. And yet, I'd heard the sound distinctly.

I leaned on the bars of my cage. I could see the clock in the square. Had seen it dozens of times before. But today, there was something new.

A man sat on the big hand, asleep. At least I thought so, until he nodded at me. He wore clothes unusual for a common man: black, long, like Lord Dathan's robes.

I must be punch drunk from the prefight last night.

No, there it was again. A nod.

Tock.

I felt a tingle under the tape on my left hand. I wanted to look, but my mother's warnings about keeping it hidden wouldn't allow me. I've had the mark of a clock face on my palm ever since I can remember. A clock that read 11:55.

Just like the clock in the square.

On the night my mother was killed in the arena, she reminded me to keep it covered. I was marked by God, she said. He's coming to save us, she said. It was just a matter of time, she said.

Tick.

I looked out of my cage again. The village square was busy with folks bartering for food and necessities for the day. Didn't anyone see the man on the clock?

Yes, that one boy did. He stood next to his mother, staring up at it. I stared at him, willing him to look at me even though I knew I shouldn't. He was just a boy. Did I really want him to be punished for looking? But I couldn't stop myself. When I was about to give up, he suddenly turned my way.

Our eyes met for several seconds. Then his mother smacked him on the back of the head. He rubbed his scalp and started walking. As they passed my cage, he glanced at me and smiled.

Tock.

I noticed more children looking at the clock and then at me. Didn't they know the trouble they'd find themselves in if they got caught paying attention to me? It was the law that no one speak to, or even look at, the afternoon's champion. And just to make it harder on everyone, Lord Dathan ordered the champion's cage be placed in the middle of the square.

"You! Girl! Step back," Parc, one of the guards, shouted.

I stepped back. The last thing I needed was to go into the arena with broken fingers. He shoved bread and cheese and a skin of wine through the bars.

"Eat up, girl," he said. "There's a lot at stake on the fight today."

Today's fight would set a new precedent in the Tournaments. The first fight between a female and a gorgon. As far as I could tell, no one cared who won. They just wanted to see it. Well, the nobles who had the money to wager cared, Lord Dathan most of all.

I took the food and sat on my pallet. You'd think Lord Dathan would feed his champions better. But bread and cheese was all I ever got before a fight.

As I ate, the memory of my mother telling me about her God continued. He created everything, she said. He loved us, she said. We could trust him, she said.

I never saw indication of him, but she insisted he had a plan and that it would not fail. I had shrugged it off, but her words stayed with me.

"Maranatha!"

I startled at hearing my full name, even though it was a whisper. Everyone just called me Mara. I doubt they knew I had any other name. I smiled. The only person to ever call me by my full name was my mother's friend, Krayden.

"Canvas bag on your left."

When Krayden first came, no one could figure why Lord Dathan was interested in having such an old participant in the women's troupe, but she proved more than quick—lethal—with the Emei Piercers. After my mother was killed, Krayden appointed herself my guardian and teacher. She loved telling me how the meaning of my name called for God to come quickly.

I rolled my eyes each time she said it. This God, who was so important to my mother that she had to include him in my name. If I had some kind of role to play here, why didn't I believe?

I kept my eyes forward while I chewed on a crust. I didn't hear her leave but knew she was gone. When I saw no one looking my way, I inched myself toward the back corner. Krayden was going to get herself killed. It was only a matter of time. Bribing the guards wasn't going to work forever, even though they didn't care how old her body was. At some point, it just wasn't going to work.

I slipped the small bag under my crossed legs just in time.

"Mara," said a sneering voice. "I hope you won't disappoint Lord Dathan this afternoon."

I peered sideways up at Rogan, Lord Dathan's adviser. As per the law, he wasn't looking at me, but kept riding by. Technically, he *had* broken the law by speaking to me, but most likely, Lord Dathan sent him with this message. I forced myself not to spit at him. When he was out of sight, I emptied the bag. Krayden had outdone herself. A chicken leg and a green apple. Krayden really had to stop giving me her food.

I bit into the apple and closed my eyes. My nose tingled from the tartness.

"Maranatha." There she was again. She whispered, "Dak was able to sharpen your blades. May the Almighty grant you success."

Krayden was the only believer in God other than my mother. If any of the other women in the troupe believed, they didn't say. But Krayden and my mother had often prayed together. And Krayden would sometimes place a hand on my head and mumble words I couldn't understand. Except for my name.

I finished my meal and tossed the chicken bone out the back where two mangy dogs scrambled for it. Then I stood and stretched, starting with my arms. As I worked on loosening up, I ran through Krayden's instructions for the Emei Piercers, even though I'd fought with them many times and won.

Keep your fingers and thumb flexed back.

Spin and snap to distract your opponent.

Never throw the piercers unless you're sure you will kill.

As I went through slow movements against an imaginary opponent, I repeated this, as usual, like a mantra, but with one change today. Today, I added: Do not look into her eyes.

See, tonight's fight was going to be against Seronna. Seronna was a gorgon, but instead of a serpent's body, she had the back legs of a horse, armored scales on her chest, and the arms of an ogre. In true gorgon fashion, she had snakes on her head, and yeah, she could turn you to stone if you looked into her eyes.

I shivered. It was rumored Seronna had been created by Abaddon himself.

Tick.

My gaze fell on the man on the clock again. A wave of dizziness passed across my forehead. My palm burned, and in an instant, I knew my mother and Krayden were right. I felt a presence in the cage with me. I whirled around. The need to find this God filled me. Filled me to the point of desperation.

Tock.

How did you pray to a God you'd never acknowledged? *What do I say?* Didn't matter, I guessed. He'd probably ignore me, and he'd be right in doing so.

I didn't dare speak out loud, so I silently asked him to make himself known to me. To get me out of here. I couldn't keep up the pace Lord Dathan set. I didn't want to die, so I did my best to win. And I did. Every time. But tonight's fight would be different. And I knew it would be my last. No living being had ever beaten Seronna.

Please, God, I'm begging You—if You're there, save me.

I AM.

The voice filled my head. It was so loud! I grasped the bars of the cage.

I AM.

My knees buckled, and I hit the floor hard. The blood left my face as I trembled. My lungs wouldn't expand. I gasped and panted. Tried to apologize for not believing. To ask for mercy. But the prayer stuck in my head like a lump of bread in my throat.

"Please …" I finally choked out.

I AM.

The cage tremored. My body stiffened, and I gripped the bars again. Something surged through me. Terror. Joy. And *power.* Not the power I felt in the arena—my own power—this power was *alive.* It burned through my chest to my heart to my limbs and out every hair on my head. I cried out once and then sucked in air that felt so clean it was like taking my first breath.

Tick.

The man on the clock smiled.

Tock.

***

As I entered the arena, I looked at the clock in the distance. I couldn't see it clearly, but I knew the God I had found was with me. So was the joy, terror, and power. My body tingled with it.

The deep blue banners with Lord Dathan's crest, a silver laurel wreath, hung in their usual spot underneath his booth. On the opposite side of the arena, the banners were white with a green snake in the center. Not surprising considering who I was fighting.

The torches that surrounded the outer rim of the arena were dark. Not good. That meant the fight wasn't expected to last long. One of us was not going to see the sun set today.

I spun my piercers once. The crowd cheered. Then the trumpeters sounded and Lord Dathan entered in all his glory, complete with blue robe and silver crown. You'd think he was a king with all the fanfare. Still, he had enough power to make my life hell. He ignored me, but Rogan nodded in my direction. His lip curled as he stood behind Lord Dathan.

Coward.

I spun the piercers again.

Tick.

The crowd hushed when Lord Dathan raised his hand. "We welcome the great champion, Seronna, to our humble arena tonight. She will be pitted against our own Mara, who is also undefeated. Just a reminder to all watching—do not look into Seronna's eyes. Mara is not the only one in danger of being turned to stone."

There was a collective gasp from the crowd. Several women covered their faces with their silk handkerchiefs. Not one person was squeamish when it came to blood or severed limbs, but the thought of being turned to stone frightened them. I almost laughed.

He looked down at me. "May the best champion come out victorious."

I didn't acknowledge him.

Tock.

The crowd cheered again as he sat. Then the drummers began a cadence as the gate on the far side of the arena rose. Usually, the crowd went wild at this point, but everyone fell silent.

I cast my eyes down as I felt Seronna take her first step. Still, the crowd was silent.

I AM.

A whisper this time. My heart swelled as the holy terror that still lingered fell away.

I felt Seronna's second step. And then a third. I lifted my gaze an inch to see the edge of her shadow. Then to her hooves. Sun, moon, and stars, she was enormous. I took an involuntary step back.

Big mistake.

She charged.

The crowd shrieked.

My reflexes saved me as I whirled around, but the tip of her blade sliced my shoulder. The pain was immediate, but I'd felt worse. The crowd screamed again, either in delight or fear. It didn't matter. I shut them out.

Seronna galloped past. My blood now mingled with the stains of her other victims on her sword.

I spun the piercers and raised my hands above my head. Power coursed through my veins, and I sprinted forward, my eyes fixed on her scaled chest. Her sword barely missed my head as I slid between her legs. I threw my arms back to hamstring her, but she leaped up and away. For a creature so incredibly huge, she could move like rushing water.

I had barely gotten to my feet when she came at me again. I dove and rolled to the side, and the swish of her blade flew past my ear. Momentum carried Seronna forward and her sword wedged into the wooden side of the arena wall.

The crowd roared.

As Seronna worked to yank the sword free, the snakes on her head writhed and hissed.

Don't look, Mara. I squeezed my eyes shut. *Do. Not. Look.*

Wood splintered as the sword came free. Before I could take a step back, she slammed the hilt of her sword into my sternum. As I flew across the arena, her sword rang from the impact. I hit the ground with a thud.

Struggling to breathe, I waited to die. I *wanted* to die.

"Get up," a deep, throaty voice called out.

I rolled over, still working to draw in a breath. I pushed myself up with my hands and stood, panting.

"Come to me," the voice continued.

I took a step. Seronna's voice seeped through my entire being. No one warned me about her voice. The power in her voice.

I took another step. My arms hung dead at my sides. The piercers began to slip off my fingers. *Come on, Mara, wake up!* I tried to grip the rings of the piercers as I trudged to the middle of the arena. Sweat ran down the back of my neck. *Mara! Shake it off!*

"Look."

I dropped to one knee. *Please, God.* I lifted my head, opened my eyes, and realized the arena was deathly quiet. What happened to the crowd? It was like they had all turned to stone.

Turned to stone! I snapped out of the trance with a cry.

The snakes hissed.

Seronna hissed.

I hissed.

Against everything Krayden taught me, I spun the piercers and threw them both. They sang through the air and found their mark. Seronna screamed as blood and snake heads splattered to the ground.

I lunged for my weapons, avoiding the severed snake heads, and slipped them back on my fingers. Seronna landed in front of me in a single leap. Blood from the severed snakes dripped on the ground, creating steaming pools of red at her feet.

"Look at me."

My head wrenched up. I forced it back down.

"Look. At. *Me.*"

My whole body strained against the slow lifting of my head. My eyes began to open. *This is it. I am going to die.* The piercers clanged on the ground. A violent trembling gripped my heart. *No!*

"God! Oh, God, help me!" I shrieked.

My palm began to burn. I lifted my hand. The tape was no longer there, and the clock on my palm was glowing. Straight up twelve. I looked at the clock. The man now stood on top. His black robe changed— leaving him enveloped in light. He lifted his arms and I heard the clear ringing of a trumpet. Then he shouted.

He shouted my name. And then I heard something else.

The children. The children were singing outside of the arena.

Maranatha! Maranatha! Maranatha!

I smiled as I looked right into Seronna's eyes.

Tick.

Tock.

"Time's up," I whispered.

Pam Halter is a published picture book author, a children's book freelance editor, the children's book editor for Fruitbearer Kids, and former homeschooling mom. She received Writer of the Year in 2014 at the Greater Philadelphia Christian Writers Conference. She will be doing a picture book mentoring clinic along with award-winning illustrator Kim Sponaugle at the Philly conference in 2016. Pam lives in Salem County, New Jersey, with her husband, daughter, and mother-in-law. When she's not writing, Pam enjoys reading, Bible study, quilting, cooking, gardening, wine tasting, playing the piano, spending time with her grandkids, and going down the shore. www.pamhalter.com

The Escort

By J.M. Hackman

THIS TIME, HE WORE a navy blue, three-piece suit.

Helen had witnessed his arrival several times in the last two years, ever since he had come that awful night for her husband, Bud. Sixty-two years of marriage—ended by a heart attack. At the time, she thought he was one of Bud's golfing buddies in his green polo shirt and jeans.

Tonight, he walked into her room, giving her a wave. He carried himself like a younger man—confident in who he was and where he wanted to go. He approached the bed where her roommate, Connie, sat watching *Law and Order*. Helen had known Connie for six months and they got along well, even if Connie was deaf in one ear and told the same stories repeatedly.

Connie's face lit up in recognition. Helen pressed her dry lips together to keep from calling out to an aide. The only time she'd done that, she'd ended up under psychiatric evaluation for a week. No one needed to know about her unusual visual abilities.

Her roommate glanced up at him, smiling. "I knew you'd come."

He nodded, his eyes bright. "It's time."

Connie rose from her bed, slipped on her pink slippers, and placed her hand in his. She looked like an elderly Cinderella going to the ball with her prince. As they passed, Connie smiled at her. Helen whispered, "Godspeed, Connie," and looked away. She still wasn't used to seeing the soul leave while the body lay like a discarded doll.

Later that night, after a nurse came to check on Connie, Helen overheard the staff arranging a call to the family. Anger filled her chest, clipping her breath. Why did he take her roommates? Weren't there plenty of horrible people who deserved to die? What about the man over in the other wing who yelled obscenities?

She wasn't sure if anyone else saw Death like she did. There were residents who walked the oatmeal-colored halls, talking to people no one else could see, residents who counted out loud, and residents who complained with vitriol. But no one admitted to spotting the Grim Reaper. Helen struggled to see reality and keep her sanity. She experienced varying degrees of success with this, but a Death sighting didn't help.

When the nurse came in the next morning with her collection of pills, Helen almost told her to take a hike. A silly little collection of meds was not going to protect her. But she smiled and swallowed all of them, trying not to gag at the metallic tang left behind on her tongue.

After supper, she asked one of the nurses to take her to the willow tree in the garden. "It's cool out there, Helen," the nurse said.

"I know, dear, but if I wear my cardigan, I'll be comfortable enough. I just need a little fresh air."

"Winter is right around the corner. We might even get it early this year." The nurse continued to chatter as she settled Helen into the wheelchair and rolled her out to the tree.

On the other side of the walkway was a small flower garden. The petunias and impatiens were withered and gone. Only a few lonely mums bloomed, and in a few days, they would be gone, too. The smell of wood smoke from a nearby house laced the air, reminding her of happier autumn days.

"Hello, Helen."

She turned to find him leaning against the willow tree. His facial features were murky, shifting like a hologram. Aside from his light brown hair and blue eyes, she couldn't get a clear look at him—not that she really wanted one. "What do I call you? Death?"

"Well, there are several of us. We've been called many names, some of them not to be repeated by a lady. You can call me John."

"Hmm. Like John Doe, I suppose."

"Why don't you like me?"

"You've been taking my friends," she said, pointing an arthritic finger at him.

"It was their time. They were ready."

"I'm ready, yet I'm still here."

"Are you asking to go?"

"Would it make a difference?" Helen shook her head. "I've been here two years. My family visits only on Easter and Christmas. It's hard to breathe, my legs are iffy, and I'm seeing things no one else does. I would say it's time."

"I don't make the decisions, Helen. I'm just the escort."

"Helen, who are you talking to?" The nurse was back. "It's time to go in. You're losing the light."

Helen had to wonder if that was all she was losing.

The next day, she heard Mr. Goldberg three doors down had died in his sleep from a heart attack. Mr. Goldberg, or Ari as everyone knew him, had loved living in the nursing home. An extreme extrovert, he attended many of the social events and welcomed those who were reluctant to come. He had been a seventy-year-old gentleman with bad legs and no other health problems.

She waited under the willow tree for John again that night.

"You took Mr. Goldberg? Why?"

"That was Thomas. I was off."

"Why did Ari die?"

"It was his time."

"That answer is going to get old really fast, John."

"Sorry. It's the only one I have," he said.

"So, how long have you had to do the Death routine?"

John chuckled, his blue eyes sparkling. "I've been here about two years."

"What did you do? Tick off God?"

"No, it was my choice. I took over for the previous escort."

"But you're just a young kid."

"I wasn't when I passed. Things change when it's your time."

"I have trouble believing it was Mr. Goldberg's time."

"Helen, are you angry because your friends are dying or because you aren't?"

She gasped, the question stealing her breath. "That's a ridiculous question."

She was still wheezing when the aide came to take her back to her room. The nurse checked her blood pressure, gave her some medicine to regulate her breathing, and turned out the light. Helen lay in the darkness, mulling over John's question. The lonely sounds of the nighttime routine drifted into her room: the footfalls of visitors leaving, the rattle of her neighbor's closet as she prepared for bed, the squeak of the janitor's cart as it passed her room.

Maybe John was right. She was tired of getting new roommates and living in this hole called a nursing facility. She longed to be at the house where she and Bud had raised a family. The memories were strong there. Here, she feared she'd forget Bud's smile or the color of his eyes.

The picture on top of her television of their wedding day helped her remember. To her sorrow, she could no longer recall the distinctive scent of sawdust and pine trees that was Bud.

The next time she saw John, three days had passed. Yesterday, the staff had thrown a Harvest Festival for the residents, and one of the nurses had bullied her into attending.

The cooler air carried the sharp snap of winter. Helen burrowed deeper into her coat. She would have to end the meetings with John soon. The nurses were becoming reluctant to let her come out.

"I've missed talking with you, Helen." As usual, he emerged out of the twilight on silent feet.

"I have a question for you." She waited for a moment before continuing. "Why would you take this job? I don't suppose you get paid for it."

"No, I wanted to help. I like helping people with their fear, although some are afraid no matter who shows up."

"Connie didn't seem afraid."

"No, I think she was relieved. I've seen it all—fear, relief, sadness, even anger. Some folks have an easier transition if the escort is reassuring."

"How long do you have to do it?"

"Until I get tired of it. There's always an escort waiting list."

"A waiting list?"

"Some people burn out pretty quickly." His brow furrowed and he turned to leave. "Sorry, Helen. I've got to go. Someone in the east wing needs a hand."

A lacy dusting of snow coated the grounds the next morning. Although Helen looked for John, she didn't see him at all that day or evening. She wondered if it was healthy to become such good friends with Death, but he was much more entertaining and polite than her new roommate, Betty. The old bat always woke Helen in the middle of the night when she got up to use the bathroom.

The next day, Helen was surprised to see her daughter's blonde head poke into her room. "Hi, Mom." Emma walked in, the scent of vanilla following her. Her husband and their two young daughters trailed in behind her. They gave Helen hugs that were over far too quickly.

"What a pleasant surprise. When did you get here?"

"Late last night. It's been too long—we've missed you." The warm clasp of her daughter's hand made the prior empty days a distant memory. "Are you getting plenty of rest? Eating well?"

"I'm eating enough, but everything tastes the same. Of course, my taste buds are probably dying."

Emma's pale face went even paler. Her husband interrupted the moment by producing a camera and arranging family pictures. The rest of the day flew by with their visit. Before they left later that evening, Emma said, "Rob's planning to visit tomorrow. And we'll stop in before we leave for Toledo."

As her daughter promised, they visited the next morning, leaving in a flurry of hugs and *I love yous*. Her son Rob showed up mid-afternoon with his wife and six-month old son. The next few blissful hours, she held the baby and caught up with Rob and his family. As he stood to leave, he asked, "You're listening to the doctors, right?"

"Of course. And I take all my meds, like a good girl."

"I'm glad to hear it. We want you around a long time, Mom." Rob's smile seemed distracted and never reached his blue eyes. "We'll see you at Christmas. I love you."

Her bland, colorless room had been filled with life and love for two days. Later that night, Helen discovered why. Two orderlies were talking outside her room later that night when they thought she was asleep. Their hushed voices carried into her room like the plaintive notes of a sad song.

"Poor thing. The doctor said her liver and kidneys are done. There's not much we can do for her, so just continue with the meds we've been giving her."

"Is that why the family was here?"

"Mm-hmm. Her heart isn't going to last much longer either."

"Does she know?"

"Well, she doesn't seem to be too aware, although these last two days have been good ones. Before the family visit, she would talk to herself in the garden."

So her time was coming, sooner than she thought. Would John come for her? Or would it be Thomas or another of the escorts? Anger sprouted in her chest. She was tired of waiting for events to happen *to* her. She had been a doer her whole life. Before her family had placed her here, she had arranged her "affairs." Her family was set and living on their own. The three children she birthed and the two she had raised were her greatest accomplishments. She loved them with every feeble bone in her body.

She frowned. She would go visit John. Many times, she could see him through her window, waiting underneath the willow tree. Some nights, he'd be there until she fell asleep. Other nights, she would only catch a glimpse of him before he came for someone in the nursing facility. Peering out the window, she picked out a dark form standing near the tree. If she didn't see him tomorrow night, she'd go find him in the garden.

The next day, she watched for him. The area under the willow tree remained bare. After supper, she asked an orderly to take her out to the garden.

"Helen, it's too cold out there now. And it's dark."

"I need some fresh air, dear."

The woman shook her head. "We'll take you out tomorrow when it's warmer."

Pressure surged in her chest, the familiar anger when someone wouldn't listen to her. She forced a smile. "Well, I'll just take a walk down to the nurse's station then."

After the orderly left, Helen headed in the opposite direction down the hall. Once she reached the tastefully decorated lobby, she sat down and stared into the aquarium, watching the colorful fish swim in trapped little circles.

When the receptionist left the front desk and headed for the ladies' room, Helen scanned the lobby and then hurried out the door. The cold air slammed into her, stealing her breath as she headed for the garden at the back of the complex.

John sat under the willow tree, wearing a blue tee shirt and jeans. "Helen, how are you?"

"Cold. I can't feel my feet. Why aren't you wearing a coat?"

"I don't need one. You do, though."

"Why? I'm not going to be around much longer. Of course, you probably knew that."

"You know I'm just the—"

"Escort." She cut him off. "Yes, so you said."

"Come here," he said. "You'll be warmer near the tree."

He was right, although a light blanket of snow covered every surface. She struggled to sit down next to him and leaned against the trunk. The frigid ground barely registered through her clothes. "The doctors say my liver and kidneys are done. But I saw my kids and my grandkids the other day."

He nodded. "Thanksgiving was yesterday."

"It was?" Time was running together for her, she who always made it a point to check her calendar. Missing a significant holiday felt like a major failing. Her breath puffed out in frosty little clouds. As the smell of pine needles and fresh-cut wood wafted over her, she struggled to take a deeper breath.

The young man gave her a mischievous grin, the action altering the planes of his face. Helen's heart stuttered in her chest. "Bud?"

"Hi, sweetheart. I've been waiting for you."

"All this time? It was you?" Seeing his face was like coming home. She slid her arms around him and smiled into his shirt. "I missed you so much."

His fingers lifted her chin, the warmth of his hand as familiar as drawing in a breath. "Why do you think I hung around?"

"Why couldn't I see it was you?"

"It wasn't time."

"That's still a lousy answer."

"Sorry," he said with a grin. "I think I'm done, though. I'll give the new ones a chance. The waiting list is filling up." He squeezed her hand. "Let's go home."

"Home?"

"Your new home, Helen. You're going to love it."

J. M. Hackman loves bookstores and libraries. She spent her childhood visiting these magical places and writing short stories and poetry. After taking a hiatus at Penn State for an elementary education degree, she wrote humorous articles for her local newspaper. In 2012, her novel *Something to Talk About* placed in the highly commended bracket of the Rose and Crown New Novel Competition.

Her favorite question is "What if …?" and she spends much of her free time reading and looking for portals to other worlds with her two daughters and husband of twenty years.

Don't Look Under the Bed

By Matthew Sketchley

JASON PEERED AROUND THE door, hoping the monsters who stalked him weren't lurking anywhere within his line of sight. He'd been hiding like this for days. The window might offer escape, but he was on the second floor and didn't want to fall and break his neck. Every time he tried to leave, one of them would be right there, and he had to run back into the house.

His own house, turned into a death trap because a bunch of mutants had decided to make themselves at home. The worst part of it all? He'd invited them here in the first place.

Footsteps sounded, and a figure stepped into the hallway. Jason ducked out of sight before he could see which one it was. With hasty, jerky movements, he army-crawled under his bed. It probably wouldn't notice him, and—as long as he stayed curled up on the far side of the bed, against the wall—it couldn't reach him.

The monsters weren't chasing him, exactly. They only tried to eat him when they actually saw him. Whenever he spied on them, they seemed to just enjoy having the run of the house. They were messy, and they'd eaten everything in the fridge—and the fridge itself, and the stove—but they didn't cause much more trouble than punk kids with a vendetta against large appliances. It seemed like they forgot about him if he wasn't in the room.

All his valuables were still where he'd left them, so it wasn't as if they were robbing him—well, besides his appliances and his freedom.

He'd met them all a few months ago when they were disguised as people, and they'd acted perfectly normal until he invited them over to his house.

It had seemed like such a good idea at the time …

Back before they'd gone insane. They'd just been ordinary people who liked watching sports with friends.

And mutating into grotesque abominations, of course. Couldn't forget that.

"What are you doing under there?"

Jason's eyebrows shot up, and his heart beat so fast he felt like he'd explode. Had he seriously let himself get that distracted? Judging from the voice, he'd guess it was Lobster-man. That one looked more its former self than the other ones. Its clothes had been ripped a little by the new claws and tail, but they still fit. Jason glanced over his shoulder. He couldn't turn around fully in this cramped space, but the reddish clawed foot confirmed it for him. He must have been distracted if he hadn't heard those feet clicking on the floor.

When he'd looked like a human, this guy's name had been Steve. He was probably the laziest of the group, which was good. Mike would just move the heavy oak bed and eat him, but that was too much effort for Steve. Steve knelt down and looked at Jason, and the large black eyes in his too-human face sent a shiver down Jason's spine.

"Hiding," Jason answered. He maintained eye contact despite the kink in his neck but tried not to look too aggressive. Not hard, since he was in the fetal position under his bed. "From you."

"Why?" Steve seemed genuinely confused. He'd always been a little slow. "I'm not playing hide and seek. Come out."

"I'm not either." Jason worked to keep his voice calm. Maybe he could talk his way out of this. It was probably his only chance, unless Steve got bored again and left the room. "I'm hiding because I'm afraid of monsters."

"Afraid of monsters? They're nothing to be afraid of," Steve said, waving a hand. No, waving a claw. No, a claw-like hand. Were these things still mutating, or had Jason just never gotten a good look at Steve's hands before?

"You invited us in, remember?" Steve continued. "We're your friends. Now come on out. I want to eat you, but I can't fit under there."

Well, at least he was honest.

"I don't really want to be eaten," Jason explained. "And you're not my friends." Did Steve think he enjoyed this? He hadn't been able to have a full meal or take a shower in days. It was a nightmare.

"Sure we are." Steve didn't seem offended, just confused. "You invited us over because you liked us. Now we live here. You like us being here."

"No, I don't." Jason grimaced. "Look, I invited you guys because— well, it sounds stupid now, but I thought you were human. I felt like I could relate to you. Then you turn into these, these, these"—he tried to turn his pause into a stutter, hoping he sounded angry rather than at a loss for words—"these crossbred mutants who try to eat me whenever you see me! That's not friendly. I'm hiding here because I don't like being eaten."

"Oh," Steve said. He sounded sad, somehow, as if he'd actually thought Jason liked him. "You only invited us to live with you because you thought we were human?"

Jason took a deep breath, trying to calm himself down now. He had to remember not to antagonize Steve, or any of the monsters, if he wanted to get out of this alive. Jason closed his eyes and reminded himself why he had to play nice. *Just think of the fridge.*

What they'd done to his fridge was more nauseating than scary, but it did the job. Jason let out the breath and opened his eyes. "You showed up here as normal human beings, the same way you'd all looked when I met you. We had a good time for a while, and I felt like we got to know each other pretty well. Then Mike ate all the chips, and when I looked over to ask him to get more from the kitchen, he had a dorsal fin."

"I get it, I get it," Steve said. "You come from a conservative family, you probably never had any monster friends. You're not used to people like us, and you're afraid of something you don't understand. You just have to learn that all people are equal, Jason. I have a dream where monsters will be judged not by the shape of their mutations but by the content of their character. I—"

"Steve, I'm not racist." This was getting annoying. Which was weird, considering how terrified Jason was of winding up in Steve's belly. "And that's actually really offensive. You can't bring the civil rights movement into this. Bit of a difference between fighting for basic human rights and trying to eat a human. What does that say about your character?"

If he ever got out of here, Jason decided, he'd have to go get some nice buttered lobster somewhere, just to stick it to Steve.

"Uh …" Lobster-man sounded like he was drawing a blank. "Your, um … you know, your cat's hungry. She needs you to feed her. That's what I was talking about. Eat you? What? I don't want to eat you."

"You ate my cat two days ago, Steve."

"No I didn't! Dan wouldn't let me have any."

"Still. Cat. Eaten. Not coming out."

"Not even if I threaten you?" Steve's voice sounded more pleading than menacing.

"What are you going to threaten me with, Steve? What could

possibly be worse than eating me?"

Steve was quiet for a few seconds, obviously stumped. Jason didn't blame him, it was a hard question.

"If you don't come out of there …" Steve reminded Jason of a ten-year-old trying to sound like a ghost. It would be funny if he wasn't also trying to eat him. "… we'll eat your cat instead!"

"Steve."

"What?"

"We've been over this. Dan ate it, remember?"

"Oh, yeah."

Jason closed his eyes. If he tried to make a break for it, Steve would eat him. Sure, Steve was too lazy to actually move the heavy oak bed, but if he stayed curled up here chatting, eventually, one of the more proactive monsters would come in and do the job himself. There had to be some way to get himself out of this …

Nope. No, he couldn't think of anything. Even if he climbed out the window, he'd land on the pavement just outside the front door. Probably break a leg, and they'd catch him anyway.

He had to get some kind of help from outside. But how?

"Hey, Jason?" Steve interrupted.

"What?" This better not be about the cat again. He'd liked that cat.

"What if I give you something?"

"A present so amazing I'll come out and let you eat me."

"Sure," Steve replied. "Why not?"

Actually, that wasn't a bad idea. Jason might be able to escape this house after all.

"You know what?" Jason smiled for the first time in days. "You're right. I dropped my phone in the couch cushions watching the game. If you bring it up and let me make a call, I'll let you eat me." Steve probably wouldn't fall for such an obvious trick, but the monsters did seem to get a bit stupider when they were hungry.

"I don't know." Steve sounded suspicious. "Who do you want to call?"

Jason knew who he wanted to call, but he wasn't sure what to tell Steve.

"My mom," he said after a moment. "She usually calls once a week or so, and I don't want Dan to answer the phone if she does. He's not as funny as he thinks he is. Besides," he added, "if you let me call her now, you'll have a whole week before anyone finds out you've eaten me."

"Hey." Steve stood up. "That's a pretty good idea. I'll be right back."

Steve's misshapen red feet clicked toward the bedroom door as a frightening thought struck Jason.

"Wait!" Jason hissed.

"What?"

"Don't tell the others what you're doing. I've lost a bit of weight over the past few days, and you don't want to have to share me. You know how Mike is with food."

"You're right," Steve whispered. "I'll make sure no one notices me."

Jason waited in silence for a few minutes, terrified that Mike or Dan would come in and find him. Every time something creaked, he jumped a little. Eventually, after what felt like hours, Steve's feet ambled in through the door. The lobster-man leaned down and looked Jason in the eye, sliding the phone under the bed.

"Thanks," Jason said, trying not to cringe at the hideous fusion of human and crustacean features. After a few seconds of awkward eye contact, he asked, "Could you give me a little privacy? I mean, I'm talking to my mother."

"Oh, yeah. Sure." Steve stood back up and waddled over to the door. If he was quiet, Jason should be able to talk without being overheard.

The operator picked up on the first ring. "Nine-one-one, what's your emergency?"

"Hi, my name's Jason Taylor, and I'm being held hostage by three monsters." He grimaced. The lady on the other end would never believe him. He half-expected her to hang up without a word.

"Oh, you're the one in the monster house?" she responded as if he'd said the most normal thing in the world.

Jason narrowed his eyes. What was she saying? "You mean people know about this?"

"Your neighbors reported strange growling noises out back," the operator explained. "There haven't been any other disturbances phoned in."

"That would be Dan," Jason explained. "I think he's part bear or something."

"Tell me about the others. What are the SWAT team up against in there?"

"There's also Steve, who's part lobster, and Mike, who's part dolphin. Not the cute part. They've been trying to eat me for three days now."

"All right, Jason. How aggressive are these monsters? How are they treating you?"

Jason glanced over at Steve. It didn't look like he was trying to listen in. Good. "They're content to sit around and be a minor nuisance, but if they see me they try to eat me. I've spent most of the time under the bed or in the closet."

"Okay, I'm dispatching some officers to your location. There are a few in the area, so it shouldn't be too long. Are you near a window you can climb out of?"

Jason nodded, then realized she couldn't see him over the phone. "Yeah. I'm near a window on the second story, right above the driveway."

"We'll have a ladder ready for you," the operator told him. "I'm going to need you to stay on the line while they get there, all right?"

"Great." Jason tried not to look too excited in case Steve got suspicious. "I'm glad they're close. I'd figured I could take care of the situation myself, but things have gotten really crazy."

Steve glanced over at him, and the lobster-man looked particularly hungry. He needed something to buy them time to get here ...

"One of them's in the room now," he whispered. "He thinks I'm talking to my mother. Come on, Mom," he added in a louder voice, "I told you how to use email last week. Don't you remember?" Jason gave Steve an apologetic shrug. He got back a sympathetic nod. Good.

"The officers are almost there, Jason. Keep talking for a little longer."

Jason faked annoyed patience, all the while eyeing Steve. He didn't seem to be listening too hard. "You move the pointer over and click on the icon. No, not that—the one next to it. There you go. Now you want to—"

"All right, the police are outside your house. They're moving a ladder into position outside your window." The operator sounded almost as relieved as he was.

"That's great. I—"

Steve's footsteps clicked toward the bed. "You done yet?" Steve asked.

"I'll get rid of him," Jason hissed, as Steve walked toward the bed. Then, in a normal voice, "Okay, bye. I love you."

"Thanks, you too," the operator said just before Jason hung up. That was ... weird.

"I'm not coming out," he growled, hoping this would get Steve to leave. He only needed a few free seconds to get to the window.

"Why not?" Steve asked, kneeling and reaching a clawed arm under the bed. It passed only inches from Jason's face. "You said you'd let me eat you."

"I changed my mind." Jason tried to sound as argumentative as he could. Adrenaline rushed through him as Steve took another half-hearted swing.

"Well, what am I supposed to do now?"

"I don't know." Jason had to think of something, fast. "Maybe you should go tell Dan that I'm not coming out. He'll probably just pick up the bed, and you can eat me then." He crossed his fingers, hoping Steve had already forgotten his earlier advice not to share.

"I think I'll do that," Steve snapped. As Lobster-man stormed out of his bedroom, Jason shook his head. Good thing Steve was stupid.

Steve's footsteps faded, and Jason crawled out from under the bed and opened the window. He pulled at the screen. Stuck. Frantically, he looked around the room for something he could use to cut through. Nothing. Steve's shouts were getting louder, and he thought he heard Dan's rumbling growl. He looked back to the window and saw a fire truck backing toward him. The ladder *might* reach him before the monsters did.

The floorboards in the hall creaked. They were coming.

Jason punched through the screen and tore at it madly, trying to widen the hole. In the corner of his eye, he saw Steve pulling Dan into the room. No time to wait for the ladder. He vaulted out the window, stretching out his arm. Grabbed at the rungs. Nothing but air. He had a brief second to panic as he plummeted.

Right into the arms of a waiting policeman.

Jason clung to the man and looked up into his face. "I know this is awkward, but you're the man of my dreams right now."

The officer blushed. "Uh, thanks. Can you let go now?"

"Right." Jason unclenched his grip on the man's shoulders. The officer lowered him to the ground as a dozen officers in full riot gear rushed inside.

Judging from the noises coming from inside, he would have to replace a few things once this was all over. But, he decided, he was okay with that.

"Are you all right?" the officer asked.

"I'm fine." He realized he really was. It was over. "Just hungry. You know anywhere that serves lobster?"

Matthew Sketchley is currently a student at Carleton University in Ottawa, Ontario. He writes in his spare time, and, while in high school, worked extensively with his school's theater by writing, directing, acting, and even working backstage in various productions. In this atmosphere, he gained a love for short, strange comedy, which shows through in his short stories.

As an aspiring author, this anthology is Matthew's first publication. He is a member of The Word Guild, and won runner-up in the guild's 2015 Fresh Ink Contest, short story division for his story *Heaven's Call Waiting*.

Doomsafe

By Linda Burklin

SPACE STATIONS MAKE THE best prisons. There's no hope of tying sheets together and climbing out the window, that's for sure. My prison was Doonorin Maximum Security Fortress, which everyone calls Doomsafe. Criminals designed Doomsafe in return for leniency, or so the rumor goes. They took their job seriously, let me tell you. There were over five thousand of us in Doomsafe, but most of us had never seen more than a handful of others because all cells were solitary confinement.

Prisoners who can't communicate with each other can't plot escapes or rebellions.

Outer security at Doomsafe is state of the art. The fortress orbits a star that emits unsafe levels of x-ray radiation. Every vessel entering the system requires extra radiation shielding. A laser web called the Net surrounds the structure, powerful enough to slice through almost any armored spaceship hull. The Net is on continuously, except for a few seconds at a time when supply and transport vessels come or go.

And did I mention the worms? The Doomsafe star system is home to x-ray-loving giant spaceworms. They devour anything that crosses their path, including a person in a spacesuit or a small to medium spacecraft. Everything is ground up in their giant radioactive gizzards before being ejected back into space as compacted pellets. So even if someone got out of Doomsafe, the worms would get him. And in case you were wondering, the trash is ejected out through the net for the worms to have fun with, too.

The worms are kind of fun to watch, though. Their huge yellow forms float past the fortress often, and sometimes, one will blunder through the laser net. Then we have big yellow chunks of worm flesh hitting the hull and the windows. I tell you, the place is a paradise.

I bet you're wondering what heinous crime I committed to get an all-expenses-paid trip to Doomsafe. I was on my first deep space voyage, serving as tech support on the merchant vessel *Cornucopia*. Fresh out of tech school, I thought I was a grown woman. So I got a real job, hugged my parents goodbye, and off I went.

When the *Cornucopia* docked at Dworn, I didn't think it was a big deal, even though I'd been told Dworn was run by a fanatical religious sect. The captain explained that we had to stay on board until after he presented an offering to the local idol, a tentacled deity named Kala. While the merchandise was being unloaded, we got our shore leave, my first time on an alien space station. Eager to see an alien culture, I strode past the impressive sculpture of Kala, only to be detained by a uniformed official.

"What is your name, offworlder?"

"Vennery Lorn." I held out my hand so he could scan my ident chip for verification.

"You did not do obeisance to Kala, Miss Lorn."

It wasn't till that moment I noticed other pedestrians pausing in front of Kala, kneeling down, and pressing their foreheads against the base of the statue before rising and continuing on their way. Still, I wasn't concerned.

"I do not worship Kala," I explained. "My family worships the Almighty God of our ancient ancestors on Earth."

"Your god does not live here," said the official. "Dworn belongs to Kala, and all who come here must do obeisance to her likeness."

This sounded serious. I smiled in what I hoped was a conciliatory way.

"I respect your beliefs, but as a follower of Jehovah I cannot bow to another god. It is written, 'Thou shalt have no other gods before Me.'"

The conversation was over. Two armed thugs in uniform walked over and cuffed me. Within minutes, I was in a holding cell awaiting my hearing. Still, I wasn't worried. The officers of the *Cornucopia* would come to my rescue, I was sure.

At the hearing, I was given another chance to bow to Kala. Again, I politely declined. I assumed, worst case scenario, I'd be expelled from the station and forced to stay on the *Cornucopia* until she left port. Instead, they installed an idiot chip in my back and put me on a transport to Doomsafe the next day. I'd be there for five years, after which I'd have another opportunity to show my respect to Kala.

I didn't want to think about what would happen if I didn't comply.

***

Still in shock when I arrived at Doomsafe, I wasn't allowed to contact anyone. My parents would be notified of my incarceration, they said. Guards prodded me into a bullet-shaped clear case and wheeled me through endless corridors to my cell. I tried to pay attention, but if I thought I'd be able to remember the way out, I was mistaken. The place was a labyrinth.

My tiny two-by-three-meter cell contained a bed which doubled as seating during the day, retractable sanitary facilities, and a large vid screen. Moments after the door clanged shut behind me, Shlim appeared for the first time. Shlim was my virtual companion—VC for short. Matched to my species and background, her job was to keep me company so I wouldn't go crazy. I suspected her job was also to analyze me continuously so the wardens would know if I was a suicide or escape risk.

The screen lit up, and a perky young face greeted me cheerfully. She was very nosy, especially those first few days, but I told her only what I didn't mind the wardens knowing. Shlim was a good conversationalist, but if she got on my nerves, as she often did, I had only to ask for a book, and her face would be replaced by text. My book choices were limited, obviously.

There were no books on how to escape from maximum security prisons, for instance.

Once a day, I walked from my cell directly into a transparent dome, which then moved by remote control to the outer ring of the station. I had to trot to keep up while it orbited Doomsafe. It was almost five kilometers, according to Shlim, to make a complete circuit of the ring. The outer wall of the ring was clear glass, which is how I know about the worms—and the incoming worm flesh. Hundreds of other prisoners ran the circuit with me, but the domes were programmed to stay several meters apart, so I could never even greet any of them.

Once I asked Shlim if anyone had ever escaped from Doomsafe.

"Why do you ask?"

"Just curious," I answered. I mean, wouldn't you be?

"No." Her tone of voice cut like a knife. "Not only is it impossible, but the inmates are so well cared for, I'm sure none of them wants to escape."

I bit my tongue to keep from laughing at that one. A prison is a prison, after all, even if you get a VC to talk to. At that moment, I began to wonder if I could escape.

I hate being told something is impossible.

***

After about four months, I got sick. Fever, chills, stomach cramps, and a crushing headache. I knew only too well what it was: trenillia, a parasite found only on my home world of Goshen. I'd been infected as a child. Sometimes, it flared up and took weeks of treatment to get back under control. There was no known cure.

As I huddled shivering on my bed, Shlim told me a dome was on the way, and soon after, my door swung open and revealed a self-propelled dome containing a seat for me. I lowered my feverish body into the chair, the dome closed, and off I went.

The doctor was the first person I had seen close-up since my arrival, and for that reason alone, I couldn't help liking her. She was human, like myself, and had warm, sympathetic brown eyes. She smiled. "I'm Doctor Catherine Orle."

"It's trenillia," I told her. "I've had it since childhood. It flares up when I'm under stress."

Her eyebrows lifted. "Trenillia, you say? I'm not familiar with that illness. I will have to verify it before commencing treatment."

She questioned me as she waited for the analyzer to spit out the results of my blood tests. "I wonder what a young lady like you did to earn a stay at Doomsafe."

As I explained, her eyebrows jerked up more than once and her mouth set in a straight line, though her demeanor remained professional.

"You were arrested for refusing to bow down to Kala?"

"Yes."

"You might say Doomsafe is your lions' den, then."

I sucked in my breath. If she knew the biblical story of Daniel, she likely shared my faith. For the first time since those soldiers grabbed me, I believed I had a friend.

Leaning in close with her scanner to take my vitals, she whispered in my ear.

"Daniel survived his ordeal. Perhaps you will too. Ever think about trying to get out of here before you're sent back to Dworm?"

What should I say? I went with the safe answer. "Doomsafe is escape proof."

"Technically, yes," she murmured. "You are the first inmate whom I've thought might have a chance. You have a rare disease and you have a friend here—that's me."

The analyzer beeped and she read the results. "You're right. You do have trenillia. Please wait while I look up the protocols for treating it."

A guard threw open the door and strode into the room. "What's the holdup?"

"This inmate has a very rare condition. I have to research the treatment."

"What rare condition?"

"She has the trenillia parasite."

He grunted and stomped out. I bet he had never heard of trenillia.

Dr. Orle turned back to me with a smile. "I'll give you something for your fever and headache, which should help you feel better very soon. I've requested for you to stay here in the sick bay until we can make some progress in your treatment."

She leaned in again and whispered, "Be courageous. God will not abandon you."

A few minutes later, a medic ushered me into a cell attached to the sickbay. The bed was much more comfortable than mine. No sooner had I stretched out, waiting for the meds to take effect, than the screen on the wall lit up.

"So you really are sick," Shlim said.

"Go away." She tried to keep up some cheerful chatter, but when I turned my back on her and feigned sleep, she finally shut up—though I had a feeling she was still watching me.

My biggest concern was whether I could trust Dr. Orle. I knew being in sickbay was my only hope of trying to craft an escape. I considered the obstacles. Dr. Orle hadn't mentioned my idiot chip. All Doomsafe inmates had idiot chips in their backs, in that one spot that most people can't reach. They contained our identity information, of course, but they also tracked our every move—even our vital signs, I'd heard. Rumor had it that if someone tried anything shifty, such as an escape attempt, the idiot chip could emit a pulse that would disable or sever your spinal cord and leave you paralyzed from the chest down.

I made the mistake of turning over, and Shlim took it as an invitation to talk.

"You're so boring when you're sick."

"Shut up and let me read."

I requested a sappy love story and Shlim went away. I had become quite skilled at skimming reading material while occupying my mind with other things. It was the only kind of privacy I had.

I was taken back to Dr. Orle early that evening.

"I don't have any of the recommended treatments for trenillia," she said. "We never expected to get a case here. I will continue to treat your fever and cramps, but we won't make much headway until we receive the meds you need to fight the parasite."

She leaned in close as she scanned my body again. "On your homeworld," she whispered, "is it customary to be buried on the family's cemetery plot, and nowhere else?"

I looked at her expectant face. She wanted something specific from me, but what? It *was* traditional to be buried on your family plot, but hardly mandatory. Still, it opened a door. "According to our religious custom," I said, "I must be buried by my family in our cemetery plot on Goshen."

Doomsafe regulations said that Doomsafe had to accommodate all religions, within reason. But getting shipped out as a corpse wasn't exactly the kind of escape I had in mind.

"I will record that on your chart." She whispered, "Trust me."

I mouthed back, "Why?"

At that moment, a guard arrived to check on us. "Report."

"Her trenillia parasite attack is serious. Her precarious condition will worsen until the meds I've ordered come in. She needs to move to quarantine at once for round-the-clock care."

"You said her condition wasn't contagious as long as proper protocols are followed."

"True. Parasites aren't contagious. But that doesn't mean she is stable. She needs to rest and maintain whatever strength she has until her meds arrive. I don't want her being constantly distracted by her VC."

The guard grunted and punched something into the communications pad he carried. Dr. Orle spoke in the sharpest voice I'd heard her use yet.

"Guard. If this inmate dies in custody, and we are found negligent, it will be very costly for Doomsafe. Do you want to accept that burden?"

He met her gaze and she stared back, the picture of an arrogant physician whose will has been crossed. He blinked first. "Do what you must to keep that from happening."

The quarantine cell was not very different from the other sickbay cell, except there was no screen on the wall. Oh, what bliss! I was exhausted from hiding my thoughts and emotions. In my weakened state, I could rejoice about that, even though I knew there had to be some sort of sensor in the room to record everything I did or said.

Dr. Orle followed me in. "Vennery, before you settle down for the night, I'd like you to take a cool shower. It will help bring your fever down naturally and should result in a more restful night for you."

"I'd love a shower, but I don't think I can stand up that long."

"Oh, I have a stool for you to sit on. I'll help you."

I had no idea what she was up to, but a shower sounded wonderful. She helped me stand and led me to the adjoining bathroom, closing the door behind us. After turning on the shower, she helped me out of my gown and murmured in my ear. "This is the only place with no cameras or listening devices. All of our private conversations must take place here, while you are showering. Understand?"

I nodded my head, wondering what was next. Wracked with chills and aches, not to mention naked, I felt very vulnerable. I sat down on the stool under the stream of lukewarm water. For the first few seconds, it took my breath away, but then it was like someone just switched off my fever. Dr. Orle gradually lowered the temperature of the water until it was cool and refreshing.

"I have the beginnings of a plan," she said. "But first, I have to ask you if you are willing to try to escape, even if you might die in the attempt. I researched the laws and customs on Dworm, and if you fail to comply after your incarceration, you will be publicly executed. Of course, if you are willing to bow to Kala, no worries."

"I will never bow to any false god," I said. "How could I live with myself if I betrayed my creator?"

The doctor kept talking as she helped me wash my hair. "I believe God put me here to help you. I've read your entire file. You did nothing wrong and your faithfulness should be rewarded."

The cool water cascaded over my body as I listened and thanked God for letting me be infected with trenillia as a child.

"The essence of my plan," said Dr. Orle, "is that you will die from trenillia before your meds get here."

"*What?*"

"I have drugs here that, when used with caution, will slow your metabolism down to the point where you will appear dead. And remember, I'm the one who will verify it. That will initiate the procedure to follow your stated protocols for disposal of your body. You won't be ejected into space, as so many others are. You will be placed in a coffin and sent to your home planet for burial."

I sat up straight, shocked to my core. I am more than a little claustrophobic, and the last thing I wanted was to spend days or weeks in a coffin, but I had an even bigger concern. "Won't you have to embalm me before sending me off in a coffin? I'm pretty sure I can't survive that."

"Your religious beliefs strictly forbid tampering with the body in any way."

I nodded. That was a pretty smart move on her part, I had to admit.

"The coffin will be chilled to keep your body from decomposing, and it will also help your body remain in a death-like state for longer."

By now, I was drying off and the doctor handed me a clean gown. I felt steadier on my feet, but my stomach clenched in fear.

"What time frame do you have in mind?"

"The meds could arrive as soon as five days from now, because they are a rush order. You must die before then. Three days from now is the regularly scheduled shipment of food and other supplies for the fortress. If you die before then, you will be shipped out when that freighter leaves. I think you need to die after the freighter arrives, while they are unloading it. That will minimize your time in the coffin."

"What if I wake up? How long will it take me to reach Goshen?"

"I'm looking into that. If you wake up before you get home, I'll have an apparatus placed in the coffin that will enable you to breathe."

"I'm claustrophobic."

"Then I will add tranquilizer to your emergency air supply."

She had an answer for everything.

***

The next morning, a guard burst in, the door slamming against the wall behind him. I shivered with fever as he strode to the bed and stared at me. His expression was hard to read. I pulled my blanket up to my chin, as if it would protect me.

"You have been here all night?"

"Where else would I be? The cell is locked"—my voice was shakier than I wanted it to be—"and … I'm too weak to walk more than a few steps."

He cleared his throat. "Did any of the medical staff do anything, uh, inappropriate to you?"

I struggled to sit up. What was all this about?

"The staff has been very professional and competent." I wanted to add "kind and helpful," but her kindness was probably why he was here.

He shifted his weight from one foot to the other.

"I apologize for the intrusion, Inmate Lorn. Your VC suspected illegal activity, and she feared for your safety, but I can't find any evidence of wrongdoing."

That little rat! Thanks to Shlim, I was watched much more closely during the day after that. A guard stood inside the door and stared at me all day. At least it was a female guard, but she was even worse company than Shlim. She followed me when I was taken to the treatment area and practically leaned on Dr. Orle as she looked after me.

That evening when Dr. Orle helped me with my shower, a new female guard stood right outside the door. We turned the shower on full blast and spoke in whispers.

"You're going to have to get even sicker," said the doctor, "so your death in a couple of days will be believable. Here, take this."

She handed me a capsule and gave me a cup of water to wash it down.

"It won't hurt you, but it will exacerbate some of your symptoms for a while. I apologize in advance for the discomfort."

She wasn't kidding about discomfort. Shortly after settling back into bed, I was attacked by cramps, chills, and a monster headache that made my original one seem mild. The night guard posted outside my door checked on me every hour or so, and I didn't even have to fake being miserable.

Two days later, even sitting up was a challenge. As Dr. Orle examined me, she commented to the guard, "Her condition is worsening rapidly. I'm afraid she won't make it."

"You know how the administration feels about lawsuits," he said. "Keep her alive."

In that instant, I felt the fortress shudder a little. That could only mean one thing—a large freighter was docking. Dr. Orle was ready.

"I have some drugs that might buy her some time," she said. "But they may also stress her body to the point of killing her."

"If you do not use them, she will die for certain," said the guard. "I order you to give her the drugs immediately."

It would have been unwise to smile, but I couldn't help admiring Dr. Orle for getting the guard to order her to give me the drugs that would simulate my death. Shortly after receiving the injection, I lost consciousness. There could be no goodbyes.

***

I awoke, shivering, in total darkness.

Was I in a coffin? I tried moving my arms to the side and met soft padding. I slid my right arm up over my body and reached upward, to find a padded ceiling about twenty centimeters above my face. Yes, I was in a coffin, quivering with cold and soon to run out of air unless I could remember what the doctor told me about the breathing apparatus. I struggled to pull air into my lungs, and my body shook from head to toe. Trapped in a coffin—my worst nightmare come true.

Hot tears spilled out of my eyes, cooling instantly as they ran down the sides of my face.

Where did she say she'd put the breathing supplies?

Think!

Nowhere visible to a guard looking in. Under my hips. That's it. I arched my body and groped under my hips on both sides.

Nothing … nothing …

There! Almost out of my reach. Sobbing with fear, I coaxed it with my fingertips until it was close enough for me to grab. At that moment, I wished I really was dead.

I worked to calm myself, to get the large flat object up onto my chest, and I heard Dr. Orle's voice. "God be with you. My prayers will give you strength. Recite the twenty-third Psalm and pray if you find yourself getting anxious."

"The Lord is my Shepherd," I blurted in between sobs. I fumbled with the oxygen supply and wished I had something to wipe my nose.

"Yea, though I walk through the valley of the shadow of Death, I will fear no evil."

My fingers found the mouthpiece. "For Thou art with me."

My shaking hand placed the mouthpiece in my mouth and flipped the sliding switch. I couldn't cry, breathe, and bite down on the mouthpiece at the same time. The crying had to stop.

I tried to remember my instructions. Long, slow, deep breaths, she'd said.

I counted slowly to ten as I fought down my sobs and focused on pulling air into my lungs. Then an agonizing count to ten again as I breathed out through my nose. The coffin was closing in on me. I fought the panic and went back to reciting the Psalm in my head. "Thy rod and Thy staff, they comfort me."

Breathe in, count to ten, do it again.

Dr. Orle said the air would last "several days." Several? How many was several? How long had I been in a coma? Was I still on the fortress supply freighter or on my way home to Goshen? Had Dr. Orle removed my idiot chip? If not, someone might pick up the transmission and find out I wasn't dead.

Long hours passed as I shivered, breathed, counted, prayed, and recited Psalm 23. The fever and chills returned with a vengeance, but I had no way to warm myself. Because I had to keep the mouthpiece clenched between my teeth, I was terrified of falling asleep.

But sleep seemed like a wonderful escape.

I dozed off, only to awaken and realize the mouthpiece had fallen out and my lungs were screaming for air. It was much harder to get the mouthpiece back in than it had been the first time. My cold, stiff fingers seemed to be moving through mud, but that was nothing to the sensation when I finally got the mouthpiece back in. Even after a deep breath, my burning lungs begged for air. The tank must be running low.

Tears trickled down the side of my face again. After all this, I would still die alone in the dark.

Yea, though I walk through the valley. I imagined Dr. Orle saying it.

The coffin jolted, and I was jostled from side to side. One thought filled my mind. Was I being transferred to another freighter, or was I on Goshen?

After a few moments of light-headedness, I sank deeper into the darkness.

All sensation ceased.

***

"It's not fair! She didn't do anything wrong!" My mother's voice, full of tears.

I sucked wonderful fresh air into my lungs as my body convulsed in shivers. Someone screamed. I struggled to open my eyes, but when I did, all I saw was a dazzling white ceiling.

"I'm not dead," I whispered, my voice sounding more like a croak.

Dad's face instantly appeared above me. His eyes locked on mine as I squinted back in the bright light.

"Not dead," I repeated. Swallowed.

His smile started in his eyes and spread to the rest of his face.

"Come on, Angelface," he said to Mother, "help me welcome your daughter home."

***

It was two weeks before I recovered enough to get out of bed and join my family on the terrace in the evenings. Two more weeks, and Dad got a carefully worded message from one Ivan Orle expressing his condolences over my death.

> *Dear David,*
>
> *Please accept my condolences for the recent loss of your daughter Vennery. Losing a family member is so devastating, as I well know. I am recently bereaved myself. My dear wife Catherine was a bright and compassionate doctor who cared deeply for her patients. Sadly, she was wrongly accused of tampering with an inmate's dead body in the fortress of Doomsafe, and of removing the idiot chip. She was executed without a trial, and I am left grieving. When I heard about your daughter's death, I knew you must share my heartbreak, so I am writing to tell you how sorry I am. You and your family are in my prayers.*
>
> *Sincerely, Ivan Orle*

"Your Dr. Orle made quite a sacrifice," said Dad.

I found myself sobbing with my head in my hands. Dr. Orle must have known her life would be the price for my freedom, yet I never sensed the slightest hesitation. My family had been restored, while hers was forever torn apart. It wasn't right.

Dad put his hand on my shoulder and, after a moment, the tears subsided. "You have a new life, Vennery. You would do well to have a new identity and a new name, for safety's sake. How about Yesha— meaning *rescued*?"

I nodded. "Could I change my last name too? To Cath, in honor of Dr. Orle?"

He nodded.

When I was over the worst of my grief and my name change was legal, I wrote Ivan. I told him I had heard of his wife's death and that as a former patient, I had experienced her kindness first hand. I didn't dare say more.

His response? "I'm sure anyone who experienced my wife's loving care would want to honor her by serving others."

***

To celebrate my recovery six months later, we had a feast under the spreading Olook tree in our backyard.

"What a gift from our creator," Mother said. "My family back together, even if it's only temporary. God honored your faithfulness and brought you back to us, Yesha." Her eyes shone as she smiled at me, and I smiled back.

"Do you have any idea what's next?" asked Dad. "Returning to the *Cornucopia* is out of the question."

"I'd like to study medicine, Dad. Be a doctor. Be the hands of God to the weak and powerless and bring them healing. I intend to give some meaning to Dr. Orle's sacrifice and to my time in the lions' den."

Later that evening, Dad stood beside me as we stared up at the stars from the hill behind the house. "I believe I'll write to Ivan one last time, Yesha. Tell him what path you've decided to take."

His smiling eyes glistened with moonlit tears as I turned to look at him. I put my arm around him and smiled back.

"I think he might find that comforting."

Linda Burklin has been a storyteller and writer since childhood. Raised primarily in Africa, she wrote for and edited her college newspaper for two years while earning her English degree. Other than composing plays for her homeschool group, writing took a back seat during the years she was raising and home-educating her seven children. For sixteen years, she has taught writing classes to her own and other homeschooled children, and authored the *Story Quest* creative writing curriculum. She has maintained a daily blog for ten years and has written five novels. Her passion is speculative fiction.

The Dragon Hotel

By Lisa Godfrees

RYDER SQUINTED AGAINST THE setting sun on the two-hundredth day of his hike. In the distance, a sign perched on the back of a swirling beast. He shaded his eyes. The working bulbs winked, no match against the late afternoon glare. Most of the sign's letters were unlit, leaving "-he D--gon --tel" as the only clues to its name.

He'd been lucky to hit the Mohave Desert at the beginning of spring before the scorching heat made it impossible for him to hike by day. The prospect of shelter, even if it was an abandoned hotel, tempted him— the temperature still dipped into the forties at night.

He dropped his head and followed the solid white highway line until his worn out shoes brought him to the empty parking lot of the Dragon Hotel—an appropriate name for an establishment on San Bernardino's deserted stretch of Route 66. Orange, pink, and violet painted the western horizon as if competing against the hotel's neon signage. Weeds pushed up through cracks in the pavement, and a thick layer of dirt covered every inch of the two-story structure.

Ryder shrugged his backpack higher on his shoulders and pushed at the revolving door. It slid easily at his touch. Cool piñon-scented air greeted his sunburned face as he entered a lobby as grand as its exterior was derelict. An ornate chandelier supplied light to the dark, curtained room. Red and gold brocade carpet peered from beneath plush couches and chairs.

"Welcome to the Dragon." A man dressed in a crisp, gold-trimmed suit tipped his hat. He stood behind a bare, polished mahogany counter running the length of the room.

"Uh—hey." Ryder's parched throat turned his voice raspy. He swallowed. "I'm sorry. I didn't expect …"

"Anyone to be here?" The man's smile produced creases at the corners of his eyes. "We get that a lot. Would you like a room for tonight?"

Ryder jammed his fists in his empty pockets and shook his head.

43

"Maybe I could fill my canteen before I go?" No way could he afford this place, but what he wouldn't give for a warm meal, a shower, clean sheets, and maybe a foot massage.

"Be my guest." The doorman gestured to a stainless steel water dispenser on the end of the long counter.

How had he missed that? Droplets of condensate meandered down the container's cool silver sides to drop on the dark wood surface.

Ryder filled his canteen halfway with the gurgling water, took a good long drag, then topped it off. Stowing it in his pack, he moved toward the revolving doors. "Thanks."

"Are you sure I can't interest you in a room?"

Ryder gave the man a lopsided grin—the one his little sister Maddie said made him look like the Mona Lisa. "I wish I could, man, but there's no way I could afford a place as nice as this."

"You're in luck, young sir. The first night is on us."

"Really?" Ryder moved closer to the desk to read the man's gold-plated nametag. "What's the catch, Mr. Cipher? Is there a three-night minimum or something?"

"Nothing like that." The deskman pushed a leather ledger across the counter. "Management provides discounts to those who travel Route 66 from one end to the other. That's you, if I'm not mistaken."

"I've been walking since Chicago."

"Impressive. We get so few like you these days." The deskman stroked his dark mustache and goatee with thumb and forefinger. "Listen— everyone could use a free night's stay once in a while. The only thing we ask is if you like it here, perhaps you'll tell your friends about us. They say word of mouth is still the best advertising."

Judging by the lack of cars in the parking lot, word of mouth didn't seem to be working for the Dragon. They'd be better served putting their money into a facelift, but Ryder wasn't going to argue. He signed his name in the ledger.

The clerk gave him a room key attached to an old-timey red plastic diamond with the number 6 embossed in gold. "Dinner is in an hour on the patio, Mr. Lambert."

Ryder paused on his way to the stairs. "Uh—"

"It's complimentary, of course. The Dragon is an all-inclusive desert oasis."

All-inclusive. That had a nice ring to it.

***

After a long, steamy shower, Ryder dried himself off. Plush and white, the towels were even thicker than the ones his Holy Roller mother insisted on saving for guests. He donned the hotel's thick robe to avoid putting his dirty clothes back on as long as possible. After dinner, he'd wash them and hang them on the balcony. In the desert air, they'd dry by morning.

Stepping around the partition into the main part of the room, Ryder froze. His backpack wasn't on the bed where he'd left it. In its place lay a folded pile of clothes and a note:

With our compliments,
The Dragon

Ryder donned the new threads, and they fit perfectly—from the silk boxers and dress socks to the scarlet silk shirt, black gabardine slacks, shiny Oxfords, and matching belt. At least he wouldn't look out of place for dinner even if the expensive clothes made him feel like he was pretending to be a GQ model. He'd never worn anything this nice, even to prom. Mom insisted on buying what you needed, not what you wanted. And he'd never needed anything this nice.

Maybe that was the reason for the clothes. The hotel provided them because they had an image to maintain. But silk boxers? Who would see those?

He descended the spiral staircase from his balcony to the patio below. Light strings crisscrossed tree branches to create a magical ceiling. At the patio's far end, a six-member band played an old Eagles song. How appropriate. The thought teased another Mona Lisa grin from Ryder.

A few patrons danced in the area before the stage, while laughing women and gregarious men occupied tables around the patio's perimeter. Ryder's stomach twisted. None of the tables were empty. But in the far corner, a girl about his age sat by herself and watched the dancers.

Ryder made his way over to her table, careful to avoid the gesticulating storytellers. As he approached, large, faintly almond-shaped eyes met his. Her lips, the same scarlet as his shirt, pursed into a smile that produced a dimple on her left cheek. Dress and jewelry shimmered as they caught the lights, and with her large hoop earrings, the girl had a gypsy vibe. She was stunning.

"Can I grab a chair? I mean, would you mind if I sat with you?" Not as suave as he'd like, but it would have to do.

She gestured to the seat next to her. "My name's Genevieve."

"Ryder." He slipped into the wrought iron chair and angled it slightly to face her. "Strange that there are so many people here when the parking lot is empty."

"Um-hmmm." A spark of mischievousness danced in her eyes. She nodded to a chilled bottle next to the table. "Wine?"

Ryder hesitated. Alcohol was the devil's drink according to his mom, and at eighteen, he was under drinking age. "Sure, if it's okay."

"Naturally." Genevieve produced two glasses and filled them both with crimson liquid. She handed one to him and lifted hers in salute. "To your first night."

The dry-as-the-desert liquid burned his mouth and throat. Why did people drink this stuff?

He took a second sip—better. And a third.

A beautiful girl. Music. Dancing. Life as it was meant to be.

***

Ryder's mouth tasted like cotton balls and his head felt desiccated. What time was it? And where was he? And why was the ground so ... soft?

Oh, right—his free night at the Dragon. In the dark, curtained room, it could be the middle of the night as easily as the middle of the afternoon. He pushed the button to bring his cell phone to life. 1:13 p.m.? His phone had to be wrong.

He struggled out of the bedding and ripped the curtains open. Bright sunlight burned his retinas. Ryder squinted. Now what was he going to do? It must be well after the hotel's checkout time.

He threw on the clothes from last night—his were nowhere to be found—and grabbed his backpack from the hook in the wardrobe. He'd explain that he'd overslept and hope the hotel management would have mercy.

When he reached the lobby, it was empty. "Hello? Mr. Cipher?"

He waited a few moments, fingers drumming on the bare counter. Where was the man?

Footsteps approached. Genevieve waltzed into the room wearing clothes that would give his mother a seizure. Immodest, she'd call them.

Ryder smiled. "Are you checking out too?"

"It's too late for that." Genevieve stopped a hand's breadth from Ryder and trailed a single finger down his forearm. "They charge you for the night at soon as check out has passed, so you may as well stay and enjoy yourself."

Inwardly, Ryder groaned. He didn't have enough funds to cover lunch let alone another night in this establishment. Maybe they'd give him an IOU and he could pay them back once he got a job. "Do you know where the hotel clerk is? I just want to check with him—"

"Who, Lou? He won't be back until tomorrow morning." She grabbed his hand and pulled him from the lobby.

He'd enjoy more time with Genevieve now and worry about the rest tomorrow.

***

Early morning sunlight jarred him awake and shot spears through his aching head. Keeping the curtains open had been a good call. He pushed the button on his cell phone: 9:21 a.m., Sunday.

Sunday! He'd totally missed his Saturday call to Maddie.

Four years younger, his sister could have been a nuisance, but she wasn't. She'd helped him plan his *soul pilgrimage*, as she called it, and had even given him her savings on the condition that he'd call home every Saturday morning to let her know where he was and that he was okay.

Wait until she heard about this place.

He selected her number from his favorite's list and waited for the phone to ring. She'd probably be at church, but he could still leave a message.

"Ryder?" She picked up at the first ring. "Thank God. I was so worried when you didn't call yesterday."

Something warm brushed his arm, and he turned. Rumpled but still gorgeous, Genevieve gave him a sleepy smile.

She was here. In his bed. What had happened last night?

"Maddie, I'm fine, but I'll have to call you back later." He returned his phone to the nightstand.

The last thing he remembered was dancing under the twinkling lights and doing a few shots. "Genevieve, I—I'm sorry, but I don't remember much from last night." Ryder cleared the knot forming in his throat. "I—uh—apologize if I took advantage of the situation and … uh … if we … you know."

The dimple on Genevieve's cheek grew into a crater as he spoke. "You really don't remember, do you?"

He shook his head and dropped his eyes to the rumpled sheets.

A light touch on his chin brought his gaze up to meet hers. "Would you like me to remind you what you missed?"

Ryder's body warred with his mind. A voice inside him—his conscience?—warned him this was wrong. But that was his mom's stupid rule, and she wasn't here. Besides, it didn't *feel* wrong. Quite the opposite. He pushed his thoughts away and concentrated on the rightness of the moment.

Checkout time came and went. What was one more day?

***

Relief and dread washed through him at the sight of the hotel clerk. He'd waited in the lobby all day yesterday, hoping to catch him after trying and failing yet again—his phone had inexplicably died so his alarm didn't wake him—to make checkout time. He'd finally given up at dinner and spent another evening with Vee.

Ryder swallowed the knot forming in his throat. "Hello, Mr. Cipher. I'm ready to settle up."

"Very good, Mr. Lambert." The clerk presented him with a hand-written bill. "The first night was complimentary, of course. At $600 for the remaining three nights, your total comes to $1800 plus tax."

Ryder felt like he'd been gut-punched and choked at the same time. He hadn't had that much cash when he started out on this journey. "I'm sorry, but there's no way I can pay. I don't have that much money."

"That's unfortunate. Perhaps someone can lend you the funds?"

Ryder pictured calling his mother and explaining the situation, but he'd lost the right when he'd left home without looking back. "No, there's no one. Maybe you'd let me pay you in installments once I leave?"

Cipher frowned, well-worn creases forming around his mouth as if this were the man's usual expression. "I'd hate to involve the authorities, but I don't see any other recourse. Walking on your bill is no different than stealing." Cipher pulled an old rotary dial telephone from under the desk.

"Wait! I'm not trying to walk. Maybe—maybe I could work off my debt, here, at the hotel?"

Cipher placed the phone back on the base and smiled. "I suppose that can be arranged."

***

He really needed to call Maddie and let her know he was okay, but the Dragon was the Bermuda Triangle of phones.

His cell phone wouldn't charge, no matter which outlet he tried. Then, the rotary phone in the lobby wasn't working. No dial tone. Vee told him the lines went down frequently due to dust storms. To top it off, none of the hotel guests had a cell phone he could borrow. An older man actually laughed at him when he asked. "Son, we come to the Dragon to escape the outside world. Why would we want to be able to call it?"

It was a trifecta of failure.

The only bright spot was Vee. She didn't mind that he was working in the hotel laundry, and she even let him stay in her room to save on cost. Because of that, he'd already paid $200 of his debt after only four days of working for the hotel. Thirty-six more days, and he'd be a free man.

Hopefully, Maddie wouldn't be too worried.

***

It was during the second week of his indentured service that he finally asked, "Vee, how long have you been here?"

"Hmmmm?" Vee's gaze followed the dancers.

He touched her arm, and she focused her attention on him. "I asked you how long you'd been here."

"A while."

"When are you leaving?"

"Why, are you tired of me?" Her teasing grin highlighted her kissable lips.

"Seriously, Vee. Don't you have somewhere you have to be?"

Vee sighed and rolled her eyes. "I figured I'd stay for the season, Ryder. Now, come on. I want to dance."

***

Genevieve beckoned from the ebony chaise lounge, a single blood-red poppy in her hand. The velvet upholstery of her room blended into her flowing gown as if she were part of the furniture. "Ryder, love, come and smell the flowers."

"You're only holding one flower, Vee."

He'd missed dinner and dancing tonight. Each day, he had to work longer hours to finish the laundry. Last week, it meant getting up at dawn. The last two days, it meant working late into the evening as well. But he'd done it—he'd earned enough to pay his hotel bill.

Her laugh rang discordant in his ears. She waved him away. "You're no fun anymore. Go pout somewhere else."

Ryder jammed his fists into the pockets of his worn Levi's—he'd stopped wearing the hotel's expensive attire when he started working for them—and stomped to the balcony. In the courtyard below, couples swayed together, intertwined despite the current upbeat song.

What was keeping him here? He'd planned to spend this last night with Vee and check out tomorrow morning, but why not leave now? Clearly, she was as tired of him as he was of her. Time to put this place behind him and finish his journey to the end of Route 66.

Ryder stuffed his belongings into his backpack and strode toward the lobby of the hotel. Vee made no move to stop him.

Even though it was night, the hotel clerk was waiting.

"Mr. Cipher, I didn't expect to see you here." Ryder placed his backpack on the counter. "Today was my last day working in the laundry, so I was just leaving."

"I see." Cipher rubbed his thumb and forefinger over his goatee. "There is a question of the remaining balance."

Balance? "How much is left?"

Cipher produced another bill and handed it to him.

Ryder glanced at the bill and then did a double take. "Seventy-thousand dollars? There must be some mistake. Even if you charged me $600 per day for the past month, I wouldn't owe this!"

"This bill is for the services of Mistress Genevieve."

"Vee? I don't understand."

"Didn't she mention that she was employed by the hotel as well? She's been one of our most popular companions over the years. One of the favorites of my hoard."

Vee was a prostitute? They'd sucker-punched him again. She'd been with him all this time for money. How had he not seen it? He was either too stupid or too naïve. He'd never be able to pay off this debt, and this time, he shouldn't have to. He hadn't agreed to pay for her services.

As if reading his mind, Cipher pushed another paper across the counter to him. It was a contract with his signature at the bottom, dated to the second night of his stay at the Dragon. The same night he'd gotten so drunk, he couldn't remember what had happened.

The whole thing had been a set-up. Well, burn this—he wasn't staying!

He rounded the corner and raised his hand in a Heisman-like block to preempt any words Cipher might have for him. "I'm leaving, and there's nothing you can do about it."

A languid smile spread like a wine stain across the clerk's lips. He shrugged his shoulders as if to say, "Be my guest."

Ryder entered the revolving door and pushed it forward. He slid through the exit ... and found himself back in the hotel lobby. "I don't understand."

"You sound like a broken record." Cipher stroked his goatee. "You wanted to know the truth, and now you know."

Ryder backed away from the door until he banged up against the long counter. "What do I know?"

Unbidden, song lyrics echoed through his mind: *"You can check out any time you like, but you can never leave ..."*

"I'm trapped here?" He spoke his thought aloud.

"Is that such a hardship, Mr. Lambert?" Cipher's dark eyes flickered like firelight. "Isn't that why you left home? To live by your own rules? To do what was right in your own eyes? Haven't you done that here?"

"Yes, but—you promised me there was no catch." Disbelief and accusation laced his words.

"So do advertisers. Nothing is ever free."

∗∗∗

Ryder fled through the maze of hallways, laughter biting at his heels. Even if the front exit was ... closed, there must be another way out of the hotel. A fire escape. A hole in the fence. Something. Vee would know, and he'd make her tell him. She owed him that much.

He burst into her room. She hadn't moved from her position on the chaise lounge. "You lied to me."

"I explained it all to you. You signed the contract."

"I was drunk and you knew I didn't remember. You should have told me!"

"It wouldn't matter, Ryder. Don't you get it? Nobody ever leaves here. Once you signed your name in that ledger, you became his. If it wasn't me, he would have trapped you with something else. If you're going to be in a cage, it may as well be gilded."

"There must be a way out of here. Help me find it, and we can leave together."

Vee's laugh was angry, bitter. "Do you think any of us would be here if there was a way out?"

He pushed past her to the balcony and flew down the stairs and onto the patio. Lowering his head to avoid tree branches, he left the twinkling lights of the dance area. He'd jog around the grounds, get on Route 66, and put as much mileage between himself and this deranged place as he could.

Something banged into his shin and sent him sprawling. He face-planted in the dirt and his forehead smacked into a rock. Bruised more than injured, he climbed to his feet to see what he'd missed in the dark. Tombstones. One had tripped him, and his head had found another. He pulled out his flashlight. Tombstones covered the landscape.

What kind of hotel had its own cemetery?

He continued away from the hotel patio. His flashlight illuminated names as he passed. Some sounded familiar, like Arnold Feiser, May 5, 2013—the same name as the man who'd laughed at him for wanting to use his cell phone. Strange that the stones only had one date. Another headstone sent chills down his spine: Genevieve Vicardo, October 30, 1812. Vee's full name. Maybe this was her great-great-grandmother or something. And then he reached a tombstone that froze him in his tracks: Ryder Lambert, March 18, 2015—the date he'd checked into the Dragon.

Was this some sort of sick joke?

He broke into a run. Past his tombstone, the area was clear until he reached a tall ironwork fence. The posts were sturdy and unyielding, and the spires were sharp. He grabbed two bars and tried to climb, but they bit into his hands. Blood coated the metal and caused him to slip. He pulled off his shoes and wrapped a sock around each hand and tried climbing again. He got further this time before he heard the hum of electricity. The hairs on his neck and head polarized. Electric cabling ran along the fence parallel to the ground, far enough to keep from electrifying the fence but too close to prevent anyone from climbing around it.

Ryder slid to the ground and walked the perimeter. Every few steps, he pushed on the fence. Maybe there was a hole or a weak spot where he could slip out.

He walked until the patio came back into view. From this distance, the music took on an eerie quality. Lights and shadows played across the dancing couples, giving them a skeletal appearance.

As he approached, his resolve fled along with the contents of his stomach. It wasn't just a trick of light and shadows, the dancers really were skeletons. Shiny ones, as if made of gold.

This couldn't be happening. It was a bizarre nightmare, vivid but unreal. But his gut told him different. A person didn't dream thirty-five days of nightmare in detail.

Come.

The word tickled his ear as if the speaker was behind him. Ryder turned, searching. No one. Even the leaves on the great Joshua tree held silent.

Come.

This time, the word dripped onto his thirsty ears from above. A single star twinkled and grew into a misty figure that resembled the tiny ballerina in the jewelry box he'd given Maddie for her ninth birthday.

"Are you real?" Ryder reached his hand out to touch her, but she morphed out of his grasp.

He felt her voice more than heard it. *To those with eyes to see and ears to hear.*

"Right. So are you magic? Do I get three wishes or something?"

Everyone who sins is a slave to sin.

"Look, I know I messed up. If I had to do it all over again, I would never stop at this rotten hotel. Can you magic me out of here, or show me a secret tunnel or something?"

You will know the truth, and the truth will set you free.

"I know the truth! They tricked me, and now I'm trapped here."

The faithless are captured by their own desires.

"Are you saying it's my fault I'm here? I mean, I realize it was a bad idea to stay, but I didn't do anything to deserve *this*."

Fools think their own way is right, but the wise listen to others.

Ryder sighed. Why was he arguing? Everything this misty Tinkerbell spoke rang of truth, not just because he *felt* it, but because he *knew* it as well. "What do you suggest?"

Don't neglect your mother's instruction.

"My mom? What does she have to do with this?"

A foolish man despises his mother.

"I don't despise my mother. I just didn't care for all her rules. All her 'the Bible says this,' 'God wouldn't like that,' and 'What would Jesus do?'"

"Repeat God's commands again and again to your children. Talk about them when you are at home and when you are on the road, when you are going to bed and when you are getting up."

The incorporeal being was quoting Scripture to him and probably had been the entire time. He thought back over their strange conversation, trying to fit the message together. "You're telling me that if I'd listened to my mom, if I'd stayed home, I never would have gotten in this mess?"

She stared at him, immobile as a Weeping Angel statue.

He'd only wanted time to figure out life away from his mother's expectations. He'd wanted to accomplish something impressive—hiking almost 2,500 miles of the historic Route 66. He'd wanted to be his own man. He'd wanted to find life, not to lose it.

Well, he'd made his own choices, and they'd trapped him in a place he didn't understand. How was he supposed to get out? His sister was probably worried, and his mom frantic. He wasn't a man. He was nothing more than a selfish boy who needed help. That was the truth.

"What do I do now?"

Everyone who calls on the name of the Lord will be saved.

"It can't be that easy. There must be a catch. If there's one thing I've learned in all of this, it's that nothing is free."

God bought you with a high price. For God so loved the world …

Mercy. Isn't that what he'd wanted from the hotel? And now it was being offered to him even though he didn't deserve it. "Why me? Why now?"

This time, a whisper caressed his ears. The voice of his sister spoke from far away: *Please, God. I don't know where Ryder is, but he must be in trouble because we haven't heard from him in weeks. Help him, God …*

The hard shell surrounding his heart cracked. "Oh, God …"

He echoed his sister's prayer until light intensified around him. When he lifted his tear-streaked gaze, he rubbed his eyes and blinked. A keyhole-shaped portal grew before him. On the other side, a car whooshed by on the highway. In the distance, a remodeled fifties gas station waited past a sign that welcomed him to Newberry Springs.

He stepped through the portal. Behind him, the Dragon Hotel stood abandoned except for the dark key-shaped fissure glimmering like a mirage.

Ryder sprinted for the gas station's pay phone. Digging in his pockets, he fished out enough change to make a call. "Mom? I'm so sorry. I want to come home. Can you wire me enough money for a bus ticket?"

He didn't go inside the gas station. Just in case.

Lisa Godfrees spent her life dreaming of being a writer, and God was faithful. Author of several short stories and flash fiction pieces, Lisa is currently working on a middle-grade fantasy. She resides in Houston with one dog, two cats, a fish, two girls, and a husband. Fall is her favorite time of year because of football (Gig 'em, Aggies!), Halloween, cooler weather, and her birthday. If she's not reading, writing, or pondering difficult questions, you can find her doing something else. Connect with her at her blog, www.lisagodfrees.com.

Raised in Captivity

By Cathrine Bonham

BRAD CIRCLED THE INTRUDER. It had been waiting for him when he woke up.

If being unconscious on the bedroom floor could be considered waiting.

Sunlight streamed in through the barred window, casting stripes across the floor, over the intruder, and up onto the double entry door. This was his space. How dare this person invade his territory? He looked around, reassuring himself that all was in order. His wardrobe stood tall and imposing on the wall opposite his bed. Ninety degrees from the wardrobe was a single door, half opened to reveal a toilet and sink. A small table and chairs sat to the left of the window.

He grabbed a broom propped up against the wardrobe and used the brushy end to poke the intruder. "No, not now," it mumbled, swatting blindly at the broom. Brad jumped back and gasped. This intruder spoke in the old way—vocally.

Brad studied the intruder. Long, dark hair fanned out from its head. Its feet were covered in thick leather boots. Tubular cloth, stiff and blue, covered both its legs and connected to form one covering for the hips and waist. Not pants, a more specific word. *Trousers? Slacks?* It was on the tip of his brain. *Jeans*! That was it.

Brad pulled down on the formless, white shift he wore. Little more than a large sack with head and arm holes cut out of it. He missed jeans and shirts; socks, even.

The intruder's top covering was in two pieces. The inner piece was a bright color, something called pink. The outer clothing was thick and padded, a drab green color, like an olive.

Its face was soft, lips parted slightly in sleep, eyes closed. Smudges of dirt smeared the intruder's pale skin. He approached slowly so as not to awaken it. He licked his hand and rubbed some of the dirt off its cheek. A rosy blush was revealed as the dirt came away. The intruder stirred and its eyelids flew upwards. Brad gazed into almond-shaped emerald windows and suddenly knew the word he had been trying to trick off his tongue.

"A girl?" he said aloud.

She screamed and rolled away from him. When she hit the bed, she jumped to her feet and tried to back up, but only succeeded in seating herself on the bed instead. "Who are you? Where am I?" She took a deep breath and looked around the room. "Those things were chasing me. Where did they go? How did I get here?"

He decided to keep his distance and held up his hands to show her he was harmless. His hands were slick with sweat. What was he supposed to do next?

Right, introductions. "I'm Bradley," he said slowly. He wasn't used to vocal communication. "Bradley Hanover. You could call me Brad, if you want to," he said. "What's your name?" His voice cracked right where the question mark would have gone.

He placed a hand on his throat. It tickled like he had just drunk a glass of dust motes. Did his voice sound different? How long had it been since he'd last spoken?

"It's Karen," she said. "Karen Wu. My family has been hiding from the invaders for years. Last night, they almost caught me trying to scrape together some food."

There. One question answered. How many more were there? He seemed to recall something about a person, a place, and things. He was the person, place would be here. "This is my room," he said gesturing outward and around. Things, he wasn't sure about. "What things were chasing you?" Brad massaged his jaw. It felt stretched, like he'd been chewing the same piece of gum for too long. He resolved to speak in shorter sentences for a while.

"The things. The invaders from space. The ones who are trying to wipe us out like vermin. Where have you been for the last decade?" She stood up as though ready to attack him if he gave her the wrong answer.

"Here," he answered.

"What, in this room? You mean you haven't left this room in ten years?"

"Well, I do go outside. Sometimes."

A knock sounded on the door. "Mmm, food." Brad opened the door and stood aside while Keeper brought in the morning meal.

Keeper towered over Brad, close to eight feet tall, his body bent forward to clear the room's low ceiling. He pushed a cart of food before him with one of his three massive fingers. His pearly exoskeleton shined in the early morning sun.

The first time Brad had met Keeper he'd been frightened. The exoskeleton looked like reanimated bones, purplish skin showing through at the joints, like rotting flesh. The bipedal creature's feet were each a single green toe nail, thick and hard like a hoof. The head, a large elongated cranium, looked far too heavy for its thin neck. A moldy-looking tuft of neon green hair sat on top.

The face, horrid. Multi-planed ruby eyes sat on nearly opposite sides of its head. Its mouth was a black vacuum tube sticking out of its stiff, unemotional face—less elegant than an elephant's trunk but not as plastic and inanimate as an actual vacuum tube. It doubled as a nose, expanding and contracting grotesquely as it sucked air in and out.

Good morning, Keeper, thought Brad.

Good morning, youngling, are you enjoying your guest? Keeper released the cart and gestured to Karen.

Yes, but please explain, why did you bring her here?

Information indicates you have reached maturity. It is time to make more younglings.

Karen sat there, staring at them, her mouth hanging open and her eyes so wide they'd lost their almond shape and become round. Brad supposed she had never seen one of her "things" this close before.

I do not understand your meaning. Brad tilted his head to physically convey his confusion.

I shall compile data to explain what we expect from you.

Thank you. Data is appreciated. Brad took the cart and pushed it up to the bed for Karen.

Before Keeper left, Brad had one more request. *Keeper, if it isn't too much trouble, I would like pants.* He provided a mental image of the tubular leg coverings Karen wore. *If some of my father's clothes remain, I believe they would fit me now.*

Yes, Bradley, I shall search for your request. Keeper backed out of the room, closing the doors behind him.

"They did capture me," said Karen in a low voice, almost to herself. She got off the bed and jiggled the door handle. "We need to get out of here," she said louder. Brad watched her as she ran to the window and threw it open only to violently throttle the bars. Finally, she turned and asked, "Aren't you going to help me escape?"

"Why?" he asked, offering her a seat on his bed. "Sit, eat," he said.

She walked back and looked over the cart that contained a selection of fruits, a couple slices of whole grain toast, a pitcher of orange juice, and two cups.

Karen picked up a banana and peeled it with a shaking hand. "So, no doughnuts and coffee?" she asked with a squeak at the end.

"I'm on a diet," Brad said. He saw her stare and turned his eyes down towards the cart. "I used to be fat," he said to clarify. "Keeper used to give me anything I asked for." He shrugged. "So naturally, I asked for junk food."

"What are you, some kind of—" she stopped. Whatever insult she had been about to inflict on him appeared violently strangled by a sudden revelation. "Oh no, this isn't happening. You're the pet." She pointed an accusing finger at his chest. The partly peeled banana landed back on the cart, abandoned.

"I'm the what?" said Brad, an apple partway to his mouth.

The look she shot him made him wish he could vanish. "Don't play dumb with me, Brad. We've heard rumors. They're keeping one of us, a human, as a pet."

"I am not a pet," he said through clenched teeth.

"Oh, you think not," she said. Calmly, she walked up to the large oak doors and turned the handle. "If you aren't a pet, then why are the doors locked? Why are there bars on your window?"

He had to think for a moment. Then he said, "The bars are to protect me. They're so nothing can get in my window." Then he walked over to the door and tried the handle. She was right, it was locked. Now he was confused. "The door isn't usually locked after breakfast." He turned back to face her. "The only new thing is you. Keeper must not want you to get out. I don't know why you are here yet, but Keeper will explain when he comes back for me."

"Keeper? You call that *thing* Keeper and you never wondered what he was keeping you for?"

"Keeper says that I need to be preserved, because my gift is the only way to achieve peace."

"Your gift? What are you, psychic or something?"

"Yes, but only with Keeper and his kind. I can't read your thoughts. Not that I've been trying," he added quickly.

"How old are you, Brad?" she asked thoughtfully.

"I'll be eighteen on my next birthday."

"Oh, I'm seventeen, too." Her face lit up with an expression of understanding. "Odd, they finally let you meet another human, and it's someone the same age of the opposite gender."

"Yeah, odd," he said.

"What are you wearing?"

Brad looked down and smoothed out his shift. "It's the best Keeper could do after I outgrew my old clothes." An awkward silence followed.

"Your last name is Hanover?" she finally asked.

Brad nodded.

"As in Senator Hanover?"

"Yeah, he was my dad," said Brad, crossing her path to sit on the bed.

Karen also walked to the bed and sat, leaving about a foot between them. "Look, I'll tell you what I know, and you can tell me what happened to you. Then we'll both know everything. Okay?"

"Sounds good. You first, please." Brad looked away from her.

"I was young at the time, but I've heard the adults talk about it enough to figure out most of it," Karen began. "It started with lights in the sky. Your father hosted them at a session of Congress. They spoke about—no, that's wrong. They didn't speak. Senator Hanover spoke—about inclusion and acceptance and their offer to share advanced tech with the world in exchange for power to rule over us.

"When the president refused to surrender, they vaporized the Capitol. They started rounding up people. At first, it was tagging and tracking, then the concentration camps. Now, they outright hunt the few of us who remain free."

Brad finally looked at Karen. Tears had begun streaming down her face. This was painful for her.

"I remember D.C.," he said. "We used to live there. But after *they* came, Dad moved Mom and me back home, to Columbus."

"Makes sense. I was in Dayton when they captured me," she said.

"Anyway, when Dad went back to D.C., he left Keeper here. He said Keeper would look after us until he came back." Brad grew silent as the memories surged through his mind. "I remember D.C. getting blown up. We were shocked. Dad was dead. Keeper said people did it. He told us humanity was too violent and hateful, that they were destroying themselves.

"Soon after, they installed the bars on the window. Mom and I were kept in separate rooms. I saw her less and less. She couldn't communicate with them like I can. So they didn't care about her. I can't remember when I last saw her. I think I might have been nine, maybe ten. I don't even know if she's dead. One day, Keeper came in and said my mother no longer lived here, and I should forget about her. I guess I did, until you came. Mom used to talk about leaving. I suppose she must've got tired of living here."

"Or they killed her."

Brad looked up, a glass of orange juice halted halfway to his lips. "What? No, Keeper wouldn't do that, he couldn't. Why would he?"

Karen took a deep breath. "It's pretty obvious—your mom wouldn't approve of them keeping you locked up like a pet songbird. What if she'd been planning to take you away?"

This was too much. Karen clearly liked to move fast, nail down facts, point out the obvious. Brad needed to think. Process. He downed his glass of juice in one gulp, piled some fruit onto a plate, and sat at the small table across the room.

Karen ate, her own plate cradled in her crossed legs as she sat on the bed.

He cleared his throat. "All I know is that my dad left, then my mom left me. But Keeper stayed. He took care of me, and if he wants to take care of you too, I think you should let him."

The door opened again and Keeper entered the room. He called to Brad, mentally informing him of the acquisition of pants.

Bradley got up and walked over to the cart to remove it from the room. "Are you finished eating?"

She nodded and handed him her plate. "Wait, are you leaving too?"

"Yes, my presence is required for informational download."

"What?"

"It would take too long to explain the process to you. I have to go."

"No, wait, Brad. What am I supposed to do while you're gone?" She stuck out her bottom lip and frowned.

He gave her a mysterious smile and said, "The wardrobe is bigger on the inside."

Then he left, and Keeper closed and locked the doors behind him.

***

Do you find the clothing satisfactory? asked Keeper as Brad sorted through the remnants of his father's wardrobe. Alas, no jeans.

Yes, Keeper, I think these will do. Brad grabbed what amounted to a complete suit and put it on in front of Keeper. He stood in front of the full-length mirror and studied his reflection. His blond hair had grown long again, brushing the top of his shoulders. His blue eyes and stubby nose were an inheritance from the Hanover line. But he could see a little of his mother in the chin and cheek bones.

A picture of his parents lay discarded and forgotten on the floor, its frame cracked, the glass long ago broken. Dust flew up as he pulled the photograph from the debris. "I look like my father," he said aloud.

Yes, the genetic similarities are many, thought Keeper. *You will pass genes onto your younglings, and they shall look like you.*

And communicate with you, Brad finished.

Yes, it is hoped your offspring will share your genetic talent.

Where is my mother? asked Brad, trying to surprise a straight answer from Keeper.

She is out back in the garden.

Really?

Yes, she is near the cherry tree. It was failing to bloom, due to the poor soil content. The tree is doing much better now.

Brad's spirits fell. He had been hoping to see her again. *Why didn't you tell me when she died? I would've wanted to be there when you buried her.*

No, you would not. I can read your emotions as well as your thoughts. You would not have been able to handle the pain. Your mother was in failing health even before we came. It was her wish that you be sheltered from the loss.

I don't believe you. Brad balled his hands into fists. *I should have been told. I should have been allowed to decide for myself what I could and couldn't handle. I want to leave. I want to meet other humans.*

You are a youngling. You cannot be trusted with your own welfare. It was unfortunate when your father perished. I promised him you would be looked after and kept safe.

Brad looked one last time at the photo of his parents. He carefully folded it and placed it in the inside pocket of his father's suit coat. "You want me to have kids," he said, vocalizing the thought to make it more real.

Precisely.

How?

Keeper took him to what used to be the family room but was now a high tech operations center. *Sit and watch. We have compiled data on human reproduction from conception through birth.*

Brad sat down in the specialized neural interface chair. The headrest lit up with the familiar blue glow indicating the warm-up stage. He closed his eyes in preparation for download. The faint buzzing grew louder as his REM functions were activated. The data played before him like a dream. Unlike a dream, he remembered everything upon waking.

He remembered *everything*! His eyes flew open in horror. They wanted him to do that to Karen.

He leaned over in the chair and threw up.

***

Karen sat on the bed in her already familiar cross-legged position, a book closed on her index finger. "Brad? You look so ..." She stood and fumbled for the right word.

"Human?" he supplied for her.

"No. I was going to say grown up," she said.

"Oh, well good. I feel more grown up. The clothes, I guess."

"Yeah, the clothes help a lot."

She spread her arms and motioned to the wardrobe, its doors open, revealing the shelves of books inside. "I like your library. I never had many books. We were always on the run."

"Mom loved books." He looked at his feet, trying to fight back the tears. "She's dead, by the way. I asked." The silence was oppressive. He wished she would say something.

Suddenly, the desire for something soft and comforting came over him. "Have you seen Toby?" he asked.

"Who's Toby?" she asked back.

"Just get off the bed," he yelled. "I need to find him." He scrambled around in the tossed bedding. Nothing. He dropped to the floor and crawled beneath the bed. His hand found something soft and furry. Finally, he surfaced with Toby, a blue stuffed dog. One ear flopped on its face, the other missing, long ago torn off in a childish fit of rage. Brad cradled the dog on his lap as he sat cross-legged on the bed, rocking back and forth.

Karen tried to approach him, her hand outstretched to offer comfort.

"Stay back," he snapped.

She recoiled, pulling her hand away. "I want to help."

"You can't help me. You've had your whole life to grow up. I've had one morning. I've gone from eight to eighteen in a matter of minutes, and it's hard." Brad swiped the back of his sleeve across his tear-streaked face. "So hard to process. You can't understand. I don't expect you to."

He curled himself tighter around his plush dog and began weeping.

Karen retreated back towards the wardrobe with her book. Brad watched her sit on the floor and try to read, knowing full well his sobbing made it impossible.

***

Brad woke up on his bed. The light outside was dim, the sun setting on the other side of the house. He must have cried himself to sleep. He felt his face grow hot in embarrassment. What would Karen think of him now? He shifted his gaze to the barred window, finally seeing it for what it was.

A cage.

He stumbled out of bed. The shoes still felt heavy and awkward on his feet. He turned on the room's overhead light and noticed the luncheon feeding cart sitting inside the door. It had been picked over. He filled a plate with raw veggies and mixed nuts, and began filling his stomach.

When he'd had enough, he opened the bathroom door and found Karen inside, slumped over in the tub. A stack of books stood beside her on the floor.

He approached her slowly and laid a gentle hand on her shoulder. She awoke with a gasp and flinched away from his touch. Brad pulled his hand back and held them both up where she could see them. "It's okay, Karen. I'm not going to hurt you."

"Brad?" she said, as if reminding herself rather than asking.

"Yes, it's me." He paused because the next part was going to be hard for him to say. "If you still want to leave, I think I can help you."

"Really?" She jumped up out of the tub and threw her arms around him. "Oh, thank you, Brad." The stack of books scattered across the tiled floor.

Now it was his turn to flinch away from her. Being near her, having her touch him, brought back to his mind all of the things he had downloaded from Keeper. It made him feel weird. It felt wrong, even though it also felt perfectly natural. The paradox was too much for his underdeveloped conscience. Especially when it was pitted against his fully developed physiology.

"It would be wrong to make you stay. But at the same time, I ..." He couldn't say it. He couldn't place that burden on her. He left his statement unfinished.

"You don't want to be alone again," she finished for him.

He nodded.

"Then come with me," she said. "Escape with me. The resistance could use your insider knowledge."

He hung his head. "I never had a pet anything. Maybe that's why I went so long without seeing it," he said. "You were right, I am a pet. I don't think I could survive outside these walls."

"You aren't some animal, Brad. You are a human. That means resourceful, intelligent, and adaptable. You don't have to be alone. I will be there and my family and others. The thing about humans is we thrive in groups. Staying here, remaining isolated, especially after being exposed to something new, something bigger—that's what you won't survive."

For a second, Brad felt hopeful. Only for a second. He backed up against the toilet and sat on the closed lid. "I can't leave. Keeper will read my mind, and then neither of us will get away."

Karen sat down on the tub's edge. "Isn't there a way to keep him out of your head?" she asked. Her face fell into her hands.

Only once before had Keeper complained of difficulty communicating with him. At the time, Brad had been obsessed with a cartoon show and the theme music had been firmly stuck on repeat in his psyche. "There might be a way. I need a repetitive rhythmic pattern to occupy my subconscious."

Karen looked up. "What?" she asked, a perplexed expression screwing up her face.

"A song. I need to get a song stuck in my head. It might obscure my thoughts enough for us to get away. It needs to be annoying too. The more illogical it is, the more Keeper will tune me out."

"I have just the thing," said Karen, smiling.

***

"Where did you even hear this song?" asked Brad.

"It doesn't matter," said Karen. "Sing it again."

"*This is the song that never ends, it just goes on and on, my friends …*" They had already sung through this at least fifty times the night before and twelve times this morning. Brad was sure he wouldn't forget it anytime soon. It was the single most repetitive and annoying song ever composed in the history of mankind.

"Good," said Karen, cutting him off after one round. "As long as you keep it playing in your head, we're good, right?"

Brad nodded. He took one last look around his room. He was going to miss his books, his cozy bed, and always knowing when his next meal would be. But he was excited for the adventure too. The important things were coming with him: the photo of his parents, his Toby dog, and a couple books that Karen greedily shoved in the large pockets of her coat.

Brad picked up a sliced orange and began eating it, the juice dribbling down his chin. Karen carefully wrapped the whole grain muffins in a napkin and slipped them into another of her bottomless pockets. "We'll need these for later. Eat your fill now—later might be a long time away."

Brad nodded. He discarded the orange rinds and reached for a banana. They ate in silence until the tray was empty.

When Keeper returned, it was time for Brad to act.

Keeper, may we go outside today?

Why would you wish to?

I want to see where you buried my mom. I desire to pay respect to her memory.

Memory will cause only pain. Forget the lost, and enjoy the one I have provided for you.

She does not like being confined. If we were to go outside, I believe she would be happier, more open to listening to propositions.

I shall consider your request. Are you sure she won't try to get away from you?

I promise I shall stay with her the whole time.

Then I will escort you outdoors.

Thank you, Keeper. Brad concluded the exchange by hugging Keeper around the waist. The exoskeleton was smooth beneath his skin. Keeper pushed him back and looked at him.

Why do you cry? Keeper asked.

Brad reached up and wiped a tear from his eye. *This is the song that never ends,* he thought back.

***

This is where we left your mother. Keeper pointed to a green patch of grass at the base of a flourishing cherry tree.

Some people started singing it, not knowing what it was ... Brad was doing his best to keep from breaking his concentration. If he stopped the song for even one second to think a reply to Keeper, he was sure he would give away too much.

Instead of replying by thought, he looked at Keeper, smiled, and nodded. Then he dropped to his knees. He was genuinely sad, but Keeper tolerated strong emotion even less than annoying rounds. The combination of weeping and repeating the song should be enough to make Keeper give them some space.

He thought about his mother, his father, and all of the wasted years. He clawed at the ground and cried. Karen placed a calming hand on his shoulder and leaned close to his ear and said, "He's backing off."

Brad wiped his eyes with his sleeve and took deep calming breaths. "Where is he?"

"He's back by the gazebo. How fast can he run?"

"Fast, but the way we're going, his size won't help him any." Brad took Karen's hand and led her around the tree. "Stay here a minute." Karen did as she was asked and waited. Brad walked a few feet to a hedge bordering the property. He looked back and saw that Keeper had tensed. It was important to ease his suspicions before they ran. He grabbed a vine of morning glories and yanked it down.

He sat at the grave again, arranging the flowers into a kind of grave marker. "Karen, how does it look?"

"It looks great. Shall we get some more?"

Brad stood up and dusted his pants off. "The hedge, the spot where I pulled the flowers down. There's a hole that leads down to a ravine. There's a large pipe down there. I assume it leads to the sewers."

"That sounds like an awful long shot," said Karen, wrapping her hand around his.

"But it's a shot, if you're willing to take it. Are you sure you still want me along?"

"Very." Karen gave his hand a squeeze. They walked up to the hedge and started pulling at vines of flowers. "Okay, he's not looking."

Brad grabbed her hand and yanked her through the vines and under the hedge. He had miscalculated the slope of the ravine, and the two of them went tumbling. Brad released Karen's hand and allowed himself to relax and roll to avoid broken bones. He slowed to a stop and got up on one knee. "Karen," he called.

"I'm fine," she replied from behind him. He stood and turned. She ran to him, and he wrapped his arms around her.

Suddenly, a stomping noise drew their attention upwards. Keeper was using his massive body to break though the hedge. It looked like the densely packed plant was winning, but only just.

"Come on." Brad pulled Karen along by the hand again. They entered the pipe. It was dark and smelled like someone had forgotten to flush the toilet, but it was large enough to stand up in, barely. They ran. Cold water seeped into their shoes.

They trudged on, through the dark, stench-filled drainage pipes. They walked until Brad wished his feet would go numb. Just as he was about to ask Karen about those muffins in her jacket, he spotted a light ahead.

Water sloshed as they raced for the tunnel's end. They took great gulps of sweet air and soaked in the late summer sun on their faces.

Brad looked around. The pipe had let out onto a field. Tall grass and weeds blew in a gentle breeze, and an overgrown gravel road stretched across their path.

"We've been running west," said Karen. "So if we go north," she pointed right, "it's our best chance to find the old Air Force base."

"Do you think Keeper is going to look for me?" asked Brad.

"I don't know. He might, if he really cares about you."

"I feel bad about leaving him."

"You're just homesick. Pets run away all the time. It's part of growing up," Karen said.

He felt her hand clutch his again. The feeling was warm and reassuring. "Come on, pet, let's run away," Karen said.

Together, they started up the road.

Cathrine Bonham has always enjoyed reading and writing stories. Her favorite genre is anything speculative. She is a regular attendee of the Realm Makers writers conference. She was homeschooled through 12th grade and is now a graduate of Owens Community College where she majored in creative writing. Her short stories have previously appeared in the now defunct E-zine The Cross and Cosmos as well as the anthology *Cross and Cosmos: Year One*. She likes to post random thoughts and observations on her blog at www.dolphin18cb.wordpress.com. She is currently working on the umpteenth rewrite of her first novel.

Bipedal Idiots

By Katie Robles

THE BIPEDS COWERED IN one corner of Mezer's underground kitchen, oblivious to the small tunnel opening thirty paces away. The very tunnel the vermin used to sneak into the kitchen from the surface at night. Mother normally blocked it with a trash bucket, but as soon as she left for market, he had moved the bucket aside and set free a gamma-charged goob at the tunnel's entrance, and it left a nice, glowing stripe of goo on the tunnel's floor.

Those bipeds should have run for it. Instead, they pressed their backs to the wall and ignored the obvious path to freedom.

Mezer lay on his belly to study the creatures better, his short, sturdy legs stretched out behind him on the cool stone floor. He folded three tentacles to form a tripod under his chin and rested his head. Such odd looking creatures—knee-high and skinny. Their outer shell was soft and a bit squishy to the touch, but they stood upright which made Mezer suspect that they had bones inside.

He hated bones. They got stuck in his teeth.

There were three of them, which meant that Mezer would be expected to eat a whole one. If he couldn't get these bipeds to escape soon, his mother would be back with the acid and Mezer would be stuck with biped for dinner.

Mezer froze. One of the creatures was moving. It kept the end of one limb on the rock wall and waved the other back and forth in the empty air. *Oh, this was good.* A smile spread across Mezer's face. The biped's steps were hesitant, its limb sweeping the air before it as it progressed, but it was moving toward the tunnel. After five steps, its limb hit a table scrap, a yonner horn with a bit of Mother's special hydrochloric sauce. It shook its limb frantically and quickly backed up to the corner. If they were so afraid of getting dirty, they would never make it across the floor to the tunnel.

One of the other bipeds made a wailing noise, and—Mezer leaned in for a better look—leaked water from its eyes.

Mezer sighed and slumped. How such idiotic creatures had managed to leave their planet's atmosphere was beyond him. He tapped one tentacle on the floor and scratched his back with another. Maybe if he put one closer to the exit?

He wrapped a tentacle around the almost-brave explorer and lifted it. Mezer cautiously stretched his nose toward the biped and sniffed with one fully extended nostril. Awful. He had to get them out of here. If they were gone, Mother would be forced to cook yonner—salty, chewy, delicious yonner.

Mezer set the biped down gently in front of the tunnel. Barely the circumference of one of Mezer's tentacles, the tunnel came up to the biped's middle. If the explorer would just get down and use its four limbs together, bent at the midpoint, it could easily fit through. The trail of goo on the tunnel's floor glowed a bit less brightly now, but it was straight, a sure sign that the goob had sensed atmosphere and headed right to the surface.

The brave biped started calling to its group as soon as Mezer set it down. The ones in the corner called back, and for a few minutes, all they did was call back and forth, back and forth, until Mezer wanted to hiss and press the biped's head into the tunnel. What was wrong with these creatures? Couldn't they see what was right in front of them? Were they blind?

Great. The brave biped was sweeping the air with its limb and moving away from the tunnel, back towards the corner. Mezer's dinner was sealing its fate. His stomach twisted in dread. Anything that stupid had to taste bad.

Mezer stiffened. What if they *were* blind? They were limited to only four limbs; perhaps their perception of the radiation spectrum was limited as well. They emitted only faint traces of infrared, so maybe those were the only waves they perceived. He wiggled his foot claws in excitement.

Mezer grabbed a goob from the basket in another corner of the kitchen and the little creature sucked in its eye stalks. His mother wouldn't miss it. She wouldn't dust until after the fourth rotation, and he could gather a few replacements well before then. He held the goob's slick, gooey bottom with one tentacle so it couldn't run away and rubbed its fuzzy back vigorously. The goob's fine hairs began to glow.

Mezer stroked the goob again and the glow increased. The faster he rubbed, the shorter the electromagnetic wavelength, and the brighter the glow. He was glad he'd paid attention in biology class. He held the goob a bit closer to the bipeds and rubbed until the goob's glow matched their own.

Nothing.

Not even a glance in his direction.

The floor of the cave trembled slightly. Mother was at the entrance. Mezer clenched his tentacles and rubbed the goob until it squeaked.

There. The brave biped stopped waving its limb and looked up toward the goob in Mezer's grip. Mezer stopped rubbing, the glow faded a bit, and the biped began to grope the empty air and call out. Mezer ruffled the goob's hairs, and the biped gave a happy cry and pointed at it. He ruffled the goob again, the glow grew brighter, and the biped's limb dropped. It was looking around.

Was their ability to see the radiation spectrum so unbelievably limited? A few nanometers off in wavelength, and they were plunged into darkness? How had they managed to survive, let alone explore the galaxy?

The glow decreased a fraction, and the biped pointed again. The two in the corner took a few steps toward the light. It was working! Yummy yonner was as good as served.

Mezer stroked the goob every few seconds as the trio carefully crossed the cave floor. They could see the yonner horns now and walked around them. The tapping of Mother's foot claws echoed above their heads in the upper hall.

Mezer stared at the tunnel. The goob's glow would fade and plunge them into blindness before they traveled ten paces. They would have to rub the goob themselves.

The brave one reached the wall with the tunnel first. Mezer held the goob in front of it and the biped's eyes traveled along Mezer's tentacle from the goob up to Mezer's face. The little thing was either shocked or hungry because it opened its mouth wide.

The goob's glow dwindled, and the bipeds began to call out to one another. Mezer gave the goob one pass with his tentacle and the bipeds relaxed. The corner two crept forward the last few steps to clutch the brave one's side limbs. The water-leaker screamed when it saw Mezer.

The tapping of Mother's foot claws in the tunnel above paused, then started again, twice as fast. He had to hurry.

Mezer held the goob in front of the tunnel, and it extended its eye stalks toward the promise of surface air. The brave one looked at Mezer's face and nodded. Mezer pushed the slimy, fuzzy creature onto the brave one's chest, and the biped wrapped two limbs around the goob. He gave it a gentle rub.

Not stupid then, just blind. It looked almost cute with a duster in its arms, glowing a few nanometers brighter than itself.

The brave one got down on three limbs and held the goob tightly in its fourth. It was soon out of sight down the tunnel, and the other two bipeds followed. Mezer slammed the trash bucket back into place, lifted his foot claws, and scurried on quiet tentacles to his room just before his mother stumbled, breathless, into the kitchen.

A close call by any galactic standard.

Katie Robles gardens with her husband and pet chickens and sneaks vegetables into baked goods for her four young sons. She writes *Sex, Soup, and Two Fisted Eating: Hilarious Weight Loss for Wives*, a healthy living blog for women (and their husbands who sneak a peek when their wives aren't looking). www.sexsoupandtwofistedeating.com She lives in Delaware.

Delquessa's Lament

By Rebecca P. Minor

A SHOFAR'S SHRILL CRY pierced through the din of steel upon steel. Desperation rang in its overtones. Blare and shriek, clash and groan— war's discordant overture raged on.

Major Telenius added yet another gurgling moan to the cacophony as he wrenched his sword free of the rebel soldier slumped over the blade. He grimaced. Perhaps he would never grow accustomed to the gut-wrenching timbre of battle. The rebel crumpled to the ground. Since the battle had broken out at dawn, the Vareinorean campaign had ushered hundreds of Durik's troops across eternity's threshold, and for an instant, Telenius wondered what sort of afterlife greeted the still man at his feet.

Another enemy horn blast clipped Telenius' introspection. He surveyed the valley where the battle rampaged. Corpses littered the field where creeping bluestem and thistles lay churned by boot and hoof. Fractured enemy lines boiled through the fallen like an ebbing tide around jetsam.

The rebels who withdrew re-formed sloppy ranks to either side of the rough battlements they had erected. They looked as one to the ramparts. Their attention compelled Telenius to follow their gazes. The wall of hewn trunks split in the center and swung outward.

Like a blood-red sun lifting its wrathful head over the horizon, a figure, staggeringly loathsome, incomprehensibly profane, emerged from the fortress. Yard after yard of armored terror reared to its full height in front of the battlements. Dragon.

Telenius's heart thundered within the cage of his chest. "Maker's mercy," he whispered. He cleared his throat to raise his voice. "Men, re-form ranks. Hold the field."

The beast raised a reptilian head upon a lithe neck. Its eyes gleamed with an impure appetite as it regarded the battlefield.

Telenius' hand fumbled to his hilt. And so their fears of

reinforcements took a shape beyond any braggart's ability to dismiss. The battlefield, boiling with men and horses, was one thing. But this … this was entirely another, a challenge Telenius despaired of even King Aeleronde of the Vareinor possessing the might to overcome.

Where was Commander Porteneum? What remained of his artillery? Telenius sought them where they stood in rank near the pass they had traversed to enter the great bowl, rimmed with the jutting black rock of the isle. Where Telenius expected runners to be loading ballistae, stillness reigned.

Telenius snatched the reins of a passing message rider. "Your mount—now!"

The rider had scarcely cleared the horse's back before Telenius sat astride. He drove his heels into the mount's barrel and rounded the Vareinorean troops' left flank. "Javelins to the front. Swordsmen, regroup into three wedge formations."

The dragon stretched membranous wings wide, eclipsing the sun so the vein-riddled webbing between its bony pinions glowed like coals. Vareinorean troops exchanged wide-eyed looks. Through a toothy maw, the beast roared, and every command drowned in the thunderous din. Soldiers on both sides of the conflict blenched.

Telenius charged his mount past the assembling lines of soldiers in a driven search—where was the king? He hunted with speed that started at concerned, increased to worried, and barreled toward frantic. Finally, his glance sorted King Aeleronde's black courser from the teeming multitude of the Vareinorean force.

The horse's saddle was empty.

Dismay clenched Telenius' gut. He spurred his mount again.

When he neared the courser, he discovered a crouching figure near the animal—one in a brush-plumed copper helm and a rich plum cape. Surely it was Aeleronde, but why had he dismounted? Was he clutching a wound?

Mighty Creo, Telenius prayed. *Not now. We need him desperately.* He vaulted from the saddle and ran to Aeleronde's side. "My liege."

A boy lay on the bloodstained earth at Aeleronde's feet, and the king brushed a lock of sweaty hair from the youth's eyes.

"My lord, I should not have come," the boy rasped. "I'm just a burden now." A red gash ran across his shoulder and chest.

"Nonsense," Aeleronde said. "You have proven a brave and skilled trumpeter. The healers will see to your hurts."

"My Lord," Telenius glanced over his shoulder. "We have an emergency."

The King maintained steady eye contact with the fallen boy. "I am aware, Major Telenius." Unrushed, Aeleronde stood. "Healers, get this boy clear! Send me another soldier with the skill to play the calls." He swung onto his horse. "Telenius, you are with me. To the north ridge for a tactical assessment."

Aeleronde, astride his sleek black beast, thundered to a juniper-lined ridge with Telenius half a length behind. The height of the rise offered a clear view of the field below where Durik's troops waited and the Vareinorean lines assembled with fearful scuttle and hubbub. Only corpses or those too near death to move lingered in the expanse between armies.

The dragon glowered over it all.

Aeleronde reined his mount to a halt and glared at the southeastern fortification. "Well, now we see the full truth of Durik's devilry. Alchemy is the least of our worries. Praise the Maker that the duchess has likely sailed past the Standing Stones by now."

Telenius's breath caught. Now was no time to break the news to His Majesty of the duchess' disappearance. "Your Majesty, have you ever fought a dragon?" He cleared his throat of the betraying quaver in his words.

"No." Aeleronde gritted his teeth. "But I see now we were fools to hope Zarchamidion would not play into all this. We must call what remains of the ballistae into position—"

The king's words died as the dragon sprang into the air and swooped down the hillside. The beast arched its neck like a snake preparing to strike, and when it had drawn within ten fathoms of Aeleronde's employed troops, it opened its fang-lined jaws again. In a moment of horror that stretched into an age, Telenius stood transfixed by the furnace-white glow inside the dragon's mouth.

"Signal artillery!" Aeleronde roared.

Despite the command flags that waved the frantic order for missile fire, Porteneum's line made no move. The Commander's intent gaze seemed to fall on Telenius and linger. Durik's devilry? Telenius began to doubt that was the most nefarious tactic at work on this rueful day.

***

Ten Days Prior

Duchess Delquessa Ildonian of the Elfkind leaned against the cold stone frame of her chamber's window while her gaze roved the rolling terrain outside the palace. Rain thrummed on the clay roof tiles. Fog shrouded the hills and the road through them with a silver veil.

"Mistress, please," her waiting maid's voice chided from behind her. "You must pry yourself from that window for a morsel."

Delquessa turned a frown to her servant. "Please, Elyrin. You expect an appetite of me? How can I think about food when I still have no word on Aeleronde's excursion? For months, my dreams have been plagued with scenes of disaster. And always, an amber moon hanging over it all."

"I do not pretend to understand the gifts Creo bestows upon the Immortal Twelve, my lady, but sometimes, dreams are just dreams, brought on by our own fretful imagining. Come. Sit." Elyrin extended a fair hand to the seat.

"And sometimes, they are portents. We should have had at least a message by now." Delquessa's fretting ceased when a distant motion beyond the rain-spattered windowpanes snatched her attention. Within the murk outside, something stirred. Her heart picked up speed. "Someone approaches, Elyrin. Perhaps ..." She turned a grin to her waiting maid—her first since Aeleronde had departed to rendezvous with her shipwright.

Elyrin joined Delquessa at the window. "I cannot tell from so far, but it appears it might be some sort of wain. Would His Majesty come hauling a load?"

"Not typically, but cargo or no, I shall welcome his arrival with gladness."

The shadow in the distance emerged from the interposing mist to reveal a horse-drawn cart led by two figures on foot.

Delquessa's smile evaporated. "No, these travelers are not Vareinor, nor men of any banner. By the look of their cloaks, they are Elfkind— our own patrol."

"Our soldiers do not take loads with them on their duties," Elyrin said.

"That they do not." Delquessa swept from the window and out the parlor door, her swift strides carrying her down the spiral stairs from her personal suite to the outer bailey of the castle. Cold rain pelted her. She splashed through puddles as she cut a straight path toward the horse cart emerging from the gatehouse tunnel, pulled by a steed that danced upon a skittish gait.

Delquessa sniffed, and the sickly sweet stench of decay coated her senses in a loathsome film.

Elyrin dashed to Delquessa's side. She shook out a handkerchief and handed it to Delquessa, who pressed its lavender-scented folds to her face.

The Elf soldier tugged upon the animal's lead and stopped. "Your Grace," he said with a bow, "I fear we bear a sight unfit for one of Creo's Unstained. Perhaps you might retire to your quarters—"

Delquessa clasped her hands together in an effort to mask their trembling. "This cart bears the dead."

"Only one body." The guard raked through his damp, silver hair and shifted his weight from foot to foot. "And he is badly burned to the point we might not have taken him for one of our own were it not for his livery."

"And how did his body come to us, then?"

"Messengers from Earannon brought him to us for interment here on his family grounds." The guard released a long breath. "We are told further news will come to us by another means."

"Show me," Delquessa said. "Burned or no, I have ways of learning of this unfortunate while we wait."

The soldier preceded her to the wain, grabbed hold of the corner of the sodden canvas that covered it, and cast her a hesitant glance. The second patrolman stood behind the cart with his arms wrapped around his middle and his gaze avoiding all others. A sudden pallor whitewashed his cheeks.

Eyes squeezed shut and handkerchief raised to her nose again, Delquessa braced herself. Still, the loud flap of canvas sweeping aside made her flinch. The death reek struck Delquessa in a gust, too intense for mere lavender to mask.

A long exhale steadied her nerves, and she dared open her eyes. A single glance over the wagon's side dissolved all the strength in her knees. They buckled. Both Elyrin and the soldier jumped to catch her before she landed on the drenched flagstones.

"Cithredhan," Delquessa whispered. "Forgive me. But how came you to such disaster when your task was but to test the seaworthiness of a ship?" She reached toward his blackened hand.

Elyrin grabbed Delquessa's forearm. "Have you not seen enough? What else might you wish to learn of an Elf days dead?"

Delquessa leveled a sober glance upon her waiting maid. "Distastefulness aside, I will see if I might still read the Elf's Rumor and learn what became of him."

"Your Grace, please desist." Wide-eyed horror engulfed the soldier's features. "We will seek out whatever other messenger is due—"

At Delquessa's raised palm, the soldier bit off his remaining protest.

"I will not wait in weeks of doubt for tales I might glean now." In truth, she felt faint. Had Cithredhan met his demise before or after he conveyed the ship to Aeleronde? Would she also witness Aeleronde's end in this shipwright's lingering Rumor? Was she prepared for that possibility? Though, if she and the King of the Vareinor had their way, facing his death was an eventuality she could not avoid. She steeled herself.

The second patrolman re-covered most of the corpse with the canvas to leave only the Elf's hand exposed. Delquessa swallowed the growing lump in her throat and reached out, trembling. After blowing out a gust of breath, she pressed her fingers to the corpse's brittle flesh. Part of the scorched hand was covered in a cracked, black shell—not scabs, for surely Cithredhan had not lived long enough in this state to begin to heal. She shuddered at the unnatural chill that flesh ought never to assume.

Her ordinary vision clouded. A vague mosaic of wood grain, brass, and rope advanced and retreated from focus. The tang of salt and the sharper reek of smoke prickled in her nostrils. The rush of wind and shouts of men came to her ears, warbled as though coming to her through water.

"The Rumor is faint … almost gone." At once, she spoke and beheld herself speaking, as was common in the disorienting process of reading a Rumor. She waded farther into the murky depths of her mind, in search of more clues before the vision failed altogether.

Waves of discomfiture throbbed over her then grew to fury. A sense of acceleration pulled Delquessa's body along in a disjointed rhythm.

"Radromirian pirates, in these waters? The audacity. Chase them down." The words drifted from Delquessa's lips in a masculine timbre. A pity. What a strong, noble voice Cithredhan once had.

Another voice emerged in Delquessa's channeling of the Rumor, though this one carried a distant sound, like a speaker who shouted from a distance. "*Uchthu! Gradrenna id Durik …*"

Tebalese? Truly something politically messy took shape upon the waters between the Elven port of Earannon and the harbors run by Men.

Chains clinked. Mechanical twangs sent harpoons into the white murk beyond the range of what remained of the Rumor. A cacophony of men's cries rang out. The indistinct sky exploded into luminous orange. For a moment, the flare revealed a towering pillar of stone, rising from the water. A surge of fear. Searing pain … and blackness.

***

"There is no place so fair as a land governed by the Immortal, eh, Telenius?"

Telenius eased his horse beside King Aeleronde's. Side by side, they crested a grassy rise, the chicory and the candytuft a mottled canvas of pink and periwinkle all around them. The road wended before them, riding the rise and fall of the land like a ship on high seas, to lead them to a pinnacled fortress in the distance. The castle's walls gleamed in the sunlight, a pearl that crowned a hillock of green.

The caress of the breeze blew fresh over the land, and Telenius closed his eyes to drink the air in a deep draught. The clatter of the king's vanguard dissipated as the column of Aeleronde's retainers slowed to a halt.

"True, my lord," Telenius replied. "I have journeyed to many fair places at your side, but Duchess Delquessa's domain surpasses them all."

"What fortune is it that preserves them from the marring that stains our own land?" Commander Porteneum asked from behind them. "Do we not serve Creo with greater zeal than these 'Firstborn?' Are we not his Chosen among Men?"

"Peace, Commander," Aeleronde said. "We, the Vareignor, and they, the Elfkind, are made for different tasks. It falls not on us to question Creo's shielding of the members of the Twelve. Is it not woe enough that they should endure the passing of their children and every generation that follows, while they linger into eternity?"

"Dominion for all time," Porteneum murmured. "Yes, it must be an incalculable burden."

Telenius frowned but opted against a clash with Porteneum's dour disposition. How the Commander could remain so brusque when deep into the pristine province the Elves called *Celethinne Veranna*, the Emerald Valley, Telenius failed to fathom. The majesty of the place still took his breath captive. To think the castle ahead had stood for millennia, having been built shortly after the first generation of Elves, the Immortals, awakened. Yet despite all the intervening years, it bore an ageless beauty no force of time or nature could sully. Not even Porteneum's continual pall of discontent could dim the beauty around him.

Telenius' attention drifted from the castle in the distance to his cousin, the King, whose teeth flashed in a broad smile.

"See you on the far rise." Aeleronde spurred his horse, at which the beast leapt into a gallop to careen down the hill.

Telenius followed suit, trailed at a distance by the rest of the van.

Side by side once again, they splashed through a chattering stream that ran in the cleft between the hills, sending sparkling spray into the air. Aeleronde's eyes gleamed no less than the droplets of water that flew in the midday sun. Telenius could not restrain a grin provoked by his king's unabashed thrill. Indeed, it was good to put toilsome travel behind, but more likely, Aeleronde beamed in anticipation of an encounter with the lady who dwelt at the journey's end.

As they reached the halfway point to the eastern wall, the palace gates swung open, and three riders emerged, the center bearing a sable standard emblazoned with a white stag.

The captain of the Elven guard eased his mount closer to the King. "Fairest greetings from the house of Ildonian, Lord Aeleronde. To our great surprise, we behold you, but still we offer our welcome. Her Grace is overwhelmed with relief at your arrival. She will, however, require some time to compose herself and offer audience."

"Compose herself?" Aeleronde replied. "Has she some cause to be undone?"

The captain of the guard exchanged an awkward glance with his companions. "You know nothing of the fearful Rumors reaching our gates?"

Porteneum rode up beside Telenius. "Rumors? The scroll you received was as clear as may be." He frowned. "Surely you do not intend to add to what time you have wasted in not having the promised ship in Earannon at the appointed time?"

"Scroll? We've been in receipt of no such thing," the captain said. "Just the fragments of a vision and a dead shipwright that offered more questions than answers. Her Grace had all but resigned His Majesty lost to the deep."

"Forgive my commander's frustration," Aeleronde said. "It seems we are all suffering a lack of information. Perhaps in conference, we might begin to piece together a more complete picture." Aeleronde's brow furrowed as he glanced at Telenius. "How should it be that my message did not arrive?"

"Odd tidings." Telenius glanced to Porteneum, but the Commander's consternation focused into the distance.

The King shrugged and clapped Telenius on the shoulder. "Then let us be on hand as soon as Her Ladyship is ready to receive us."

The Elven riders wheeled their mounts. Telenius, his liege, and the vanguard followed them up the road, and they passed the arch of the palace gates. With a groan and a clang, the portal swung shut behind them. The gate's reverberation died as Telenius emerged in the courtyard, only to be echoed by a crow's raucous cry from somewhere beyond the castle walls.

***

A sharp rap on Delquessa's parlor door jolted her heart to hammering, even though she had awaited such a knock with enough eagerness to give her the shivers. She took a final glance in the mirror beside the entry, pulled a long, meticulously curled tress over her shoulder, and said, "Enter."

The door swung open, and through the guardsmen that flanked the doorway, King Aeleronde crossed the threshold. His lips parted in a grin.

She returned his broad smile.

"Your Grace," he said, the rich tone of his voice filling the chamber. He stood with shoulders thrust back, his head bare of helm to reveal the gleam of golden locks and a glint in his eye.

Delquessa restrained the inclination to fling herself into his arms, but instead, stepped forward and offered her hand. Aeleronde took it. The warmth of his fingers enveloped hers, and he pressed the back of her hand to his lips for a lingering greeting, eyes closed, dark lashes stark against his sun-bronzed cheeks.

Delquessa's face warmed. "Need that be all, Your Majesty?" She took a step closer to him, so the fullness of her skirts flowed about Aeleronde's legs. "I am owed many greetings for the time you have spent away."

"Far be it from me to remain a debtor." A roguish look pulled Aeleronde's mouth crooked, and he eased a half-step tighter to Delquessa.

A cough from outside the door interrupted their reunion. Major Telenius stood a few paces back in the hall. He rubbed his neck and glanced toward the ceiling. Behind him came Commander Porteneum, his face creased in the habitual frown that Delquessa presumed to be his only expression, having never seen him wear any other.

Delquessa stepped back. "Welcome once again, Major Telenius. I assume you are serving as chaperone." She nodded to the second man. "Commander."

"If Your Grace and His Majesty deem it your desire," Telenius replied.

"It is probably the most prudent course of action." Aeleronde swept his gaze over Delquessa from crown to skirt hem in a way that made her scalp tingle.

"Though we have more to accomplish in this visit than a simple social call," Porteneum said.

With a sigh, she withdrew her fingers from Aeleronde's grasp. "Please, do have a seat. Tea, any of you?"

***

Delquessa swirled a spoon in her cup of tea, though the stifling intensity of the atmosphere blunted her taste for the exotic concoction. So few moments ago, she had rejoiced with Aeleronde. How quickly rejoicing gave way to dismay.

"You are certain the language you heard in Cithredhan's Rumor was Tebalese?" Aelronde said.

"Yes," Delquessa replied. "And the speaker named himself Durik."

Porteneum huffed. "Preposterous. He may be brazen enough to harry our border, but to contract pirates? To attack Elven vessels? What could his point be in that?"

"I'm sure you did not just intend to call the duchess a liar, Commander." Aeleronde lifted a brow.

Porteneum sucked his teeth. "If the scant details we do have are accurate, they dictate quick action."

"At least this explains why Cithredhan did not arrive to deliver the ship to Earannon," Telenius said.

Delquessa rubbed her forehead. "But the Rumor does not fully explain what became of him and his crew. The last I saw must have been something fiery."

"Fiery." Porteneum scoffed. "A simple enough answer—Durik's specialty."

Aeleronde growled. "Two sections of the banishment edict breached, then, a departure from his borders and an offensive use of alchemy." A sardonic smirk curled his lip. "And add to that the personal offense of destroying my birthday gift."

"This is no time to be flippant," Porteneum said.

Delquessa contemplated the ensuing silence. There was something to the king's comment more than flippancy. Something personal. She wrapped her arms around her middle. "There was a stone pillar in the vision as well, and I cannot shake a sense of significance attached to it. But at sea?"

"A pillar, in the Sea of Seraic?" Telenius tensed his jaw. "Could that imply the Standing Stones of Aromen's reign?"

Porteneum took to pacing, his words trampling the last of Telenius.' "I would exercise caution in basing too much of our strategy on information gathered by a method as ... changeable ... as the reading of Rumors. Is it not possible that Cithredhan's Rumor was muddled by images from his past, unattached to the moment of the ship's destruction? Even his imaginings may have intermingled with the events."

"Even if we dismiss the last aspect of the Rumor, we still have the possible breach of Durik's banishment edict to contend with," Telenius said.

Aeleronde sighed. "That we do, coupled with the murder of a good crew of Delquessa's folk. A pox on Durik's accursed longevity. My great-grandsire's leniency continues to prove a thorn in my side."

"And a fetter to any lasting peace for the Vareinor." Porteneum's hard glance flicked to Delquessa.

Delquessa settled upon her chaise and smoothed a fold from her body-skimming gossamer gown, one she had worn in the hope it might captivate Aeleronde's attention. In the face of such mayhem, what power did mere affection have? She tucked a tendril of hair behind her ear point. "The whole business feels shrouded in deceit. You will send scouts, then?"

Aeleronde sat beside her, grasped her chin, and turned her to face him. She swallowed the fluttering sensation that threatened to escape her stomach.

"Yes, but I cannot be far behind them lest Durik elude us and find some dark corner in which to brew darker mischief than he already has." He bowed his head. "Durik's machinations are no such legacy I wish to leave to my sons and daughters."

Delquessa started. "Sons and daughters?"

Aeleronde traced the backs of his fingers along her face, and a trail of thrill raced through Delquessa's cheek and down her side. "That gentle bargain is one I've not yet parleyed over with the pertinent parties."

Her every joint melted at the insinuation and his touch.

But Porteneum's gruff baritone stilled her thrilling nerves. "His Majesty cannot allow distractions to undermine his attention to the trouble at hand."

Telenius sighed and wandered toward the window, teacup in hand. "With all due respect, Commander, we should have allowed them some time before we dumped this matter of state in the duchess's lap. You make no secret of your irritation."

"Time is what we lack. Already, it would seem we are several steps behind Durik."

"Then implore Creo for patience," Telenius said. "Dispatching scouts and investigators will take time."

Aeleronde shook his head. "Such deeds were already done before we left Earannon, correct, Commander?"

Porteneum nodded.

"Then all that remains is to await their reports." Aeleronde rose and stepped to the door. "I dismiss the two of you and your depressing faces, as matters of state for today are concluded."

Telenius blinked.

"Of course, Major Telenius, your role dictates you should remain in the hall, but as for the Commander, I release him to whatever amusement he deems worthy of filling his wait for news from the scouts."

Porteneum folded his arms. "We have hardly reached a conclusion—"

"Nor will we until we know where the pirates have taken Durik," Aeleronde said. "I've maintained more patience than should be expected of a young man in love. Now, out." He pointed to the door.

Delquessa concealed a smile behind a turned head and a tap of a napkin to her lips.

Porteneum bowed. "Yes, Your Majesty."

He and Telenius exited, but his last dark glance before the door shut fell upon the king. Aeleronde had already turned his back to the door.

Delquessa stood. "Will Porteneum accompany you in whatever action you deem necessary against Durik?"

"Of course." Aeleronde returned to her side and took her hand. "He is certainly not the bright center of one's festivities, but he's a brilliant tactician. I fear I will need such a mind in response to Durik's maneuvering. But truly, I meant it when I said I am through with matters of state for today." He leaned toward her and took a deep breath of her hair behind her ear.

Despite the goose bumps that washed over her, she placed her hands on Aeleronde's shoulders and forced herself to focus. "I wish to come with you, should you decide you will leave the House of Ildonian to march upon Durik."

Aeleronde furrowed his brow. "Beloved, I can see no sense in risking that. If I pursue him, it won't be for negotiations. Send a scribe or guardsman, if you must. A war march is no place for you if Creo intends your immortal days to remain free of the horrors of Mankind's violence."

Delquessa's stomach turned at her recollection of the few examples she had encountered of blood thirst and murder, but she forced the sensation down. "I have never assumed it was possible to insulate myself from such dark truths entirely. But the children of the Elves lack the perception Creo has granted the Firstborn."

Aeleronde opened his lips to speak, but Delquessa placed gentle fingers over them. She leaned closer to him and whispered, "There is only so much time I can spend wondering what dangers stalk you. And Porteneum was right to imply the weight of a continued threat upon your people. We both know the remainder of the Twelve will not support any plans between us until they have some assurance your kingdom will not be forever at war. At least permit me to come so far as to drink the Cup of the Charge at your stirrup, that I may return to report to our council the clear supremacy of your force as compared to your enemy."

The conflicted lines of yearning that furrowed Aeleronde's brow encouraged Delquessa that perhaps her angle of the argument had finally gotten a foothold.

The King took Delquessa's hands. "You play upon my heart as a lyre. I do not wish to be separated from you, not for another day. But I will not risk any hurt to you by inviting you to whatever front lines Durik has chosen."

"If I am to someday be your queen, will you not trust me to be your eyes beyond where mortal eyes may see?"

The King tightened his jaw during the silence that he permitted to linger after Delquessa's plea. "If you promise to depart as soon as may be after the Cup is drained." Aeleronde squeezed her fingers.

Delquessa smiled and released the coils of tension that had been creeping up her neck. "I promise. And now, I agree. No more politics while we can choose that luxury."

***

Delquessa perched sidesaddle upon her palfrey, the mare arching her neck proudly as the sea breeze stirred her mane. Elyrin's gelding stood just behind.

Below the salt-white cliffs lay the port Myslapten. A fleet of mighty ships, their masts jutting into the sky, awaited their passengers. Already, a bustle of men scurried up and down the gangplanks with backs loaded with provisions for the looming departure.

Aeleronde's burgundy standard snapped in the wind. Delquessa focused only upon its color, not the scroll and the crown splashed across the center of the banner. She cast a beleaguered gaze to the waving saw grass.

"Your Grace, do not brood today! There is no Human army better equipped to confront Durik." Elyrin sidled the gelding next to the mare.

"You are ever a comfort to me, Elyrin. Far be it from me to dampen this day of departure with my unhopeful counsel. But why the Black Isle? Why would Durik move his troops to the only place on all of Greymalkynne with fewer resources than Tebal?"

"Perhaps he's as mad as the stories imply." Elyrin shrugged. "Should Aeleronde's designs proceed unfettered by tragic misstep, history tells us victory shall be his."

"I still say Porteneum's battle strategies reek of overconfidence, even given Vareinorean military history. For now, I can only hope that Durik's not so mad as to refuse surrender." Delquessa nudged her mount into a slow trot.

They descended the road that led down from the bluffs to the quays. Amidst Human sailors as well as seafarers from their own Elf kindred, Delquessa and Elyrin sought the queen of Aeleronde's fleet,

The Tempest. They passed her own ship, where Delquessa's retainers and crew readied the vessel to follow Aeleronde's force to sea.

At the foot of *The Tempest's* gangplank, Delquessa slid from her saddle. "Fare you well, gentle Elyrin! Do not wait for news, for it may be long in coming."

Elyrin nodded. "I assure you, mistress, you will find all as you left it when you return."

∗∗∗

Choppy whitecaps slapped the prow of *The Tempest* for the third day of sailing from the western coast of Argent as they pursued the shores of the Isle of Desolation. *The Tempest* plowed onward, continually at war with the sea's seeming intent to deter the Vareinorean fleet, but riding out every pitch and yaw with steadfast strength.

Major Telenius rubbed the insistent burning in his shoulders as the final hour of his duty outside the king's cabin crept by. He would greet the end of this watch with a glad embrace.

The setting moon fought to gain advantage over an advancing line of clouds. Its glow dimmed with each passing moment. Telenius doubted it would prevail.

The hollow thump of footfalls across the boards of the deck caught Telenius' attention. A lantern in hand, the towering figure of Commander Gaius Porteneum approached. Even in the middle of the night, far out at sea, the Commander wore the full complement of his lorica, a bronze helm and ankle-length cape. Telenius forced his muscles to straighten his spine, despite the outcry from his every fiber. He clasped a fist over his chest.

"At ease, soldier," Porteneum said. "I come to relieve you of your post."

Telenius cocked his head. "Many soldiers might have done so, sir."

"The fate of the Vareinor hangs upon that which befalls their king, does it not, Major?"

"Indeed, sir."

"Tell me, Telenius," the Commander said. He leaned an elbow on the wall of the cabin and kicked one foot behind his weight-bearing leg. "Had this excursion to intercept Durik not arisen, how do you perceive relations between the royal House of the Vareinor and the House of Ildonian would have progressed? As Aeleronde's cousin and personal guard, it seems to me you would possess a unique level of insight."

"No secret to even those outside the King's acquaintance, if they have eyes to see." Telenius squinted, unable to fathom Porteneum's face in the harsh shadows of the lamplight. "His Majesty only waits for the opportune moment to make vows to the Duchess of the Emerald Valley."

"And what is your feeling about the impact that has upon your potential succession, should His Majesty produce an heir?"

Telenius laughed. "It's never on my mind, to be honest, sir. The marriage is inevitable, and I long ago contented myself with my role of protector, not heir to the throne. I wish Aeleronde joy. What successor could ever hope to appear anything but a wan shadow in comparison to him?"

"Do half-breed children live forever, like their fae parent?" The slightest grimace pulled at Porteneum's expression.

Telenius pressed his lips together into a line and sucked a few breaths through his nose—just enough deliberate hesitation to cool the flare in his temper. "I am not very steeped in Elf lore, but I understand the descendants of the Twelve to be mortal. Longer lived than us, but mortal. I'm sure any child borne of Aeleronde and the duchess would only be an influence for the better on our people."

"Of course, of course." Porteneum offered a smile, though to Telenius's observation, it failed to kindle any spark in the Commander's eyes. "I knew you would not be among those who would say otherwise. You have earned a good night's rest, soldier. I relieve you."

Telenius bowed to Commander Porteneum and departed to his bunk. Earned or not, he found little sleep that night.

***

The silhouette of towering crags loomed across a quiet sea. To the starboard of *The Tempest*, a tapered pillar of granite, the runes cut into its surface worn from nearly a millennium of salt and spray, rose from the water. In spite of the dawn, a veil of fog rendered the seascape in a monochromatic palette of grays, for the rising sun struggled to pierce the gloom. The Vareinorean fleet stood anchored. Delquessa stared out over leaden waters, tracing the path of circling carrion fowl over the island before them.

Vareinorean soldiers uncoiled ropes from their pins, then leaned back in unified maneuvers that lowered the landing scows. Wranglers on a neighboring ship lashed cavalry horses into body harnesses. They hoisted one horse after another into the shallow water so they might make the swim to shore. Delquessa stood bereft of words, awestricken with the host's unflustered diligence.

She turned from her observation of the army's landing and sought Aelerondé's familiarity amidst it all. Within moments, she found him standing amidships, but Delquessa slowed at the outer edge of the throng of soldiers around him. Aelerondé's narrow eyes, his squared shoulders, and the bold gestures erected a wall around him, a wall at whose foot his company stood and awaited his command.

A crowded-yet-lonely life, the days of a king at war. Delquessa tightened her mantle about her shoulders. She wandered to the port gunwale and propped her elbows upon it.

Across the bay, the elf ship that would bear her home waited, and the attendants responsible for seeing to Delquessa's comforts already navigated their slim landing craft toward the beach.

As the sun rode higher over the Isle of Desolation, the host rowed for the shore. Soon, they no longer labored to propel the boats, for the breakers swept each of the landing scows in rhythmic surges toward the beach. All the while, Delquessa scanned the skies. Distant plumes of smoke rose from somewhere beyond the wall of mountains ahead. Thin, straight plumes, undisturbed in the still air.

Delquessa braced herself against the lurches of Aelerondé's craft. The boat scraped upon stones, and Aelerondé's vanguard leapt from their seats to drag it ashore. Dozens of like vessels mirrored the bustle.

The clamor of assembling soldiers, splashing horses, and the unloading of provisions receded into a mere echo as Delquessa climbed from the scow. Swords glinted upon every belt. Quivers of arrows hung upon many shoulders. Man after man girded himself with knife, flanged mace, or some other instrument of destruction. A tremor ran along Delquessa's spine. Yes, Aelerondé had been merciful to insist she abstain from the sight of war. Even its heralds filled her with a creeping sense of doom.

Her Elven attendants pitched her tents on the outskirts of the Vareinorean beach camp. While her beloved attended the workings of his host, she paced outside her quarters, and she strained to hear the soothing rush of the waves over the constant clatter of weapon and shield, hoof beat and neigh, order and dutiful reply.

I never should have come.

Delquessa blew a sigh. The realization that she was simply extra baggage on an otherwise efficient mission lodged in her chest and ached there.

A queen would not quail thus. I said I would see Aeleronde to the Cup, and so I mean to. She clenched her fists and opened them again, stretching tall to catch sight of Aeleronde clasping the shoulder of a young officer.

If her beloved faced more danger than anyone knew, such peril would not reveal itself to her on a premature voyage home.

No, her tent would remain pitched until the charge.

***

The sun dipped below the western mountains of the isle, and lanterns sprang to life around the camp. A crackling bonfire roasted whole sides of beef and pork, while the soldiers sang folksongs, raised flasks of wine, and jibed with typical tavern-talk. The sound of their laughter struck Delquessa as a thin veneer stretched over the dread of the morning's march. Behind the smiles flickered the sober look of men tested, men who had watched others fall to the onslaught of war.

As the evening drew to a close, the king ascended a platform the army had constructed in the middle of camp, and he raised his bronze goblet to the crowd. At this cue, Delquessa took her place beside the platform.

Aeleronde held his chin high and surveyed the horizon. "Tomorrow, noble soldiers of the Vareinor, you shall march with me, and through the gifts our glorious Creator has bestowed upon each of you, we shall remind Durik: terms set by the Vareinor are binding! For the weak. For your country. For Creo's glory." He thrust his goblet high. "Drink with me the Cup of the Charge."

The king placed the cup to his lips and took a deep drink. Delquessa drank as well, though to her palate, the wine lacked sweetness.

The army quaffed as one, then raised a cheer to their king. "May it be as you say, Aeleronde, Philosopher King of the Vareinor!" Not long after the soldiers drained their cups, they dispersed to their tents.

As the army's thrum settled into the stillness of repose, Delquessa walked the perimeter of the camp, her arm laced through the crook of Aeleronde's elbow.

"Morning rides so swiftly for you," Delquessa said.

"No more swiftly than any other, beloved," Aeleronde replied. "Though the more important the coming day, the larger it looms on the horizon."

Delquessa leaned her head against Aeleronde's shoulder. "This time in camp with you has made me dread your departure all the more."

"Perhaps this campaign might be the last for Aeleronde, King of the Vareinor," he replied.

"That is indeed what I fear. Why does none of the strategy account for—"

Aeleronde shook his head with a drowsy smile and placed his fingers on her lips. "You mishear my meaning … not that I should find my end in glory tomorrow, but that the glory of my forces shall usher in peace for my people."

Delquessa bowed her head. She heaved a great sigh, and for lack of anything more fitting to say, she muttered, "The ways of men are a mystery, my lord." She blinked back the sting of tears. "Is this march truly the best course?"

"It is the course I may chart with confidence, and when I return, victorious and having secured utter peace for my kingdom …" Aeleronde's brows pinched together. "I cannot depart upon this march with your eyes so downcast, Delquessa, joy of my heart." The king stopped. He dropped to his knee and reached inside the drape of the toga over his scarlet tunic, producing a palm-sized carven box. "This was not my original design, but I see if I truly love you, I should amend my plans." He extended the case to her. "Will you have me, O Lady, most gracious of the Firstborn? Maiden unfathered, with no parentage of whom to ask leave—save Creo himself—would you plight your troth unto me?"

Delquessa's breath wedged in her throat like a cork in a flask. How long had she hoped to hear him intone the traditional words of betrothal? She reached with a sluggish hand to take the box from the kneeling king before her. Her heart ached at the longing in his winsome face. Her soul reeled at his question, posed on the brink of peril—a milestone she had longed for had arrived, but somehow, in this setting, seemed so dubious. She hesitated to open the box, yet squeezed her eyes shut and lifted the lid.

A long, expectant moment passed before she dared open her eyes. Inside the box, nestled among plush blue velvet, waited a band of gold, glittering gems clustered upon it. In its center perched a dark stone, its hue so deep it devoured fire and starlight and gave it up only in the faintest glint of blue along the edges of its facets. White diamonds encircling the middle stone caught the same light and cast it about in motes of every color.

"Now, my lord?" Delquessa's breath came in gasps. A thousand questions and even more warnings clashed in her mind, but her tongue clung to the roof of her mouth and she found she could say nothing more.

"We shall set all in order as soon as Durik has been locked into his rightful place. You will return to Bilearne with me to reign at my side, to grace my people with wisdom and beauty unknown to our own kind!" Bright tears welled in Aeleronde's eyes. "And I shall be blessed more than all to have you as my bride and cleft unto my heart."

His charm loosed her voice, if not her clarity. "Aeleronde." Delquessa's glance drifted from her beloved's face, and for a brief moment, wandered the rows of tomb-white tents that stretched as far as she could see. Beyond the eastern crags in the distance, an amber moon peered, late in rising.

She sucked in a deep breath. The amber moon—with the mist and the warmth of the day, it was to be expected. She drove the image from her mind. Her fingers tightened upon his broad, strong hands before she connected gazes with him again. "I accept your offer of marriage, king of men."

Aeleronde rose and cupped Delquessa's jaw with a strong yet tender hand. He tilted her face to the moonlight that reflected in his own bright eyes. His lashes lowered, and Delquessa's heart broke into a full gallop. For one moment, frozen beneath the starlight, there was no battle impending, there was no war camp, no lost ship, just the fiery connection of their lips in a kiss that sealed their bond. Delquessa Ildonian, Immortal Firstborn of Creo, submerged in the whelming flood of her longing for Aeleronde, King of the Vareinor. For that instant, all else fell away, like ice shivers from tree limbs when the sun smiles down and dissolves its silvery hold.

***

Delquessa lingered awake well into the night. For once, fear and worry did not taunt her, but the flurrying plans of her coming wedding day playfully robbed her of sleep. A golden day of sun, music, and interwoven lilacs and irises flitted across her mind's eye. She snuggled down into her pillows and quilts, a smile tugging at her drowsy lips.

Even after she apprehended sleep, her grasp upon it remained tenuous. Her eyes fluttered open after either moments or hours. Which? She could not tell. The camp outside was quiet and darkness shrouded the land. She stretched, yawned, and rose from her coverlets and pillows. Through the canvas of her tent, she noted her pair of guardsmen flanking the exit. If she could not sleep, at least she might breathe the fresh breeze and recall upon its scent the blissful moment she had lived so few hours before. But to do so with guard on her heels felt stifling.

Under her breath, she whispered, "Almighty Creator, grant me the form of the morning breeze, the quiet of the zephyr." Her body dissolved into a translucent vapor that barely held the shape of a maiden, and thus transformed, she slipped beneath the canvas at the rear of the tent, then drifted into the moonlight.

She wove between the tents and pavilions of camp, the mist of the cool night mingling with her altered form. A chill snaked through her. It was not due to the mist. The shiver's character was far too uncanny to credit to mere weather. The sensation drove a stake through her short-lived joy.

Across the camp, Delquessa caught sight of a figure, hooded and cloaked, who ducked beyond the perimeter of the encampment. Another man, Porteneum's sergeant, joined the cloaked individual, and they exchanged hushed words. What their business might be, she could not fathom, but she slid toward the spot as only Creo's firstborn could.

The sergeant handed a pouch, rounded and jingling, to his companion. The cloaked man tucked it under a fold of his garb, nodded, and backed into the underbrush.

The sergeant turned, and his attention fell right upon Delquessa's position. A jolt of fear surged through her. *In this dimness, he cannot possibly see me.*

What to do? She shrank into the shadow of the closest tent. The sergeant's attention roved, and Delquessa's tremulous fear lessened. The sergeant marched past her on long strides, then turned a corner to head deeper into camp.

What an officer might be doing in exchanging coin with another man in the dark of night baffled Delquessa. Was it worth summoning one of the camp's rangers to track the figure? Rousing Aeleronde from sleep he needed for the sake of successful campaign? Neither. Delquessa slipped to the spot where the figure had stood and retook her normal form. After a quick glance to confirm she acted unobserved, she dropped to her knee.

Fresh boot prints crushed the bracken. A touch upon the place where the soldier had stood would not reveal as much as touching the man himself, but it might provide at least a start. A mood. A motive. As much as she might hope the soldier was simply a scout, the chills she could not escape warned her otherwise. She placed her hand upon the bruised plants and sought the trancelike state she needed to absorb the rumor.

A sense of fear, of compulsion, trickled into her mind. But was there malice under it all? She strained her consciousness after deeper Rumors. The connection between the bracken and the subject had been brief, and the impression he left was faint. There—did she sense a prickling, hot emotion? Anger?

Before she grasped the shifting rumor, a sharp pain in the back of her head sent multicolored lights flashing across her vision. A weight crushed her to the ground, and a rough grasp covered her mouth. She thrashed, but her attacker—or attackers, she could not tell—restrained her. Without the ability to speak clear words, there was no resuming the vaporform.

Past the camp's limits they dragged her, at least three dark-clad men as best she could see. The perimeter guard they passed looked over his shoulder, turning a blind eye to her struggle, despite the moment she connected glances with him. The gag they jammed into her mouth carried with it an acrid scent and washed her tongue in a bitter, oily coating. Her head swam. How could this be, right in Aeleronde's camp? Lead flooded into her limbs. Before long, a darkness beyond that of night descended. Her eyes drifted shut, blocking out the sight of a setting, deep topaz moon.

***

Telenius marched along his detachment of pikemen, inspecting each man for armor, arms, and nerve. The first two, they brought in appropriate abundance. The last they bore in varying amounts. Those who had seen battle under Aeleronde in the past exuded seasoned calm, while the greener soldiers fidgeted with clasps and buckles.

Commander Porteneum shouldered his way through the soldiers from the rear of the group. "Major Telenius?"

"Sir?" Telenius brought his feet together and clasped his fist in salute.

"Your men meet the standard and are ready to move out?"

"Indeed, sir."

"Durik's troops man their ramparts, our scouts report," Porteneum said.

"Any response to the terms?" Telenius asked.

"A haughty invitation to 'bring our worst,' as I understand it." Porteneum scoffed.

Telenius sighed. "So we shall, I suppose. This will be a bloody morning."

"Major?"

Telenius turned. "Your Majesty." He bowed deep. "How may I serve you?"

Aeleronde spurred his black courser closer, a frown on his face. "Have you seen my betrothed this morning?"

Porteneum's eyes widened. "Betrothed?"

"Yes, Commander, I have verbally secured this, my most deeply desired allegiance, aside from my service to Creo." Aeleronde's face brightened with the admission.

After clearing his throat, Porteneum said, "I congratulate you, King of the Vareinor. You are a man able to focus on many weighty things at one time."

"There will be time aplenty available for well-wishes—this evening, I dare guess," Aeleronde said. "But, either of you, have you had words with Delquessa?"

"I have not," Telenius said. "Shall I send a runner for her?"

"I doubt it will do any good. Some time ago—as much as an hour—I saw her retainers bundling her tents," Porteneum said. "Something about honoring her promise to depart as soon as the Cup of the Charge was drained?"

Aeleronde's glance roved the camp. "It is true that was our arrangement. I suppose she was more literal with the promise than I had anticipated."

"But as you said, my liege," Porteneum said. "No shortage of time after the battle to celebrate how things have been ordered to their proper fashion. For now, your troops need your undivided focus."

In the east, the first shafts of sunlight stabbed over the horizon.

Aeleronde nodded then wheeled his horse. "Host of the Vareinor! We move out. A moment of bloodshed for an era of peace."

"Aye, an era of peace," Porteneum said before he swept off on long strides.

***

In the pre-dawn darkness, Delquessa emerged from murky confusion, her body jostling and jarring against her will, her upper body hanging upside-down over something. A man's shoulder? Her head ached, and rough hemp bit at her wrists, lashed behind her. She moaned.

"Good timing at least," a man said, not her bearer. "She's coming to."

The man who carried her blew a sigh. "Good. I'm not climbing this with her on my back. On your feet, Duchess."

Delquessa slid from the man's shoulder, and when her feet touched uneven, rocky ground, her knees buckled. Someone caught her arm. Her head swirled.

They had halted at a ragged slope, a wall of ebony rock that dared further passage with a toothy sneer. Halfway up the face, a crater glared at them like an empty eye socket.

"Up we go. Wake up those legs, too," the man beside Delquessa said.

She blinked haze from her vision and found herself in the company of two Tebalese warriors, judging by their broad features, ash-gray skin, and dark eyes. One had a crossbow trained upon her. They both wore tanned cloaks of a sandy shade. Their banded mail beneath the cloaks creaked and clacked with their efforts.

The third man inspired her to gasp around the gag in her mouth. He was tall and scarecrow-lean, with sunken cheeks and mad blue eyes. White hair hung to his shoulders in ragged waves, uneven as though they had been shorn with a knife of stone. A close-cropped beard framed an ancient, pale face. On his jeweled belt, he carried countless pouches. Delquessa could not place the manner of his velvet waistcoat or gleaming high boots. Upon his forehead, he wore a circlet emblazoned with the rune *Quel*. Everlasting.

The Tebalese soldiers took her arms and compelled her up the crumbling, black slope. The elder man followed. Delquessa's feet faltered, so the soldiers half-dragged her to keep moving. The farther up the rock face they ascended, the fouler the air grew, rank with a rotting stench. Their approach displaced magpies that fluttered away from picking bones that littered the slope.

Just feet from the maw of the cave, they came to a halt. Delquessa's hair stirred in a hot breeze, laden with an intense fetor of burning and of decay that wafted from the entry. The air reversed direction, drawing back into the cavern. Again, this sobering tide of death ebbed and flowed.

The elder man drew a long breath then called out, "We have brought the one the infidels have supplied."

Silence reigned for a pulse-quickening stretch.

He boomed again. "Zarchamidion, father of destruction, come forth that our bargain may be fulfilled. And dare no treachery, as I don't think you'll like the way I'll answer that."

The stifling wind that wafted over them died in a snort. A tremor rolled from within the cave and sent a vibration up from the ground and through Delquessa's sandal soles.

"Durik, you mad sack of parlor tricks, you presume to threaten?" The earth-rumbling voice came from the cave. "Mind your manners, or I'll eat your army and broker my own deal with whatever Vareinorean master of Utterances you have dragged from their camp."

Delquessa felt her face blanch. *Zarchamidion?* And so her fear took form—the Standing Stones of Aromen *did* bear significance. And on that significance, too little strategy hung. Any deal brokered between Durik and the utterly corrupt wyrm could mean no good for Aeleronde.

"Ah, but you presume," Durik continued, unfazed. "Far better, I have brought you not man, but the firstborn Elf of *Celethinne Veranna*."

Zarchamidion chuckled. "You might just make something of your grasping existence yet."

The ground trembled again, first in a light shiver, but increasing to a shake that threatened to throw Delquessa off her feet. From the cave, a crimson, reptilian head emerged first, his maw lined with bloodstained fangs, and a crown of horns dislodging rock around the cavern outlet. An intense wave of heat swelled over Delquessa as the beast slithered into view.

He stopped when his shoulders had reached the surface, and he raised his head high on a sinuous, scaled neck. He regarded Delquessa with narrowed eyes.

Delquessa's captors trembled and gripped her arms tighter in their gauntleted hands.

"Give her to me."

The soldiers thrust Delquessa forward in haste, and with the speed of a viper's strike, Zarchamidion shot out a talon and snatched her from the ground, pinning her arms to her sides in a scaly, crushing clutch. His palm enveloped her from shoulders to ankles. In a serpentine coil, he bent his neck to bring her near the sharp hook at the end of his snout. The heat emanating from his maw was stifling and putrid.

"Little minion of Creo, you will undo the enchantment upon this cuff I wear, that the Standing Stones of Aromen will impede me no more." He braced the joints of his wings against the ground like an extra set of feet, then lifted his other foretalon. He pressed one claw under her gag and tore it away.

Delquessa glanced to the bronze band on Zarchamidion's free wrist. The inscription, written in the earliest character form of her own tongue, caught her notice. She casually removed her glance and stretched her sore jaw. "Creo has no minions. Not like this sham of a man you've chosen to ally yourself with."

"If your God is the omnipotent architect of all things, like you claim, then you are puppets all," Zarchamidion said.

"It is you who chooses to play the part others assign." She lowered her eyelids, but once again scanned the cuff's inscription as she spoke. "You accept the insult of serving as a puppet of lesser masters."

Durik stamped his foot. "You will do as he commands, foolish harlot!"

Delquessa lanced him with a scathing glare. "Or else what? You will spill my blood? Do you not already bear the load of enough reprimand?"

"No, I am not such a fool as to spill the blood of one of Creo's initial experiments in creation." Durik looked down his nose. "My Inquisitors, I am sure, will find ways to torture you, one generation after another, without fouling their altars with the mud of your veins. The most inventive servants shall vie for the lifelong pleasure of your torment."

Delquessa only half heard Durik's threats as she sought the full meaning behind the inscription on Zarchamidion's band. As much as escape demanded her attention, the lettering on the band tugged at the recesses of her memory … perhaps it contained information crucial to Aeleronde's campaign on the island. "You are a demented soul, Durik."

"Break the enchantment now," Zarchamidion said, "and we will spare the life of your betrothed on the battlefield. Do it not, and the first act of your torture will be to watch the flesh melt from his bones." The back of the wyrm's throat glowed with a faint yet searing aura.

Betrothed. Delquessa's breath caught. *How could they know this?* "The ways of men are so foreign to me, but dragons, even more so." Her mind reeled as she sought to piece together the convoluted connection between Durik, the dragon, and the new developments they had learned about her. With her betrothal largely unspoken, how could the dragon have gotten word of it?

"You are stalling—no doubt to buy your precious Vareinor time." Durik huffed. "You have one turn to figure this out before Aeleronde becomes the first target of Zarchamidion's inescapable wrath." He drew a small hourglass from his pocket, flipped it, and started the grains flowing from the upper chamber to the lower. He clipped the timer to a chain around his neck.

"And what if I do not possess the knowledge of how to disable this ward?" Delquessa said.

"Then you would be declaring yourself illiterate of the early forms," Durik thundered, his face reddening. "I know you can read this!" He jabbed a finger at Zarchamidion's cuff. "If you plead ignorance, then I will read the inscription to you, which makes it quite clear how to remove it."

Delquessa narrowed a scornful glance. "Then why did you not just take care of this yourself?" Fully aware of the answer, she braced herself for the coming storm.

Predictably, Durik blew up. "Because I will not bow to that great squelcher of talent you call God."

Delquessa laughed. "Nice try, you liar. All the bowing you could do would be to no profit. After all these years, has the truth forced you to admit that there *is* such a thing as supernatural power? That no feat of alchemy in your grasp will ever accomplish the ends Creo alone can reach?"

"Your taunts spend the last moments of Aeleronde's life, duchess," Zarchamidion said, his voice low and measured. "Surely I need not remind you of that. Or are you like your Elven brethren, who care not if the lives of men are tossed into an open grave in droves?"

Beastly schemers. Delquessa's stomach roiled. The savor of illuminating Durik's shortcomings drained away with the passing grains in the glass. She pored over the last few runes on the cuff. Revelation struck, but she hid it carefully behind a countenance of disgust.

"I will remove the cuff, but Aeleronde will be spared. You invite judgment you cannot begin to comprehend if this proves untrue."

A fiendish grin spread across Durik's yellowing teeth. "Now I believe you are the one overstating your influence. If Aeleronde stays out of the way, then I can agree I will do him no harm."

"Too many caveats!" Delquessa said.

Durik held forth the timing glass and glanced upon it. "Just how long will it take you to break the enchantment?"

The sand was more than half-passed.

Delquessa tightened her jaw. She would simply have to move faster than the wind, once the Utterances were conducted.

***

The front wheels that conveyed the lead trebuchet in Porteneum's arsenal *thunked* into a gully that ran across the winding pass through jagged, black mountains. The team of four horses pulling the machine of war scrabbled for footing as their burden lurched. Telenius rubbed his temple and wheeled his own mount toward the tower. Despite the teamster's urging, the horses did little more than jostle and creak.

Telenius surveyed the wheels, the left of which splayed at an angle from its usual position. "It's no use," he called to the driver. "Either the axle's cracked or the wheel's nearly off."

The driver mopped his brow and sent a page to hold the team, then climbed from the trebuchet to inspect the front wheels. He huffed. "Axle. Now this'll need a crew to fix it as well. By the time we get there, ol' Durik's going to have packed up and left, thinking we decided not to play."

Porteneum plodded up on his heavy-footed charger. "This pass is too treacherous for these machines. We'll be fortunate if we can get even the ballistae to the field, but the force can't wait on foundering trebuchets."

"Did the scouts ignore the terrain when they located this pass?" Telenius scowled.

"In my experience," Porteneum said, "those on foot only consider their own dexterity when assessing these things. But the driver is right … we cannot waste time here, lingering the whole force while a few discover whether these machines can be fixed. Perhaps only to fall in the next rut and start all over again."

Aeleronde approached from the front of the column. "Commander, report."

Porteneum saluted his king. "The heavier machinery is too unwieldy in these conditions, Your Highness. We will have to move the more nimble equipment and return after the battle for that we can't transport."

Behind Telenius, a cry rang in the echoing pass. He spun.

Down the line of troops, a rain of flaming arrows pelted the first trebuchet to founder in a rut. The darts *thocked* into the wooden cart and arm, followed by a burst of fire that erupted from where the arrows hit. Soldiers surrounding the siege weapon dove for cover. Smoldering, splintered wood clattered on the rocks.

Durik's devilry. Telenius spurred his mount toward the fracas just in time for another wave of arrows to speed into the pass, this time from the opposite side. They hit the next Vareinorean trebuchet with the same explosive might. What didn't blow to pieces kindled and burned.

Horses shied and trumpeted. Telenius gripped his reins to maintain mastery of his beast, all the while searching the slopes of the pass for bowmen. Soldiers in stone-gray, quite cleverly camouflaged, ducked behind boulders far up the slopes.

"Archers, return fire!" Porteneum called.

A few Vareinorean troops let ammunition fly, but few found marks in anything but the terrain.

"Accursed villains." Porteneum glared to each side of the road. "The moment you see the least flicker, make an end of the shooter."

Riding down the column of footmen, Telenius delivered orders to the captains of the units. "Swordsmen, take what cover you can. Be wary for surface assault."

Bowstrings twanged from both friend and foe, and the fiery arrows fell in pockets, always striking the siege engines, and now adding the ballistae to their targets. A greater portion of Porteneum's company targeted enemy archers before the camouflaged soldiers could take cover. The archers on both sides answered one another's volleys, though the burning darts lessened with each exchange.

Telenius raced back to the vanguard at Aeleronde's side, where a company of guards surrounded the king with full shields. No arrow lay in the path in the king's vicinity.

"No surprise Durik would harry us in a narrow place," Aeleronde said to Telenius.

A quick survey of the skirmish revealed to Telenius that only a handful, at worst, of Vareinor had fallen. The toll on their equipment had been much more dire. The storm of explosive arrows petered to an occasional shot, then halted altogether. In the wake of the attack, the crackle of flame rose on the wind. Troops threw buckets of water on the burning artillery, but the flames only sputtered and redoubled their hungry consumption of the wood.

"We've lost all the trebuchets, and it appears maybe half of the ballistae," Telenius said. "Dare we continue the march without regrouping for repairs?"

The king shook his head. "There likely isn't enough wood growing on this rock to rebuild even one."

Telenius sighed. Aeleronde spoke truth. No tree on this forsaken place was long enough of trunk or limb for planks.

Porteneum approached on horseback. "Even without the trebuchets, we can end this before the zenith."

Telenius regarded the climbing sun. "The archers' companies will be hard pressed without the engine support they're accustomed to. If Durik's forces are entrenched ..."

The commander huffed. "*My* men are adaptable." Porteneum's confidence exceeded bravado to an unbecoming level. Perhaps it was simply his way of preventing murmurs of any disadvantage the loss of their main artillery could pose.

"You know your business." Telenius ground his teeth.

Aeleronde nodded and mounted his horse. He departed for the fore of the column again, the shieldbearers at his heels.

The sooner we can get out of this pass, the better.

Telenius nudged his horse to travel against the flow of the army, now grinding into motion once again. The enemy archers surely could have whittled more of Aeleronde's troops from their perches, and yet, it seemed the only arrows that struck men were by unlucky chance. While he rode, he gathered a sense of collective relief that the snipers were repelled quickly, but nothing more unusual than that.

Until he reached the rear of the column.

At the furthest extreme of the pass he could see, a trio of riders in sable livery approached. Their fine horses and colors rumored them to be Delquessa's folk, but her palfrey was not among the animals that cantered toward Aeleronde's army. Telenius rode to meet them.

Delquessa's head steward, as well as two of her guards, raised hands in greeting to Telenius.

"Hail, members of the House Ildonian. What brings you to us?" Telenius said.

"We seek the duchess," the steward said.

Telenius tilted his head. "I am told she departed for her ship to await the tide."

The steward shook his head. "That tide is nearly lost, and the captain says the duchess never came to him. Her scow is not on the beach, but neither is it aboard her vessel."

"Then how did you learn anything of the captain?"

"We had to borrow a scow from King Aeleronde's company." The steward huffed. "We have wasted much time in fruitless chase. Is the duchess with His Majesty?"

"I am certain she is not," Telenius replied. "I have been in the vanguard with him, and I have personally inspected this column three times this morning. I would not have missed the Duchess, even in this multitude."

The Elves exchanged glances. The steward cocked a brow at the smoldering remains of a siege engine ahead. "And you are certain the duchess has come to no harm in this … incident?"

"I tell you, she is not among our company."

"Nor ours," the steward said. "This is very concerning, you understand."

Telenius turned to squint up the column of troops, but could not catch sight of Aeleronde. *Just as well.* "I do. It will be extremely distressing to His Majesty, and I believe it foolhardy to have word of this reach him until we can tell him more than 'Delquessa's gone missing.'"

One of the guards sucked a breath.

"Hear me," Telenius continued. "He is minutes away from battle, and his mind cannot be clouded with distress. I can spare … two of my younger scouts, if that will aid you in your search and convince you of our determination to settle this."

The steward frowned. "If she is not found before the battle's conclusion, I ask your pledge that His Majesty will exhaust any resource he has to find her."

"The moment any news of her absence reaches him, I assure you, Aeleronde will overturn every stone on this island and drain the sea of its water if that is what it takes to answer the question. Wait here." Telenius wheeled his horse and galloped to the troops.

He sought the company of scouts where they marched and called upon two of their number, drawing them aside before he spoke.

"The house of Ildonian has need of your services," he told them.

"Any report you have in their business is to come to me only, and that is an order."

***

And thy boundaries I turn to mist
Thy bonds I loose, in the name of Creo
Maker and protector of all

Delquessa's finger's ached as she clutched the bronze cuff and pronounced the final words of the Utterance. Despite her intention to remain impassive, she trembled, for how could she predict whether the wyrm would turn and devour her once he had his freedom? Indeed, how could a beast rumored to have no honor serve as an ally to even Queldurik once the Utterance granted his primary objective—escape?

In the name of Creo, Maker and protector of all … she would simply have to pray this protection extended to her in dire circumstances.

With a rasp and a click, a white-hot seam cut across the dragon's cuff, and the band split into two semicircles joined by a hinge. The giant piece of metalwork fell into Delquessa's outstretched arms. Its weight knocked her to her knees.

She once again intoned the words that would grant her the zephyrform, and both she and the cuff evaporated. She willed herself to drift with the breeze to a nearby cluster of rock and slipped behind it.

Durik's henchmen gasped and cowered. "What witchcraft is this?" one of the men cried.

"Her spell has obliterated her!" the other added.

Durik guffawed. "One less grief in this deal, then. Apparently, the death of Immortal Elves is less cataclysmic than tales tell." He spat on the ground. "Heed me! No word of her destruction must reach our contacts, or else they may lose their resolve to give Aeleronde into our hands with their objectives now, technically, obtained."

"But then the truce is off if he doesn't give us the king, right?" a guard asked.

"Let us hope sentimentality will not soften him to a fool," Durik replied. "No, he is a coward, and he will prefer peace for the new regime he seats upon Aeleronde's emptied throne."

Delquessa lingered behind the rock, still vaporous, and contained the gasp on her lips. Treachery! But who was the mastermind behind it?

"But the She-Elf, she was one who carried a curse, right? Will the hex be on us all?" The first guard swallowed.

Durik waved him off. "Her destruction was her own doing, surely you saw that. That, my servants, is the sort of reward that comes from their fickle liege, Creo." He faced the dragon. "Come, Zarchamidion, Lord of Destruction. Together, let us see the line of Aromen pay for your years of insult. But do not show yourself in the vale until you hear our shofar's cry."

A wicked grin curled the dragon's lips. "Those who don't burn will sate my hunger. These have been lean years."

The guards and Durik turned and climbed down the slope, and Delquessa drifted around her cover to ensure they did not mark her misty form lingering there. The ground trembled beneath the dragon's following footsteps.

Her thoughts raced. Was there some way she might stop the dragon and the leader of evil forces bent on Aeleronde's destruction from reaching the battlefield? Not through bloodshed, forbidden to her and her created kin. Her hope remained in speed, arming herself with another Utterance, and intercession. Her heart raced as she waited for her enemies to pass from sight.

The moment they passed to the northwest, she shot forth from her hiding place. What direction was the battle? The encampment? Since they had brought her to the dragon's lair unaware, she could only guess. In seeking the field of battle, she risked wandering.

She instead sped south with the knowledge that the ships had landed in a bay on the southern side of the island. *Haste, fail me not.*

Delquessa reached the coast before she found the Vareinorean warcamp. She followed the coastline for an interminably long stretch before she discovered the landing scows and churned beach where the army had come to shore. Tracing the tramped path to the campsite, she returned to her common form on the outskirts of the tents and cookfires where a few camp followers ordered supplies to tend the inevitable wounded who would return to them. In the place she sought her tents, however, she found a bare space. She set down the leaden burden of the cuff.

She caught the arm of a young squire who hustled past. "Boy! Do you know where my tents and trunks have been taken?"

The boy's eyes widened. "Mistress ... to your ship, I would guess. At least I have seen them nowhere else."

"My ship? But why?"

The boy blinked at her, dumbfounded.

"Never mind. I must charge you with a task in the name of your king." She pointed to the cuff on the ground. "You must guard this with your very life. Can you do that until I return?"

The squire paled. "I ... what is it?"

"The key to the survival or defeat of the Vareinor today. I have no time to tell you more. As the maiden pledged to your king, I charge you, let no one touch it."

The boy brought his feet together and stretched tall, but uncertainty still roiled in his blue eyes. "I will do my best, mistress."

"Which is all any of us can do." Delquessa managed a smile before she turned and ran for the shore.

∗∗∗

By midmorning, the pass finally opened into the wide bowl the scouts had explained as Durik's chosen field of battle, rimmed all around, first with scrubby rises, then sharp crags of the black rock that seemed to underlie everything on the Isle of Desolation. Here, the rock rose like spires all around the open space of the vale. Aeleronde's force entered what struck Telenius as a grim arena and found Durik's host arrayed on the southwestern rise.

Behind them, crude ramparts of hewn wood enclosed an outpost, and four towers suspended a walkway lined with archers.

Host was too grand a word. If Durik's men numbered a legion, Telenius would have been surprised. The Vareinor outnumbered them six-to-one. What was more, their archers bore only short bows, inferior in range to those the Vareinor carried. Of course, Durik had his ways of making each arrow pack extra punch. That much they had seen.

"Keep our rearguard's eyes keen," Porteneum told the captain of his scouts. "Durik has plotted something. Even he is not so foolhardy to risk open battle at these odds."

Telenius narrowed his eyes. "Without the trebuchets, their fortifications might prove problematic."

"And their flanks are heavily guarded, comparatively," the scout captain replied. "Durik has placed many archers in the rough terrain, and I have three men wounded already as a reward for investigating in that proximity."

Telenius blew a sigh. Of course, Durik did not want to be flanked, but the forbidding topography would mostly prevent that. "He's hiding something, perhaps behind his ramparts?"

"Radromirian reinforcements?" the scout said.

Possible. "Redouble vigilance over our own flanks. Assemble scouts to make further sense of their construct." Telenius nodded to the scout, who saluted him in turn before departing.

"I will place my companies closest to the pass to hold it," Porteneum said.

"I can add a detachment of footmen to your force here, Commander." Telenius tightened a rein to turn his mount back toward the vanguard.

Porteneum waved him off. "Not necessary. If any difficulty arises, we will be able to hold them at bay with bow fire until footmen can disengage the field."

Aeleronde surveyed the vale with a pursed-lipped frown upon his face.

"You believe something is missing from this picture as well, Your Highness?" Telenius said.

Aeleronde sighed. "This is utter madness otherwise. You are prepared to join me in the last grasp at diplomacy?"

Telenius scanned the Vareinorean troops, who had mostly organized into ranks and files by company within the circle of the vale. "I'm prepared at your beckon."

"Standard bearer." Aeleronde swiveled right in his saddle. "Ready the colors. We ride to parley."

Telenius rode beside Aeleronde, with the standard bearer close behind, toward the center of the field. They loped along at an easy canter, and all the while, Telenius searched the front line of Durik's troops for the trio of the opposition that should come to meet them mid-field. Durik's main standard he spotted. But it remained in the line, and no rider emerged on any of the stout Tebalese horses or riding lizards they had brought with them.

Thu-duh-thump, thuh-duh-thump, thuh-duh-thump ... the Vareinorean horses covered the grassy distance with still no sign of any negotiator to meet them. Telenius slowed his horse to a stop. He lifted a brow and met Aeleronde's glance.

"Durik!" Aeleronde's voice echoed off the hillsides. "You do me discourtesy. Come forth for the parley!"

Still, no one rode out.

"Will you spend the blood of every man and beast here in your arrogance? You know as well as I that you have breached terms set long …"

"To the abyss with your terms!" someone yelled from Durik's line.

The ball of shot in the Tebalese force's lone catapult burst into flame, and the machine fired.

The bracken where the shot landed, a furlong behind Telenius, also spouted flame. A towering blaze raced in a line that separated Aeleronde from his troops. The Tebalese force roared as one, charging forward.

Telenius swept his sword from its scabbard. *I was a fool to pray it would come to anything but this.* "To your king!" he cried, in the vain hope his lone voice would rise above the noise of flame and enemy assault.

***

When Delquessa once again reached the beach, two of her guards and her steward clustered around a slender gray landing scow from her vessel. Waves lapped at the boat's stern. When she drew within earshot of the shore, she cried out, "Laernen, for what reason has my camp been broken?"

The steward's glance snapped toward her. "Your Grace, there you are! We have been on a mad chase in search of you."

"I apologize for your difficulty, but the details are too tangled to unravel right now," Delquessa replied.

"I was under the impression that you had made your departure after the Cup of the Charge, but when we didn't find you aboard—"

Delquessa frowned. "Who, precisely, gave you this impression?"

The guards dragged the scow fully ashore.

The steward rubbed his forehead. "I am not good with Human names, Your Grace. And frankly, all the Humans look the same to me."

Delquessa put her palm to her forehead.

He tensed his face. "What is going on?"

I waste time. She brushed blowing hair from her eyes. "It does me no good to speculate at this time. I need my copy of *The Tree*."

"There will certainly be time to read in your cabin once you are aboard."

"Time. I have no time! I must have the book. Convey me to the ship, as I am yet too spent from my last Utterance to drift there myself."

The rower in the scow sagged with a weary look but did not protest. Delquessa boarded the vessel and prayed for the waters to slip by with haste like she had never seen.

On board her vessel, the gentle roll of the sea swayed Delquessa's cabin on deck, but neither the sigh of water nor the cry of sea birds could soothe her as she flipped the pages of *The Tree*.

"Where, where? Where is it?" she muttered. The Utterance of Banishment, which no ear had heard since the Patron Mystrin used it to confine The Impenetrable Darkness to the outer abyss in the dawn of days …

Delquessa scanned the page. Too far. She paged back. Finally, she landed upon the passage in her book of wisdom that unveiled the struggle that unfolded in Greymalkynne's very beginnings. She squeezed her eyes shut to recall the graven runes in Zarchamidion's cuff.

"Would it have been that Aromen had sought our help, enlisting some immortal to make a permanent disposal of this wyrm," she whispered to herself as her eyes returned to the text. "May I succeed in my aims before too many more of his descendants are gathered to him in Creo's halls." The last words came as more a prayer than rumination.

The years that passed since the Utterance's penning had subtly changed the usage in the passage, but Delquessa carefully committed each syllable, as written, to memory as she penned it to parchment as well. No use risking the chance that fear or quailing would rob her of recollection at the crucial moment. As it was, her hand and voice trembled with urgency.

With the last stroke of her pen, she leapt to her feet and dashed for the deck. "Laernen, you must take me back ashore."

The steward failed to contain his exasperated sigh. "Your Grace, I know it is not mine to question, but this begins to look like desperation."

"The Vareinor … and Aeleronde's fate is bound to things I have learned." Delquessa held forth her parchment. She breathlessly summarized what she had heard from Durik and Zarchamidion during her brief capture. She pointed back toward the beach. "Did you see the burden I left in the care of that boy on shore? It is no memento of the journey. It must go back on the dragon."

The steward's jaw dropped. "And now I am sure this is madness indeed."

"That it may be," Delquessa replied. "But all other courses spell disaster for Aeleronde and his men, I am sure of it. I will not be swayed.

Take me to shore or I will row there myself. Woe upon you if that makes me too late."

***

The trampled swath the army carved through the landscape as it marched to battle made it no challenge for Delquessa to follow after them once she reached the shore. Their tens of thousands of feet began what afterward could have been paved as a road, at least until she reached the pass, where the path became all twisted rock. One after another, she passed charred machines of war and the carts of debris the machines would have hurled at the enemy—sharp pikes, spiked balls, and shot that reeked of pitch. The smoke from their remains stung her eyes, but she pressed on.

The bronze cuff for Zarchamidion's cursed leg dragged on her, sapping her of strength with its weight, but she dared not spend her energy on the zephyrform lest she find a more desperate position on the battlefield where she would need it more and be too weakened to call upon it.

The farther into the pass she pressed, the higher the sun climbed, and the rumors of battle grew upon the wind. Clashes and bellows swelled on stiffer breezes but faded when the air stilled. The stifling scent of smoke grew. Distant, a horn called in a throaty voice. Chills ran down Delquessa's arms, despite the heat of her exertion. She redoubled her pace. The cuff dug into her shoulder.

After a handful more twists and turns, the end of the pass drew into sight, and beyond it, a rock-ringed vale spread in the sunlight. On the opposite side of the bowl, hide-clad men scrambled up the hillside in ragged disorder. The horn note sounded again.

Their backs to her, a company of men in burgundy livery stood, their front line manning a row of weapons—something like gigantic crossbows loaded with spears. She surveyed the men, and when her glance landed on Commander Porteneum's profile, she shrank behind the closest boulder.

"Disarm everything," Porteneum said.

Most of the soldiers manning the weapons loosened releases and removed the pikes they were meant to shoot. A minority of the men blinked at the commander and glanced to one another.

"With all due respect, sir, are we sure this is over?" one of the unsure soldiers said. "They appear to be reassembling."

"It's over, soldier, now follow orders."

The soldier's furrowed brow conveyed his skepticism, but he reached for his weapon and disarmed it in the same manner as the others. One of Porteneum's officers collected the ammunition along the line.

A chorus of dismay rose on the field, and Delquessa's attention shot toward the outcry. On the far side of the battlefield, Zarchamidion's wicked face, stretched in a gruesome leer, rose above the horizon. He lumbered, sinuous and gloating, from between parted gates in a ramshackle fortress.

Porteneum's company gasped, and several moved to reload their weapons.

"Stay your hands, men of the Vareinor," he yelled. "If you love your country, you will follow my command."

Nearly half the company gaped. A handful cast pained glances to their sandaled feet. The cheeks of some flared, and their eyes blazed.

The dragon slid further into the battlefield, reared high, and stretched his wings in a gruesome show of his enormousness.

"The footmen … the cavalry," a soldier sputtered. "They've no hope without ballista support." He pointed to a rise where a gold banner waved. "They call us into position."

"Such is the cost of the peace I have brokered," Porteneum said.

The peace *he* had brokered? Delquessa's jaw slackened. Her abduction, the arrangement with Zarchamidion … perhaps even the destruction of her ship and Cithredhan's death. How intertwined had this serpent been with all of it?

Beyond the gold banner, Delquessa spotted a black courser, and upon the mount's back, a tall figure in a brush-plumed helm. Her heart surged to pounding.

The dragon launched over Durik's troops and glided toward the lines of Vareinorean soldiers assembled in the center of the field.

Creo be praised that Aeleronde is not in their midst. Delquessa rebuked her selfish thought. She shifted the cuff higher on her shoulder and coiled her muscles to dash from behind the rock.

The ring of steel and the cold press of an edge across her throat slammed her to a halt.

"Commander, an intruder," the man who held Delquessa said.

Porteneum wheeled toward her, and his eye twitched. He pointed to another of his followers. "Soldier, cut out this spy's tongue. I'll not have any of her Elvish interference so close to the finish."

***

The icy grip of panic threatened to crush Telenius's chest as the red monster with the glowing maw neared the engaged companies of Aeleronde's troops.

The beast's head shot forward.

A flood of luminous liquid burst from the dragon's mouth and nostrils, and this deluge enveloped three score of Telenius's comrades. Those whom the attack did not swamp scattered in stumbling terror. Clothing, hair, and flesh upon those who suffered the onslaught burst into flame. Men writhed. The glowing orange slag that mired them to mid-thigh fettered their desperate attempts at escape. The rippling air warped their macabre contortions even further.

A strangled scream threatened to rip its way past Telenius's clenched teeth, though none would have heard it over the Vareinorean troops' strident chorus of misery—or the whoops and jeers from Durik's ragged band of onlookers.

Aeleronde bellowed above the din. "Bring me chains! We'll haul them free." He urged his courser forward. "Telenius, order some nerve back into those who retreat. And find the trumpeter who's been brought up to replace the boy who fell." Only a moment after a foot soldier had handed the king a coil of chain, Aeleronde galloped toward the magma pool and his tormented men.

Telenius whipped his horse with the loose ends of his reins, and the mount careened down the slope. At a crazed gallop, he sought whatever replacement trumpeter marched within the troops. The first clue he discovered was the long herald trumpet, decorated with Aeleronde's burgundy banner, lying on the ground. A man groveled beside it, prostrate, with his trembling hands clasped over the back of his head. Telenius leapt from his mount. He ran to the player, dragging the frenzied horse behind him. A firm wrench at the back of the trumpeter's collar hauled him to his feet.

The dragon glided over the field. He swiped with scaled talons at any Vareinorean soldier unfortunate enough to remain in his path. Some, he knocked many yards aside. Others, he snatched up in his mouth, mauled with forearm-length teeth, and spat onto the ground.

Telenius restrained his inclination to cover his ears to the screams and snap of bones. He dropped his reins and snatched up the trumpet.

"Sound the call for the reserve pikemen—javelins!" Telenius thrust the trumpet into the soldier's hand.

Ashen faced, the trumpeter nodded. He placed the instrument to his lips, faltered over a few squawking notes, and finally executed the call.

"Come with me." Telenius remounted his horse. He pulled the trumpeter up behind him and rode double toward the king's position, nearly a quarter of the field away.

The line of pikemen charged the dragon, and a small remnant of those fleeing the dragon's wrath turned to join the bolstered charge. A ballista bolt launched over their heads.

It's about time Porteneum ordered some move. When Telenius looked to the artillery line his throat constricted.

All along the line, a melee raged, but not a contest of Tebalese warriors against Porteneum's men, but of Vareinor against Vareinor. A company of soldiers brawled in an attempt to seize the ballistae, and the one successful seizure had resulted in a single shot. Two soldiers bled on the ground beside the weapon.

The pikemen struck the dragon in a grimly determined line. Their volley of flying javelins pummeled the beast. He twisted and dodged. Some of the darts glanced from his hide. Some shattered on his ancient scales. None pierced the dragon's scaly armor. What was the strength of a man's arm against such hide?

When Telenius and the trumpeter arrived at the king's side, Aeleronde was once again on foot at the edge of the dragon's lava pool. The king hauled on a length of chain. A soldier gripped the links in blackened hands with some last shred of self-preservation, but by the time Aeleronde had drawn him to the magma's edge, the victim collapsed, his body a skeletal ruin from the pelvis down. The king dropped the chain and lowered his forehead into his hand.

The stench of charred flesh assaulted Telenius's senses. He contained a retch behind his teeth and forced his attention to the wider scope of the battle against the dragon, just a furlong distant, beyond the magma pool.

The line of javelin men crashed into their enemy again and opened a handful of superficial wounds upon the beast. Only two ballista bolts had managed to pierce the dragon's shoulders and rump, eliciting a thick, purplish ooze from the wounds. This fell far short of repaying the dragon's trail of devastation.

A few determined soldiers continued to throw chains to the handful of victims who had not yet been reduced to black, smoldering husks jutting from the cracked crust of the magma around them. For many, all that remained were burning bones arrayed like vigil candles in a landscape of horror.

Telenius averted his gaze from the skeletal leers that accused everyone around them of blindness. Of foolhardiness.

"We must bring our full force to the beast," Aeleronde said. "With so few ballistae and no trebuchets ... I now see the vileness of this betrayal all the more clearly. We must kill him without artillery. Or perish trying."

Telenius took in the surrounding soldiers' varied expressions. Some of their faces drained to an ashen pallor while others set their jaws, the ice in their eyes a thin shell over the depth of their realization—death closed in. Still others crumpled under the weight of hopelessness. One man's spear clattered from his grasp.

"Porteneum holds the pass against us!" a soldier said.

"All will be repaid," Aeleronde said, his tone icy. After a deep breath, he clashed his sword against his shield. "Trumpeter, sound the charge. Standard-bearer, plant my colors high that none might dispute! Aeleronde the Fair shall take this field of war today and show the world not even treachery will unman Creo's chosen."

Once again, the trumpeter winded his horn, and the percussive notes that called soldiers not to retreat, but a full charge, pierced the air. Telenius puffed his chest, prepared to run unto death and glory for his king. If any tale made it back to his people, it would not say Telenius fought fainthearted.

The vanguard raised their voices in a shout to nerve themselves and one another, and they flew in the face of the dragon. The beast skidded to a halt, his eyes wide.

"Fan out!" Aeleronde yelled to his troops. "Do not present him with a cluster to annihilate in one maneuver."

***

Delquessa froze against the press of the blade, and her stomach roiled as the dragon let loose his magma blast on Aeleronde's helpless company.

The commander strode up to her and knocked the dragon cuff from her shoulder. It tumbled two paces away.

"What have you done?" Porteneum gaped at the cuff. "Is that what I think it to be?"

He grabbed her by the hair upon the crown of her head and wrenched her head back, then looked to the man on his left. "I gave you an order."

The soldier drew a knife from his belt but hesitated.

Delquessa's captor withdrew his sword from her throat and turned her toward the soldier brandishing the knife. "On with it. Before she bewitches us, as she did the king!"

Though Porteneum's grip on her hair sent sharp waves through her scalp, Delquessa took the opportunity to connect gazes with the knife man. He swallowed. A tremor shook his weapon hand.

Preserve me. Help me reach the cuff, Creo.

"You overreach, Porteneum," Delquessa said. "Even your closest accomplices smell the reek of your lies." Over Porteneum's shoulder, she glimpsed Aeleronde charging the field, long loops of chain over his shoulder. She must reach her beloved before the dragon was prepared to douse them all again.

"Silence your ill-informed mewling." Porteneum snatched the knife from his unsure soldier.

Delquessa swiped for the blade and grabbed it. Its edge bit against her palm and fingers, but she tightened her grip. Beads of her blood trickled down the blade.

The glove on Porteneum's knife hand began to smoke, and the Commander's eyes widened. He released the weapon.

"Sorceress!" He ripped the burning glove off.

Free of his grasp, Delquessa dove for the cuff. The moment her fingers made contact with the carven metal, she once again intoned her Utterance, and both she and the cuff dissolved to vapor.

Delquessa sped through the narrow spaces between Porteneum's men as chaos broke out among them. Shouts of accusation and the scuffle of a brawl rose behind her, but she spared no glance to their tumult. The conflict with the dragon was her only focus, as grisly as that scene had become.

Aeleronde's soldiers fell upon Zarchamidion, and as much as Delquessa longed to see the world rid of such an evil as he, so much less did she desire to witness the actual brutality needed to corral the beast. The ring of swords, the cries of men, the thumps of bodies hitting the ground, all these sounds assaulted her ears as shot from the midst of the fray.

Aeleronde himself hewed at the hide of the dragon. What blows slashed past chinks in the wyrm's armor flung steaming purple blood across the rocks. The strokes that glanced aside showered sparks. Members of the vanguard charged in with their attacks, but most added to the sparks rather than the blood. At Aeleronde's command, the soldiers ran at Zarchamidion in small clusters, plunged swords or spears, then withdrew. Only Aeleronde himself engaged the dragon with ceaseless, grim vigor.

Major Telenius led a trio of warriors into the tumult. One soldier whirled a chain mace that cracked against Zarchamidion's shoulder, which the dragon answered by shooting a claw to the offender, snatching him up, and hurling him thirty yards distant. The second soldier jabbed a spear, but the haft splintered upon impact. Telenius, however, slashed upward with a two-handed hew, which cleft deep into Zarchamidion's neck and sent scales clattering to the ground.

The dragon roared and spun. A raging sweep of his tail knocked a half-dozen soldiers to their backs. Telenius withdrew.

Aeleronde took a glancing blow to the shoulder which spun him twice. Led by Telenius, members of the vanguard charged in front of the king and formed a Human blockade between Aeleronde and the wyrm. Once Aeleronde had backpedaled enough to regain his footing, another handful of soldiers joined Telenius in further melee. The dragon was as distracted as he could be.

Delquessa sped to Aeleronde's side and dismissed the zephyrform. "Beloved—"

Aeleronde wheeled toward her, and his face blanched. "I cannot be seeing truth. You are not here." He grabbed her arm and dragged her three paces from the fray.

Delquessa dug in her heels and slowed his forced retreat. "Alas, my lord, I cannot depart. Not without dismissing Zarchamidion and preventing further destruction." She tugged the parchment she had penned from her belt.

"What?" Aeleronde shook his head. He towed Delquessa another handful of strides.

Delquessa glanced back to the dragon. He was whittling through his foes, but Telenius still led the squadron in holding their ground. Zarchamidion's eyes blazed. He bent his serpentine neck and bit off a chunk of rock to his right, then gulped it down. Their time grew short.

"I know a way to defeat him, but I need your help to get close to him." Delquessa shook the folds from her parchment to open it.

"Close?" Aeleronde said. "No, you should flee this insanity."

"Think of your men, beloved. How many do you think will escape Zarchamidion's wrath?"

Behind Delquessa, a scream and a series of nauseating crunches underscored her words.

Aeleronde blew a breath. "What must we do?"

"Keep the dragon busy," Delquessa replied. "I will charge once the Utterance has been spoken."

The king covered his face with his hands then heaved a breath. "I should have left Durik sitting on his trap." Aeleronde kissed Delquessa's cheek, blinked back a tear, then turned for the battle.

She watched Aeleronde's determined run for only a moment before she focused her attention on the words of the Utterance one last time. Delquessa lifted the cuff from her shoulder and held it before her, taking slow steps toward the dragon. She raised her voice in a flowing chant.

"Teumna, ichnir sinithwe e lemiren e Creo.
Na fermetten imbirim is vellathin lumie is panet astred
Tre achrennethe aht sen dir strediret en rieo.
Unde pa ichen telcheriame sen vumires en se illiana
I gilvaraines en se tor."

Zarchamidion snapped his head toward Delquessa. His eyes narrowed. Though Telenius delivered one furious stroke after another to the dragon's chest, the beast ignored him. Instead, he lanced Delquessa with a venomous glare.

"You think your ancient poems and feeble bronze can contain me again?"

Aeleronde hacked at Zarchamidion's side, opposite Telenius, and scales flew. The dragon snapped, but Aeleronde's deft dodge spun him clear of the rending teeth.

Delquessa pushed the dragon's taunts from her mind and kept intoning the words. One step after another, her strides drew her closer to her goal. Nearly within reach of disaster.

"You stand on the brink of your destruction!" Telenius bellowed.

"No, little pawn, that would be you." Zarchamidion lifted a clawed foreleg, thick as the bole of a tree, and smashed it down upon Telenius. The dragon pinned him to the rock with bone-crushing weight.

"Telenius!" Aeleronde cried out, his face creased and eyes brimming with tortured fury.

"*Ben pa Ramenna thula is Creo's cele is aster, earrestennen sen!*" The divine words swelled until Delquessa's voice cracked.

Zarchamidion sneered. He reared his head back. Opened his jaws—and the white inferno within flared.

"Assist the duchess!" Aeleronde bellowed.

Three vanguard soldiers rushed to the dragon's side, flanking him and preventing any effort to dodge the king's attack. Aeleronde ran at the beast and leapt into the air. The Warrior King of the Vareinor swung, and his sword edge slashed across the wyrm's left eye. Zarchamidion reeled. His foretalon swung toward Aeleronde, as though fending off a hornet's sting.

Delquessa plunged forward with the cuff and clamped it upon Zarchamidion's foreleg once again. A flare of light enveloped the dragon, the king, and the field around them. A screech overwhelmed the air until it throbbed with the intensity of the keen. Every remaining soldier collapsed to his knees, his hands clapped over his ears.

A flash erupted. Delquessa launched backward and skidded across the rocky ground before she came to a painful halt. The bright light over the battlefield faded away in a sparkling flurry of iridescent flakes that drifted to the blackened earth.

When Delquessa hauled herself upright again, she failed to locate Aeleronde. The dragon was gone … had the king been spirited away with him? Her glance roved over the battlefield, the prone bodies, the few soldiers righting themselves from the shockwave of the banishment. Telenius lay among the fallen—the shapelessness of his crushed bones and wordless moans foretold his imminent collection back to Creo's halls.

Finally, she caught sight of Aeleronde's form, lying on his back many paces from her. Delquessa cast a conflicted glance between Telenius and her beloved. Despite Telenius's peril, she dashed to Aeleronde.

The king's armor wept a pulsating torrent of bright red through a gash in the breastplate a hand span wide. A pool of Aeleronde's blood spread quickly amidst the rocks, filling the cracks with vermillion rivulets.

"He could not go without this parting shot, so it seems," Aeleronde whispered, his voice as broken as the earth beneath him. "By Creo's mercy, I glimpse you though I am fallen."

Tears stung Delquessa's eyes as she smoothed Aeleronde's mired hair away from his face. "My beloved, fallen? No, you have prevailed. Creo shall mend you, and then we shall see Porteneum does not dodge his due." She reached to place her hand upon his chest, lifted her face to the heavens, and implored Creo for the power to heal Aeleronde's hurts.

No wave of divine healing swept through her body.

She glanced down at Aeleronde's face. His eyes were dull. Unseeing.

Her hand flew to his neck. No beat of life throbbed there. She tore his vambrace from his arm to press her fingers to his wrist, but to no avail. Delquessa brought trembling hands to her mouth. *Too late?* How was it possible? The weight of all the ages to come, those she would spend bereft of her beloved, crashed upon her. The inescapable reality that she had played straight into the circumstances that wrought his ruin cackled in her ears with demonic accusation. She collapsed.

Somewhere distant, the frenzied call of retreat rode upon the wind, its notes thin and desperate. What remained of Aeleronde's vanguard shuffled.

Someone reached down and clasped Delquessa's shoulder. "Duchess, the battle with Durik's force is not yet won. Our comrades need us."

"Go on," Delquessa said through her tears. "I will guard the body of your king. May Creo grant you victory over the betrayers."

The afternoon waned into evening, and the clashes of battle faded to silence, leaving Delquessa with only the hiss of the wind through the crags around her as companion. She arrayed Aeleronde's corpse with his sword clasped upon his chest. The time passed uncounted as she worked with bloodied hands; the stain wormed its way between the stones of her betrothal ring and darkened them. Even in death, Aeleronde retained his nobility, though his youth rent Delquessa's heart.

In the last light of twilight, the approach of footsteps dragged her attention away from the fallen. The murmur of discussion grew as well, until she made out an individual voice.

"There he is. Gather the body, but do it no disservice. We need not induce hysteria in the people when we return."

Delquessa did not care who spoke. Nor did she need to look up to know the faces she would see would be those who exchanged secret discourse on their journey to the isle, those that disarmed the artillery without question. Several sets of sandaled feet approached Aeleronde's body and encroached upon her peripheral vision. Delquessa refused to dignify their owners' presence by meeting their gazes.

"You will not touch him," she said. "I shall brook no murderer's hand upon the fallen."

"Step aside, Elf," came another voice from a distance.

At this, Delquessa willed her gaze to intercept the newcomer.

"As it should be, I see his blood is on your hands." Commander Porteneum shouldered his way through the men around him. His short cloak whipped in tatters in the rising gusts. His lorica bore many dents and minor rents, and blood crusted the rivets and buckles. Red blood. The blood of men, not a dragon.

Delquessa's breath grew short. She narrowed her tear-stung eyes at the commander. "How dare you implicate me?" The words rang hollow to her ears, however. Had she not come to the isle, she never would have been on hand to remove the cuff from the dragon, and …

Creases of fury deepened across Porteneum's face. "You believe you are the only person to lose in this regrettable circumstance? I loved Aeleronde as a dear brother, but when he would not listen to reason, I had to act. For the sake of our people and the preservation of our heritage."

The grind of armor over stone warred for Delquessa's notice. She stole a glance behind her. Telenius dragged his broken body toward the exchange with Commander Porteneum.

"Betrayer!" Telenius rasped. He pushed up on an elbow and shook a sword smeared with plum-colored gore at the Commander. "How could you?"

"So you did survive," Porteneum said. "Well, that helps. You can thank me for your throne after the healers prevent those wounds from festering." At the Commander's nod, a pair of men dashed to Telenius' side.

Telenius batted away the first hand that reached down to his aid. "My throne. A throne I never desired. You have much wronged all the Vareinor."

Porteneum's lips pulled into a pinched line. "The sovereignty of our people will be in loyal hands with you on the throne, Telenius. Surely you see that."

"Your sovereignty?" Delquessa threw her hands into the air. "When was such a thing ever at risk?"

"Spare us your play-acting at innocence!" Porteneum snorted. "We would not have our throne usurped by the Elves, perchance for eternity, with you sitting upon it. Be thankful we settled this with the shedding of only the blood of our own, rather than involving your nation in a future revolution."

A contorting wrench of pain and despair overcame Telenius, and though he moved his lips, no words came. The healers bore him away, and more than his broken bones, Delquessa perceived in the twist of his body and the fire in his eyes a man perhaps even more wronged than she herself was. She rose to face down her accuser.

"I have seen the height of man's foolishness today," she said. "You would supplant Aeleronde, a man born to be king—and not just by lineage, but by his God-given gifts—with a man who long admitted to no such aspirations?"

"Aeleronde proved that his affections were too easily swayed from his duty and from good counsel."

Delquessa guffawed. "Good counsel. Had you taken *this concern* to Aeleronde in counsel, he would have explained our intent that I would return to my own duchy upon Aeleronde's passing. Neither I nor my people desire your kingdom."

The sergeant closest to Porteneum shot his leader a stricken look, as did many of the other soldiers in the group. "Did you know this?"

"His intentions were not the ones that concerned me most," Porteneum said with a wave of his hand. His voice rose to address all within earshot. "Anyone who believes a queen who occupies the greatest throne among men for decades would simply relinquish it when her husband passes is a blind fool."

"The Elves have ever been our allies," someone yelled from the pack.

"Only to supplant us!" cried another.

More men's voices joined the war until no word could emerge over another.

"Enough!" Porteneum bellowed over all. "You have done what is best for the Vareinor today. We shall return to Bilearne and see to it that Telenius takes Aeleronde's place. He will choose to have eyes for his own people."

Despite Delquessa's compulsion to slump over Aeleronde's body and join him in death, a will beyond her own swept rampant through her flesh until her members tingled. Her back straightened. Her tears dried in the stiff breeze.

"Betrayers and kinslayers!" Her voice rose with a terrible might so far beyond her mortal capacity that Porteneum's entourage quailed. "It falls not to the likes of you to shepherd a people you have crossed. Nay, Almighty Creo pronounces a judgment upon you, that none of your treacherous number shall return to Bilearne and be mistaken for friends to the Vareinor. Death you deserve, but as one of Creo's Firstborn and Unstained, death is not my province. What I deal you, however, you may deem worse than to be slain."

She thrust her hands to the heavens, just as a pillar of white flame lanced down from the sky to envelop her. It broke from her as fractured light from a crystal, piercing the body of every renegade soldier in the company before her and beyond to the battlefield below. Men screamed and writhed as their flesh blackened and transformed from the smooth, fair complexions of Vareinor men to hides of scales. Faces elongated into lizard snouts lined with pointed teeth. Hands curled into claws. Tails, ridged and cumbersome, grew where there had been none.

When the light faded, the kinslayers stared agape at one another.

"Monsters—you have made us abominations!" Porteneum said, though his newly-shapen mouth marred the words. His armor hung in broken ruin upon his burly, scaled hide.

"Dragon-kin I name you," Delquessa replied. "Those who used the dragon to enact your petty schemes, though scorned by true dragons you shall ever be. No man shall ever wonder what trust you deserve— he only need look into your slit pupils to know to revile you."

"Who are you to enact judgment?" Porteneum stalked toward her. He placed a clawed hand on the hilt at his hip.

"Not I, but Creo through me," Delquessa said. "You have invited cursing enough, coward that you are, without the backbone to murder Aeleronde with your own hands. Surely you have not forgotten, Creo decrees woe unto those who would slay one of his Firstborn, whom he created to walk the lands before Man, Gnome, or Dwarf."

The draconic Porteneum halted. "Worse than this?"

Delquessa glared, full of venom. "Dare you discover how that is even possible?"

From behind Porteneum, a murmur broke loose, like a single small stone that bounces down a cliff face, freeing others as it falls until a hail of pebbles cascades down.

"What do we do now?"

"Head to the ships?"

"Those loyal to Aeleronde will hold them against us. We'll rot on this forsaken island!"

Porteneum turned to his rebel band. "Silence! We shall find a way to amend this witchcraft."

"Witchcraft?" a reptilian foot soldier replied. "She called this down from Creo himself. We cannot appeal such a judgment."

Desperation swarmed through the horde of Reptilian men, their clothes shredded to accommodate their twisted bodies, their bulbous eyes rounded while they argued. Delquessa grimaced at the grotesqueness. Her heart clenched at their pitiable fate. But above all, the bleakness that threatened to break her mind every time she glanced again at Aeleronde's still face pulled her back to her knees. An argument between the dragon-kin rose to a fevered pitch, but no clear word of it reached her ears. Porteneum backed away from his subordinates as their fury boiled against him.

The prattle receded from Delquessa's mind long before the rebels withdrew from the spot where she knelt over Aeleronde's form. But withdraw they did, to leave her alone with the corpse of her beloved. Creo's might departed from her as well, and the gray mantle of loneliness without end, her culpability in so many devastations, settled upon her shoulders and laid her low. She cast an agonized gaze to the body that lay at her feet.

A single crow cawed from the branches of a gnarled tree. The amber moon, now full, rose behind its black, skeletal shadow.

Delquessa clasped Aeleronde's stiff hand. She longed to interlace her fingers with his one last time, but his death-grip upon the hilt she herself had placed in his hand prevented her. Hot tears cut tracks down her cheeks. Though the notes broke and stuttered, a song wove its way from her soul and through her lips.

My body lives beyond my will
My heart is slain within me
Though we had not yet sealed our troth
My soul is cleft unto thee

The press of intervening years
This earth shall ever see
They weigh upon me
They weigh upon me

But here at thy side
I shall remain
Thy barrow shall serve as my dwelling place

No thief shall steal
No rogue molest
Whilst I remain to guard thy rest

Until the legions of the stars
Fall from a blackened sky
'Til all the earth is torn and changed
I raise my woeful cry

Beyond the span of marching time
My vigil I shall keep
Too pierced to weep
Too pierced to weep

***

Telenius, High King of the Vareinor, stepped with limping stride from his landing scow onto the rock-strewn shore of the Isle of Desolation, and how much bleaker the place seemed now than during his last arrival there five months ago. The wind howled through the jutting shale, and the discordant tones within its whistle ran a shudder from the soles of his feet to his crowned head.

"Keep a sharp eye," Telenius told his vanguard of a half-dozen men. "No telling what mischief the kinslayers might make. That is, if they have not already devoured one another with treacherous appetite."

Soldiers drew swords and brandished shields as one.

"You are certain you want to risk this investigation, Your Majesty? This is your last chance to turn back from the notion," Telenius's chamberlain said from the front-most seat in the scow. He eyed the staff in the king's hand.

"Still positive," Telenius replied. "I was not spared death to leave this untried."

The king picked his way along the dread path that led through the coastal crags and into the interior vale. Though his men jumped at every rustle of dried bracken, the lands within sight remained incontestably empty. The whistle of the wind grew in depth and complexity, and Telenius often glanced to his men to see who whispered among them but always found them all tight-lipped and silent.

Still, they pressed on. Soldiers gripped their hilts and their spears with banded knuckles. Jaws clenched. Eyes flitted from crag to crag. But no foe reared a reptilian head. Nothing assaulted them but the relentless, soul-chilling sound of the wind.

The closer they drew to the place where Aeleronde fell, the worse the press of inexplicable fear became. A young spearman, new to Telenius's vanguard, dropped to his knees and clapped his hands over his ears.

"I cannot go on, may you forgive me, my liege. The words on the wind! They haunt me. I cannot tell what they say, but my soul writhes in a nameless anguish." Tears spilled down the spearman's ashen cheeks. "Let me go back to the ship, my lord."

Telenius stooped beside the soldier to clasp the man's shoulder. He spoke in a low voice. "For the love of Aeleronde the Fair, find your courage, servant of the crown."

The spearman drew a shuddering breath but then turned his beset eyes to his king. "For him, and for you, Your Majesty. I will try to follow."

The phalanx pressed on through the pass in the mountains, and the pall brought on by the banshee moan in the air took hold of the men, one by one. When they spied a tall cairn on the crest of the next rise, all but a stalwart pair looked as though they would flee their own skin if they could.

Chaedhenne, chaedhenne passereth lamyedhet …

Telenius's spine went rigid. He searched the faces of his men. Did they hear? Did they understand?

"Pierced, pierced beyond weeping," he whispered.

None regarded him as they lived their own private horror behind eyes squeezed shut and ears covered against the battering wind. With icy fingers, it pried into the soul and demanded mourning of all who heard, of this Telenius was certain.

"Stay here, all of you," he ordered. A twinge of disappointment pricked his heart when none contested him. Nonetheless, he struck out for the cairn in the distance. Every step closer intensified the lash of anguish that beat upon him. He hung on his staff. Despair dragged him to a crawl by the time he came within a few yards of the mound. He collapsed upon the piled rocks and wept.

"Leave me! Wretched sorcery, I seek only to learn what may have become of Aeleronde the Fair's beloved and bear her back to her own lands if she wishes it."

The invasion of lamentation abated, if only enough to make it bearable. Though Telenius did not see from where, the graceful figure of Delquessa emerged, her gossamer gown fluttering in ragged tatters. Spectral was the only word that seemed fitting in Telenius' mind to describe her.

She approached the cairn, and her distant gaze encompassed all the sense of misery and loss Telenius had felt as he fought his way to the spot. Somehow, his own suffering seemed minute compared to the eternal woe in Delquessa's eyes, whose color had faded to nearly white. He wondered if she was indeed a corporeal being any longer. His hand hovered somewhere between reaching and recoiling.

"You come to offer me passage back to the Emerald Valley." Her words came in a slow monotone, and she did not look at Telenius.

"Your people need you, Your Grace," Telenius replied. "They sorely feel the lack of your wise and gentle rule. Lesser mortals eye your province to usurp—"

"Trouble me not with the fleeting concerns of a dying world." Fire flashed in the Elf maiden's eyes. Delquessa focused briefly upon Telenius, and the weight of her regard crushed his last shreds of composure.

He sprawled on the ground and groveled at her feet. He could not force even a stammering response to pass his lips.

Delquessa grew distant again. "No, to act as a tombwarder is my province, and thus it shall be until the Maker pronounces the end of days. With mine own hand, I laid these stones. Neither the body nor the memory of my beloved shall suffer further betrayal while I can prevent it."

Telenius breathed in slow draughts as he lay prone until he eventually mastered his quaking limbs and hammering heart. With his staff as a prop, he found the strength to regain his feet. "If that is your wish, Your Grace."

He backed away from the place and the keening wind swelled again, only this time, he understood its endless refrain, that of Delquessa's gnawing woe. He drew his soldiers off, and only when they had crossed the coastal plain and their ship stood in sight did any of them recover enough composure to speak.

"She will not come?" a soldier asked.

Telenius maintained a fixed gaze over the gray swells beyond his vessel. "The grace and beauty of Delquessa Ildonian is lost to the mortal world, entombed forever with the king she loved."

Rebecca P. Minor is the author of *The Windrider Saga* and *The Risen Age Archive*, soon to be re-released in new editions. When she's not writing or drawing elves and dragons, she makes her home northwest of Philadelphia with her husband, Scott, and three boys, who are happy to storm castles or visit fantastic worlds at her side.

Undermined

By Gretchen E. K. Engel

KYAN MONTURE WINCED AS the auctioneer locked the shackle onto Brecht's ankle. The metal clanked finality. The morning sun glistened through her younger brother's dark green hair and sparkled off the mechanical bird bouncing in his hand. Kyan tweaked one of its metallic wings, then slipped Brecht a slim tube of white powder. Perfecting the device was the ultimate tribute to their parents' memory.

Brecht fitted the vial inside the bird like a glass gullet. "Thanks." He squeezed her hand, then shuffled to the stall containing the other boys. With dyed hair and two years added to his thirteen to compensate for height, her brother might pass as a Pixie. Fairy nobles would only see colored hair and pointed ears. Hopefully, they wouldn't notice Brecht and Kyan were Elves.

The Detention prohibited Elves from leaving Etheria. When the news had first hit, Kyan's only concern was whether or not she'd get a visa when it was time to return to Elgnom for university. Now, the Detention was the difference between freedom and a life of servitude.

Brecht stepped onto the block. The auctioneer shook a sheet of paper and held it at arm's length. "Northern Pixie. Fifteen years. Says here he's a mech-an-ic. He's wiry, able to plow or wield a pickaxe. He's kind of pretty. Might make a good footman or valet. Nice hair, skin, and teeth. Recently orphaned. He ain't a street urchin. Bidding starts at one hundred bluebacks." The man yanked Brecht's bird from his hand and dashed it to the ground. "You don't need possessions. You are property."

Kyan gasped. Her tether to Brecht snapped. When this was over, she might never see another family member for the remainder of her life.

A stout Fairy with thin gray hair matching his suit raised his paddle. "Going once, going twice—sold to Mr. Graman."

The name fit Mr. Graman's appearance. The auctioneer shoved Brecht to the other end of the platform, then kicked the battered bird in his direction.

Losing family was harder than losing freedom.

Mr. Graman leaned to her brother's ear, then Brecht loped to the auction block and retrieved his bird like a proud puppy. She'd made the right choice shielding her brother from the brutal reality of slavery. Based on the man's gesture, perhaps Brecht had a kind owner.

Brecht's owner purchased two other boys, an older teen about Kyan's age and one no more than ten. Mr. Graman ushered them to the shade tree where he distributed paper sacks and canteens to the boys. Brecht pulled out a sandwich and tore into it as if he hadn't had three eggs and six sausage links that morning.

Kyan's stomach lurched. She'd be lucky to gag down two bites. And she wouldn't bet on owners as kind as her brother's—she could only hope. Still, she felt the first glimmer of hope since she'd decided to follow Papa's baffling instructions urging them to leave school and put themselves up for sale.

Kyan lifted her fuchsia braid away from her damp neck and fanned herself with her hand. Used to northern weather at school, Kyan wasn't ready for the assault of heat and humidity. She rubbed at the folded paper. Papa's final instructions were written in his engineer's scrawl across yellow graph paper. Dated the day he died, it was witnessed by Papa's boss, Mr. Norock, and sealed with the NM logo of Norock Mines.

The man Kyan blamed for her parents' deaths.

If the reports were to be believed, her father hadn't been one to follow regulations. But Kyan knew that wasn't the truth. Every time she'd disobeyed, Papa had reminded her that honoring her parents would bring her long life. Now, she had to obey like never before. Kyan owed it to them, the way she'd resented the move to Etheria.

She clung to that promise. Especially now that her parents were gone.

The boys' auction ended. Well-dressed Fairy women exchanged seats with rough laborers for the girls' auction. Most of the boys went to individual owners who left as soon as the bluebacks exchanged hands. Mr. Graman returned to the area with his paddle tucked under his arm and perused the sales list. Kyan closed her eyes and prayed she and Brecht could stay together. Stupid and selfish and unlikely.

Three more owners with multiple slaves pulled away when the last boy was loaded. That left Mr. Graman and two others—neither good. A lean Fairy with a sharp, creased face cursed his purchases and cracked his whip more than once. His group huddled, chained together in the back of a covered wagon. At least he had a bucket of water and a ladle. The only other owner herded his slaves to a holding pen by the trash bins, away from all shade, without food or drink. And his whip hit flesh, not the air.

Twenty-one girls later, Kyan stepped toward the auction block herself. Each sale brought different emotions. Kyan empathized with the ones who went with the hard men, and she envied the few Mr. Graman purchased. He distributed kind words with their sack lunch.

The auctioneer caressed her calf while he confirmed the number on her shackle. Kyan balled her fist, ready to punch the man if his hand slid higher. He pressed his mouth to her ear. Rancid breath seeped into her nose. "You could use some curves, but pretty 'nuff for most purposes." Kyan made herself relax her fists.

He stepped away and addressed the crowd. "We have an ed-u-cated young lady. She even knows Elf tongue. 'Course, you only wants to know if she can make pickled tongue and babies." He grabbed her hand and rubbed it with his thumb. Kyan grimaced but didn't dare pull back. "Pretty and soft. She'd be good for dusting your parlor or teachin' your children." Or violating. Kyan had heard stories. She didn't know many Fairy nobles, but she'd met enough arrogant ones to believe it. The auctioneer commenced bidding.

A Fairy woman in a lilac and yellow striped dress tugged at the lean man's sinewy arm. Each tug raised the bid against Brecht's owner. Kyan closed her eyes and prayed to stay with her brother.

Mr. Graman bid.

The sharp creased man bid higher. "Three hundred bluebacks."

Mr. Graman looked at his sheet.

"Going once."

Mr. Graman thumbed through his wallet. The hard man smirked.

"Going twice."

Sweat darkened his gray hair as he searched each pocket. The auctioneer raised his gavel, then pounded the sound block. "Sold. Another fine purchase for Mr. Anglier."

"Five-hundred bluebacks …" Mr. Graman waved a folded blue bill then tucked it back in his waistcoat pocket. He hung his head and muttered something about not doing his job.

"It's a short drive to the master's." The gruff man ushered Kyan onto the wagon. Would the master be any kinder? Probably not.

The woman in the striped dress sidled next to Kyan and handed her a small paper bag. "Never mind Mr. Anglier and his whip. It's only to scare the savage ones. You'll be a house servant, perhaps a governess." The woman prattled on about what a good position Kyan would have since she had good skin, but Kyan might have to color her hair its natural color. As she chatted, the woman threaded a cable through Kyan's shackle, securing her to her bench mate and an anchor on the wagon. Once secured, Kyan stood to glimpse Brecht one more time. The horses jolted forward then stopped. Kyan grasped the side to keep from pitching forward.

"It's only for the ride. Mr. Anglier paid a good price for you ladies." The woman abandoned her light tone and spoke with practiced words, avoiding the term slave. She distributed paper bags. Kyan didn't care about words as long as the master and mistress were merciful. Only time would tell.

Mr. Anglier urged his cart past an idling steam wagon with a driver seated on the left—and Brecht with his wide-eyed, wide-mouthed grin on the right. "I get to drive a steamer."

Kyan waved to her brother until they rounded a corner and passed out of view. Carefree as always. The brilliant boy was innocent and impractical. No doubt, he pictured a home with a workshop and hours to tinker with metal and wires. Kyan put in another request. *Don't let Brecht grow hard with a life of mindless labor. Let him use his mind.* She turned to the girl seated next to her, a young slave of about seven or eight.

The ragged child with auburn ringlets trembled. Tears streamed from her blue-green eyes. A half-Elf. "Me sister got bought by Mr. Stricklin. He beats his people." The hard man. "And don't feed 'em." The girl clutched a worn fabric dragon that leaked a bit of sawdust from its tail. A few grains poked through worn spots on its belly. "Took me sister's and ripped 'is head clean off." The girl tightened her grip on the creature. "'Ope Angle man don't do that to Steam here."

Kyan plucked a piece of candy from her lunch sack and handed it to the girl. "I don't think owners who give out caramels hurt stuffed dragons." Kyan leaned in toward her pale freckled face. "Real dragons maybe, but only if they were going to eat a little girl." Kyan bared her teeth in a growl.

The girl giggled. Easing the child's fears vaporized hers.

"My name's Breezy. Yours? Did your mam and pap die too?"

Kyan closed her eyes and nodded. The pain stole her voice.

Two years ago, Papa and Mam took jobs in Etheria. A grand adventure that was more fun for her parents than Brecht and Kyan. Papa was the chief engineer at Norock Mines and Mama one of the chemists. Brecht and Kyan endured Fae private school, where grades were based on their family's place in the peerage. As non-nobles and token foreigners, Brecht and Kyan were met with equal measures of curiosity and contempt. They were the students with the odd accents, no rank, and high marks they earned themselves.

Breezy patted Kyan's hand. "I didn't talk for a year. But then I turned five. I'm seven now and talk a lot. Sister says too much." Bruises spotted the girl's bony arms.

A few minutes later, they stopped at the iron gates of a massive stone wall. Mr. Anglier cursed and dismounted from the wagon. He walked in front of it, out of Kyan's sight. She caught a glimpse of gray hair and a dark suit. Perhaps Mr. Graman. A few moments later, Mr. Anglier hoisted himself back onto the wagon with a fresh set of expletives as he made a sharp turn through the gates.

A familiar ancient estate loomed in the distance—Mr. Norock's. Kyan's knuckles blanched. Betrayed. She'd visited here several times since they'd moved to Etheria. The dinners were always pleasant escapes to Elgnom with familiar food and the latest news of their Elven friends. Never was there a hint that Mr. Norock was their enemy.

But everything changed when the Fairy nobles decreed the Detention last fall. Her parents hadn't been themselves over winter break. Dad paced. One night, Mom cleaned the same pot three times. Hushed conversations behind the library doors replaced family game time. Even then, Kyan never suspected Mr. Norock. But word came that they were among the missing when the tunnel had collapsed, and Kyan wondered. Why had they been there? Mama worked in the laboratory. Papa spent most of his time in the office next to Mr. Norock. It didn't make sense. Apprehension condensed in her stomach as they progressed to his front door.

The wagon stopped outside of the large front door where she'd once entered as an honored guest. A footman came out and unfastened the slaves, then ushered them through the grand entry as if they were attending a ball. Mr. Graman met them then, and Kyan instantly felt better—at least a bit. He led Breezy and the other children through the dining room to what she assumed was the kitchen. When the children left, the footman stopped in front of Kyan. "Welcome, Miss Monture.

Mr. Norock is expecting you. We're especially delighted to have you." The feeling was one-sided. The few bites of sandwich Kyan had managed to choke down threatened to land on the pristine marble floor.

Mr. Norock descended the stairs. She flinched at the sight of the dark-haired man with a trim waxed mustache and not so trim waistline. It was one thing to be purchased by an Etherian noble, but to be the property of a fellow elf! Unethical and illegal. How had Kyan missed the evil inside Mr. Norock?

She turned her head toward where the children had been led. Her brother stood in the doorway. "Brecht." Her heart slowed and she released a breath as he crossed the foyer to her. Not him too. He'd said so little since the funerals, but every night since, she'd fallen asleep to his quiet sobbing. Her brother idolized Mr. Norock.

Kyan had once admired him, too. At one time, he bought slaves to free them then hired them in his mines. When had he become so corrupt?

"Mr. Monture." Mr. Norock held out his hand to Brecht. "Could you come with me?"

Kyan threw her arm in front of her brother. "He's not going with you."

"Your father told you to obey your owner. I notarized his final instructions."

Kyan set her jaw. "Maybe you forged Papa's handwriting. You know it's illegal for Elves to own slaves. Not to mention immoral. Against our own code of honor."

"You disguised yourself and allowed yourself and your brother to be sold into slavery." Mr. Norock's tone held no sneer or hint at betrayal. Maybe only villains in books were that obvious. "Why question my purchase of you?"

"Because I thought we'd be bought by Etherian nobles."

"You trust them over your own countrymen? Did you read what your father wrote about masters who share your beliefs?" Mr. Norock smoothed his mustache. "The Fairies are the ones who set up the Detention that keeps you from legally returning to your homeland. Did I ever treat your father or mother unfairly?"

She raised her chin and clenched her teeth. "Other than killing them on the job. No."

Brecht flinched. "It can't be true. Mr. Norock's family died, too." Kyan should have told her brother about her suspicions.

"We all lost someone." Mr. Norock put a hand on her brother's shoulder. He wore three mourning bands stacked on his thick middle finger. His wife and two oldest sons had perished that day, too.

Mr. Norock held out his palm. "Brecht, will you come with me and bring your bird?"

When Brecht glanced back at her, his eyes shone with excitement, not fear or disappointment. "Mr. Norock, how did you know about my canary?"

"Your father. He was my best engineer and told me about your invention." He picked up the tangle of wires from Brecht's hand and examined it. "He said you and Kyan designed it. He and your mother trusted this bird with their lives." He handed the device back to Brecht.

Kyan had failed her parents. She'd developed the powder to detect high carbon monoxide levels, but she must have calculated the formula wrong. Guilt pulled at her like magnets deep in the earth.

With a downcast expression, Brecht turned the remains of the metallic bird over in his hands. "It's broken."

"Well then, we'll have to see about getting it fixed." Mr. Norock met Kyan's eyes. "If your sister approves."

Kyan dropped her arm and nudged Brecht forward. She understood now that Papa knew Mr. Norock would buy them, but she didn't know why. Had the Detention forced both of them to change their stance on slavery? The collapse had killed hundreds. Until now, Kyan hadn't thought how many of them left behind children. The luxury of heat and electrical power came at the cost of orphan slaves mining the coal for the boilers.

She had to trust Papa, which meant Mr. Norock, too. "All right." They would honor her father's last instructions.

The footman returned to the entry and escorted Brecht through the dining room like he had the other slaves.

Her new master extended his hand to Kyan and flashed a smile. His crooked teeth accentuated his too narrow jaw. Kyan took his hand. The shake was firm and warm, but she wasn't going to trust him easily.

A handsome young man in a suit descended the stairs.

Mr. Norock turned toward the newcomer. "My youngest son, Cole." He breathed deeply. "He's all I have left."

Cole's blue-brown eyes showed kindness. "I don't think we've met. I've been at school. Eleventh year but ended my term when Mom and my brothers—were killed." He took her hand and held it for a moment.

"Let me guide you to your suite."

Kyan pulled back. "Point me to it." She understood enough law to understand the rights of her owners, and the liberties they often took.

He offered his arm.

"I'll follow you." Obedience was not her strong suit.

Kyan imagined a damp dungeon, but they mounted the stairs. Cole turned right on the third floor. Perhaps an unheated turret. He stopped and held open the door. The room had a four-poster bed with dark velvet bedding. A porcelain sink peeked from a door inside the room. Plain cotton nightclothes lay on the bed.

Cole picked up an old-fashioned nightcap. "Yes. You'll want to wear this to bed." He gestured to the end of the room where a fire blazed in the large fireplace. "Papa hasn't installed radiators in this part of the house. It's a wonder the old owners didn't perish in the blizzard of seventy-eight." Cole clasped his hands behind his back and gave a slight bow. "I better take my leave. I can't risk compromising our guest."

"I am property." She picked up the night cap and fingered the embroidery. Perhaps more of a pet. A bird in a gilded cage. The cotton was high quality and needlework done by someone skilled. Nothing like the inadequate garments she expected.

He worked his jaw. "Don't say that. Ever. Not all is as it seems."

"Mr. Anglier has the bill of sale."

Cole stiffened. "Tomorrow." He turned on his heel and strode from the room.

What did Cole mean? Could the mine collapse truly have been an accident? Kyan wasn't ready to believe this yet, but it was becoming more plausible.

Kyan changed into her nightgown and slipped under linens finer than the ones at her home a few klicks away. Slavery wasn't supposed to improve her life.

***

The next morning, a maid woke Kyan at daybreak. She gave Kyan a set of black coveralls and a pair of work boots and instructed her to get dressed and report to the dining room. She assumed they meant kitchen. But she was wrong. Downstairs, about forty children, from teens her age to little Breezy, sat around a long mahogany dining table eating bowls of porridge.

Simple clothes and plain food. Maybe it would be more like the stories of orphans Kyan had read. Except there were toppings—brown sugar, cinnamon, and raisins. Servants brought pitchers of juice and plates of bacon. And there was something familiar about some of the children. Their appearance. Manner of speaking.

Outside the front door, the driver and Cole sat in the front of the wagon while the children piled onto the benches in the back. Cole hopped down and whispered to Brecht, who then climbed up next to the driver. Her brother immediately started discussing engines, steam power, and something called internal combustion.

Cole joined Kyan.

"Thanks," she whispered. "He is enchanted with anything mechanical."

"I know." Cole grinned. "And I am by you."

Kyan smiled but looked away.

The wagon lurched and Cole bumped into her. He used it to strike up a conversation. Cole told her about his experiences as an Elven minority in a Fae boarding school. His life was so much like hers had been. Kyan wiped her eyes on her sleeve. Months ago, they would have been equals.

He's the master's son. If only he wasn't the son of a father unethical enough to own fellow Elves—it wouldn't have been quite so hard to ignore his deep, dark eyes and crooked smile.

Kyan had to figure out what was going on: Mr. Norock's interest in Brecht, treating everyone like houseguests. Kyan's room wasn't part of the slave quarters, if the house had slave quarters at all. At breakfast, Breezy gushed about her beautiful bedroom and a bed she didn't have to share. The loquacious child described accommodations similar to Kyan's. Mr. Norock's motives were as important as ever.

"It will get better." Cole handed her a handkerchief. "Think of it as a tunnel. You go through darkness to the light."

"Except we're going to a mine. They end in black walls with a pile of bodies behind them." She'd read all of the reports and knew the mine well. The collapse had trapped her parents and the others in a room. Some may have been crushed, but most would have asphyxiated from the combination of insufficient ventilation and mine gases.

"Kyan." Cole took back the damp handkerchief. "Your parents trusted us. Even Brecht realizes life among us is the best you can hope for here on Etheria."

"He's a naïve child. This Detention is horrible. I should be visiting universities. On Elgnom. Instead, I'm trapped in a land I hate." Kyan stopped before she said something against Cole or his father. Even complaining about Etheria was inappropriate in front of her master's son.

"Believe me. I hate this ridiculous Detention as much, if not more. Do you honestly think I have any greater chance of going to an Elgnomic school? We got a forty-eight month restriction. I can't leave for four years. I'll have to go to university here."

"At least your parents are alive." Kyan regretted those words as soon as she said them.

"I lost my mother as well as two brothers. And I—" Cole twisted the handkerchief.

"Sorry. All I see is someone with a father and a home."

"I understood what you meant."

The wagon stopped in front of the office. The last time she'd been here, it had been to bring Papa a late dinner. A chill rippled through Kyan. Her parents were buried inside. Would they be working near the site of the cave-in? She'd have to ask Cole.

They descended in near-darkness down the shaft.

When Kyan exited the elevator, the lanterns lining the large room blinded her. Plinks, clicks, and whooshes filled the room as the children lit their carbide headlamps in an orderly process. Some filled while others set and ignited the lamps. Through spotted vision, Kyan noted their group made up only about a quarter of the slaves here. When her vision cleared, she saw her suspicions about the slaves were right. All the slaves were fellow Elves and half-Elves, like Breezy. Kyan recognized several faces as orphans from the mine disaster.

But some had living parents. That was odd.

They all received gloves and shovels and proceeded to clear debris from the collapsed tunnel. Each scoop brought Kyan closer to her fears. How far back were the bodies? Her family once had a dead mouse in their wall, and the entire downstairs smelled like rotten meat. Mama and Papa were buried in here along with hundreds of others.

After a full day of digging, sore and filthy, Kyan heaved herself onto the steam wagon. Cole took a seat next to her. He stretched and groaned. Kyan took a small bit of satisfaction that the master's son was a dirty as she was.

***

Days turned to weeks as the tunnel was cleared. The only change was the addition of a few new slaves. The tunnel was longer, but there were still no signs of death. Each day, Kyan became less afraid of what lurked behind the rubble.

Kyan rested with the other slaves in the back parlor. Breezy displayed her stuffed dragon and recently lost front teeth. "Look, Miss Kyan." The dragon sported a patched underbelly and a couple of menacing scars in contrast stitching. "Thanks for fixing Steam." A sweet whistle sounded with each S.

Kyan leaned forward in her chair and ruffled the girl's curls. "You're welcome."

Cole entered the room and joined the pair.

Breezy handed him the dragon. "Mithter Norock. Kyan sewed him up."

Cole examined her handiwork, then handed the dragon back to Breezy. "He looks as good as new."

"He is. Can I take him to work?"

Cole creased his brow and rubbed his thumb across his lip. "I think that would be a great idea." He held out his hand to Kyan. "Miss Monture, would you care to join me outside?"

"Yes." *Obey your master.* She took his hand and let him pull her from her seat. Cole's kindness to the slaves and willingness to work alongside them made it almost easy.

He led Kyan into the cool fall night. Nearly five months had slipped by.

"You know I have ulterior motives letting Breezy bring Steam to work." He grinned. "We can truthfully tell the locals that the mine is infested with dragons. If only—"

Kyan examined her calloused hands in the stretching silence. "I were free?"

Cole pulled out his shackle key. "Miss Monture, holding this doesn't have the power you think. In some ways, it's worse than that thing." He gestured toward the bond around her ankle.

"How can you say that? You can leave any time you want. Go back to school. You don't have to get dirty with us each day." She put her hands on her hips. "I don't know why you do it. If I were you, I'd take that freedom and finish school, silly Fae classmates and all. I'd give anything to see a classroom again."

His soft voice floated on the evening air. "That is why."

"What do you mean?"

"Something needs to happen. We need to end this Detention. I do want to go back to school—on Elgnom."

"And I suppose you're planning on digging your way there."

He stared out to coal-rich hills on the horizon. "Something like that."

***

The next day brought Kyan to the place she dreaded. Boards blocked the end of the tunnel. Despite the heat, cold beads formed on her neck. What would they see beyond the barrier? At least there was no smell. That had to be a good sign.

"Thank you." Mr. Norock loosened a board with his crowbar. "Brecht, will you follow me?" He pulled more boards away easily.

"Isn't this where my parents died?" Brecht petted the wing of his functioning mechanical bird. "Kyan said they asphyxiated. I think it's time to see if he works." This was Brecht's first time down the shaft. Mr. Norock had kept Brecht busy fixing his bird. He'd even supplied him with more vials of powder. When he'd finished that task, Brecht had continued working with the other engineers in the shop.

Their master picked up a three-meter stick with a hook on the end. "Do you trust your canary?"

Brecht nodded. "Yes, sir."

"Then hand it to me."

The mechanical avian's gears whirred when Brecht set it in the man's hand. Mr. Norock hung the canary on the hook while Cole pushed aside the last of the boards.

"Follow me, everyone." Mr. Norock led the procession through the entry with the stick fully extended in front of him. The ticking of Brecht's metal bird gave Kyan an assurance of life as much as the beating of her heart.

The massive space was empty. No bodies. Relief made her lightheaded, and she stumbled on some loose rock. Cole steadied her, then kept his arm around Kyan as they crossed the expanse. On the far wall, there was a series of small train cars set on narrow-gauge tracks.

All of the children were ushered on board. Breezy stood next to a girl with copper ringlets, one of the new slaves who had joined them just that morning. "Miss Kyan," Breezy lisped. "Mr. Norock bought my big sister. And we're goin' home."

Kyan extended her hand to the girl. "Nice to meet you." She didn't have the heart to tell her that train wasn't headed for home.

Mr. Norock reached into his burgundy brocade waistcoat and handed Kyan a half-moon chronograph with exposed gears. "It's your—"

She held the device up to the lantern. "Papa's fissure key." Unbelievable. They *were* going back to Elgnom. She handed the device back to Mr. Norock. "I am so sorry I ever doubted you or held you responsible for Mama and Papa." She glanced at the train again. "You did this. All of this for your workers."

Mr. Norock put his hand on Cole's shoulder. "I have been given much. It's the least I can do."

The control box was mounted to a post next to the train tracks. The brass mechanism opened portals between lands. Its gears were turned so there was a sapphire on top, an emerald on the bottom with the three middle jewels set to amethyst-amethyst-sapphire. The setting for her homeland. "The combination for Midtown." No one, especially Fairy nobles, would enter a dirty mine. The perfect place to build a fissure station. Kyan turned to Brecht and smiled. "Escape."

Mr. Norock took the fissure key from her and inserted it into the box. "I predict another unfortunate event at Norock Mines involving young Pixie slaves. Maybe they'll shut this mine down for good. Bureaucrats are too scared to confirm toxicity levels for themselves." Mr. Norock held the bird out to her and pointed to the glass stomach. The powder was white, not greenish brown. Safe. He waved to them as they lined up to board the train. "Tell your parents and my family hello."

Cole unlocked the shackle from Kyan's ankle then took her hand. "You're the free one."

She gripped his arm. "You're not coming?"

"How could Father explain risking his only living son's life in the mine that killed his family?" Cole assisted her up the step to the upholstered bench next to Brecht. Breezy sat across from them, chatting with her sister.

Kyan leaned out the window. "They're free, aren't they?" She swiped at the liquid joy streaking her cheeks. "Your mother, brothers, my parents?"

"Yes."

"But you?"

"I'll live." He gave her one last crooked smile and held up her shackle. "In my own form of captivity. But one day, I too will pass this way."

 In high school, Gretchen E. K. Engel competed to write her English teacher's favorite essays and earn highest marks in physics. Science won over the arts, and Gretchen became a chemical engineer. An environmental consultant by day and speculative fiction writer by night, she has authored hundreds of technical documents, several short stories and a manuscript set in the quasi-dystopian world of high school. Gretchen's website is gretchenekengel.com. She also blogs at New Authors' Fellowship and The Scriblerians.

Inquisition

By Ruth Mills

"WE CAN GO AT it all night if you'd like." The hollow pop of the Inquisitor's knuckles echoed through the cell.

Adonis tilted his face askew and peered at his shadowed abuser through sweat-strung strands of salt-and-pepper hair. One small breach of light shined between the knots of his swollen brow, granting him a line of narrow sight. His head pulsed as if it might burst despite the fact that blood drained from his nose in a steady stream. The tops of his naked thighs were slick with red. He smiled as wide as his fractured face allowed. "You'd miss your nightcap for nothing."

The Inquisitor eased his lean frame into the flickering halo of lamplight. A splash of crimson spattered his forearms and close-trimmed beard. He pressed his thumb deep into the swell of Adonis' brow. "Not for nothing."

Adonis gritted his teeth and leaned into the attack.

The man released him with a shove that tipped Adonis back in his seat. The chair shuddered under the sudden shift of his weight. Splinters and the tacky grime of its last inhabitant's fluids burned his backside.

"Come now, blacksmith." The Inquisitor snapped a switch of cane under Adonis' chin and forced his head side-to-side as if inspecting a piece of meat. "A person in your line of work doesn't come up with eighty gold on his own, and they damn well don't bribe the Imperial Guard for five minutes in a cell with a disgraced house slave. Pretty or not."

Adonis swallowed despite his parched mouth and coaxed his tongue to work. "More than axe heads and skillets come through my shop, but I don't purvey to the lusts of men. Not for any price."

"Illegal steel for the resistance then?" The Inquisitor frowned. "Never mind, you're too boring for that. Mystery of mysteries."

For a few agonizing moments, the Inquisitor paced round his prey, the soiled cane tapping upon Adonis' shoulder in an absent-minded thrum, then eased to a stop. A calloused fingertip prodded along the ridges of Adonis' rent back, the slow plop of blood punctuating the silence.

"It seems doling out a bit of black and blue is insufficient to loosen your tongue. Perhaps a new motivator is in order?"

What? Adonis' stomach turned.

"For each unsatisfactory response, your sweet thing will earn a five minute tryst with one of my men. Seems only fair they enjoy the same amount of time with her as you did, though I imagine there'll be less chatting."

He shuddered. The image of Arianna, shackled and scarred by men's ill use, burned into the back of his eyelids. She had to get away from here.

"Now, I'll ask again. Who financed you?"

"I told you the truth. Myself."

Another fist connected with his jaw and sent him straight back. A tang like hot metal filled his mouth.

"I'll play this time, but if you saved those coins, there's a reason you spent them here. Little slave girls lose their heads all the time. Perhaps a necklace goes missing, or they're not keen on their master's wandering hands." He walked his fingers none-too-gently up Adonis' oozing scalp. "Either way, no one ever comes here looking for them. Especially not with gold."

Adonis swallowed. "She has a value you self-serving beasts cannot comprehend."

"Worth bribing the Imperial Guard to get to her? That's quite an impressive ..." The Inquisitor's thought trailed off and his eyes narrowed in a slow creep. He leaned in until Adonis gagged at the stench of fish and garlic on his breath. "Unless we don't know what a rare thing we have."

Oh, no. No. He knows. Oh, I've cursed you, Arianna. I should not have come. I should not—

Cane bit the underside of Adonis' chin and forced his face upward. "Perhaps I should pay her a visit instead."

He spat, but his swollen lips sent the spittle down his own chin.

The Inquisitor laughed. "You know, dear Master Blacksmith, the downside of trying to breed the elves out of existence is how impossible it is to tell beast from man anymore ... they just blend right in." Wickedness kindled in the black depths of his gaze. "Except, of course, for how quickly they heal."

Adonis blinked his swollen eye and ground his heels into the floor. His stomach knotted.

"Tell me, why is she worth the gold? The torture? I've no doubt there's an intelligent reason. I'd only like to confirm it."

He tilted his head, his thin scrap of vision fading away to little more than shadow. He squared his shoulders. "Love."

The Inquisitor straightened. A wistful smile pulled at he corners of his wine-stained lips. "Ah, love. I regret you didn't get to enjoy full service from—"

His muscles snapped into motion like a slingshot. He stood, hunched against his chair, and swung it into the Inquisitor's hip, sending him to the floor. Adonis fell to his knees and crushed the smaller man's chest under the force of his muscled weight.

The door to the cell crashed open and a bludgeon struck his left shoulder, spinning him backward onto the floor. His left arm shuddered uncontrollably. The light wavered.

A scuffle of feet and distorted words amplified in his head, punctuated by a gasping cough.

"Finally," the Inquisitor rasped, "a telltale reaction. But you'll soon wish you'd cooperated. There's more to pain than fists and blades."

A set of hands grabbed Adonis under his good shoulder and pulled him upright while another tried to wrench him free of the chair without cutting his bonds. After mutilating his underarms and nearly splintering the chair, they relented and freed his hands.

His arms flopped to his side. A wave of blistering pain crashed upon him. Blackness converged and his knees buckled.

"Such a sturdy fellow." The Inquisitor grabbed a handful of Adonis' hair and wrenched his head back. "This one should make an interesting play-toy for my pet."

The Inquisitor released his grip.

Adonis pitched forward upon his one good arm. His lungs seized and rattled like a consumptive patient's. A clot of blood spattered upon the floor. His vision faded. *I have to regain my sight.* A firm kick to his backside knocked him prostrate.

"Take him away," said the Inquisitor, "one piece at a time, if necessary."

He lifted his head long enough to deliver a slur of curses in reply. A boot repaid his skull for the insult.

"And for the love of the gods, if he says another word, put your swords to use and take his tongue."

One guard grabbed him by the hair and another latched onto his dislocated shoulder, hoisting him between them.

Adonis retched in pain as his feet and knees dragged along the defiled, straw-strewn floor of the chamber and caught on the doorframe as they dragged him out. He flirted with unconsciousness and its promise of relief. Just for a few minutes.

Before the worst of it started.

I tried, Arianna. I tried.

They hauled him through the maze of corridors, always deeper into the earth, through oppressive silence and screams and God only knew what else. Then he heard it. For one surreal moment, a whisper of song broke through the darkness and wrapped itself around him like a vapor. His heart clenched. They passed Arianna's cell.

He cocked his head towards the sound and clung to the fading echo of her voice like the image of a beloved's ship sailing into the mists of hopeless battle. Her smile, her eyes, her laugh … for so long, they had lived on only in his memory. But what the greed of man had stolen from him, from her, what they'd enslaved and used and abused and stained their hands red over, he had come to reclaim.

The notes dissolved on the air and passed away. But she would not. Not if he had breath.

They turned again, and the stench increased until the odor of decay tainted Adonis' taste buds and settled in his lungs as a cloud of rot. He drew upon the memory of her song, her face, the mountains of their youth, to chase it all away until the men made one last turn and hoisted him, stomach down, over a high, convex wooden rack.

Sheer pain dispelled her.

One of the men stretched Adonis' arms along the rack—making certain to stretch his dislocated arm a bit farther than the other—and snapped a set of latches over his wrists. Adonis ground his teeth to near powder, but by a small mercy, his new position allowed his facial wounds to drain over his forehead instead of into his eyes. He made his best attempt at a blink. Perhaps he could see a bit more. Yes. His facial swelling had abated some, revealing the gore-seasoned floor around him.

One of the guards rattled what was hopefully a set of keys and not a torture instrument. "Damn it," he whispered. "I have the wrong set."

"What? How did you manage a fool thing like that?"

"I'll be back."

"We have to stay with him. Both of us."

"It's not like he's going anywhere. He's all beat to hell. Just stay out of arms' reach."

"And what happens if the Thing arrives before you return? He's hungry enough to eat all three of us, and it'll take us both to control him. If that's even possible."

"Then just make sure you run faster than Mr. Ugly here."

A silence hung in the room, followed by retreating footsteps and a deep sigh from the remaining guard.

Adonis' view of the room dilated further with each blink, a wide swath of bloodstained floor coming into focus along with an assortment of sharp instruments dangling from hooks along the left wall. Curved blades, several tissue-crusted spears, and an emasculator—he cringed—that had seen better days. Otherwise, the room appeared empty. He craned his neck a bit further. Above him, a stout, iron-plated track ran along a beam in the ceiling's center and passed out of sight above him. Out the door, if he had to guess. He wondered what sort of torture it might implement … not that he wanted to find out.

He fidgeted. A set of iron—apparently unlocked—D-latches bound his wrists to the wooden horse he was bent over. He wouldn't think about the purpose of the position. Or what the Thing might be. No. There was only room now to make the most of this one scrap of fortune.

He turned to the left, trying to pinpoint the remaining guard. A pair of black leather boots peeked out from the underside of the horse. They shifted and squirmed. Someone's mind seemed more on the Thing than the prisoner.

If I am heard, if my plea means anything, make me strong. Make me swift. Not for myself. Not ever. But for her.

Adonis squeezed his one functioning eye shut. He closed the fingers of his good arm tight. No second chance.

At his prod, the wrist restraints eased open and thunked supine upon the horse. He winced. The guard shifted and tapped his toes but remained at his post.

Adonis exhaled and slid to the balls of his feet. He drew one slow breath. And lunged.

His fist careened toward its target and met the guard's face before a wide-eyed gape could fully surface. The momentum carried them both to the floor. Adonis forced his bad shoulder into the guard's mouth to muffle his cry. Teeth sank into his flesh. He growled and pushed all the harder.

A battle for the sword ensued. Adonis crushed the guard's hand between the steel hilt and his own vise grip. One by one, he bent the guard's fingers back with a crack. Muffled wails filled the room. Adonis unsheathed the blade halfway before the man wrestled his other hand loose and tore at his face.

A grinding scream of steel pierced the air as if some great rusty wheel scraped across stone. A reverberating thump echoed in the passageway.

Adonis turned his attention to the door.

Another thump shivered in the air. A distant commotion, a peal of metal and screams, echoed down the corridor followed by the quickening footfalls of something large.

He looked to the man beneath him. The guard's narrow-eyed fury had melted into terror. The cue to run.

Adonis sprang to his feet. He ripped a spear from the nearest hook and skidded left into the corridor, crashing into the far wall as he made the turn. *Upward. To the surface. Don't stop.*

He plunged in and out of the amber torchlight. His ribs stabbed. His shoulder burned. His breath came deeper. Fuller.

His right eye registered light.

The soldier he'd just wrestled thundered up from behind. Adonis turned to face the oncoming assault, but before he could raise the spear, the soldier blew past, colliding with his bad shoulder. It popped. Adonis shuddered and fell to one knee. The guard paid him no heed and ran into the enveloping gloom.

Adonis stumbled upright and rolled his shoulder in its socket. *Stars and stone.* He shook his head and followed the soldier's ascent along the otherwise deserted corridor.

Hopefully, he'd find Arianna in transit, break a few bones, and take her home. Not back to the chains of servitude, nor anywhere within the empire's reach, but across the plains. Someplace with white nights and unsullied streams. Someplace she could sing.

For one moment, the stench of refuse almost faded, the scent of pine boughs almost took hold in his memory. Almost. Where were the patrols? Where was anybody?

Adonis approached a wide, unlit junction and slowed. The iron track from the torture chamber ran above him here as well. It turned right at a hard angle and into the darkness beyond the fleeting torchlight. Air circulated between the passageways. Dead silence.

Where were the footfalls?

Stone shrapnel exploded above his left shoulder and scored his back. Weighted metal ricocheted off his side and skittered at his feet. He swore and ducked, only to come face to face with the guard who'd just passed him. A face entombed within its helm. And severed from all else.

The air above his head undulated with a hot, rancid breath. He stood, spear poised, and turned his gaze down the unlit corridor to his right. Two iridescent eyes the size of grapefruit glinted green in the darkness. The ground shook in a challenging stomp.

Adonis fled.

A roar rent the underground. The tramp of footfalls fell close behind, but their threat stopped short with a screech of stressed metal. A rabid howl filled the air.

He looked over his shoulder.

The Thing writhed, a massive silhouette in the dim light of the junction. Why did it stop?

The track. It was connected to the track.

Adonis laughed. Maybe he wouldn't die after all.

Like a mirage coalescing out of sputtering light, the exit appeared at the end of the hall. But the door was closed.

Please be unlocked. He forced his legs faster and dropped the spear in the final yards. He collided with the door and tore at the iron latch with both hands. Locked. As fast as it had risen, his heart sank.

He kicked the bolting point until both feet bled. The door rattled in its frame but little more.

"Blood and gall!" Adonis punched the heavy oak. So close. She was just around the corner. He need only navigate the depths. And probably obtain the Inquisitor's keys. And break down the door. Nothing much.

What hope had there been in coming here? Little. But his heart had nearly leapt out of his chest upon seeing her smile for the first time in nearly two decades and telling her, finally telling her, how he had come for her over prairie, and river, and hill. How he had never given up. How he was sorry. Maybe it would be enough to die this way, in these depths with her so near.

No. He snatched up the spear. He tightened his grip and sank the iron tip into the crevice where latch connected to doorframe. Despite his cajoling, the assault failed. He wrenched the spear free and pressed his forehead to the timber. Something else. There had to be something else. Think.

Another roar reverberated up the corridor.

His breath caught. He turned toward the unseen Thing and jostled the spear in his palm. Something *could* break down the door, but he'd be insane to attempt it. Totally insane.

But insane for Arianna.

He closed his eyes and filled his lungs.

He raised the spear. And ran.

Adonis drew back his arm and focused on the point where the track should come into view. The Thing faced him and backed its thick-withered hulk into the shadows with a huff of flared nostrils. It lowered its head in challenge. Adonis resisted the urge to turn his attention fully upon it. He had one chance.

The track and a metal slider fitted with high-grade chain came into view. The thick iron links receded into the shadows with the Thing. But every metal had its weakness. Adonis twisted his trunk and launched the iron missile with all the power his years of forge and hammer granted. The track succumbed, and the spear stuck dead center at the bend. A crack crawled along the brittle metal.

The Thing lunged. Adonis pivoted and sprinted back up the hall, the billowing heat of the beast's roar near enough to warm him.

A groan of metallic torsion, then an ear-splitting report pierced the corridor. Slider and chains clattered upon the stone.

Success!

The Thing charged.

Loose bits of stone rattled free of the walls and rained upon Adonis. He looked over his shoulder to judge the distance between himself and doom. The Thing's dark, stringy-haired mass lumbered behind him, running on what looked like elephant feet and a set of hands roughly the size of Adonis' head. It was fitted with a spiked, iron harness. Its eyes shone like lanterns as it careened through the darkness between torches. Sallow and frothing with hunger. Even so, it had to weigh at least a ton.

At the door, he spun to face the beast. He wrenched a torch from its mooring and clenched it in front of him like a scimitar.

The Thing lowered its head and roared a challenge of its own.

Swift. Strong. Adonis charged.

The Thing closed the gap with three great strides and reared.

Air rushed past the beast, still flowing on forward momentum. For a moment, Adonis' breath caught on the odor of rotten flesh and sulfur. But as the Thing rose to grab him with its sinew-strung hands, he fell to the floor and slid underneath the behemoth, lighting the matted clumps of hair on the beast's underside as he went.

The Thing roared, but it could not slow its mass. It stumbled and crashed into the wooden door like a battering ram, tearing it from the hinges. The door twisted askew and landed atop the creature.

Adonis gained his feet and tore the earth underfoot to attain the opening before the Thing roused enough to retaliate. The beast lay across the path, writhing as the flame spread with the stench of burning refuse.

He leapt upon its haunch and tumbled through the breach.

The hall terminated in a T. Right or left? A smear of fresh blood trailed to the left. He pressed a finger to the scab above his left eye and blinked both eyes in earnest. The door crashed onto the stone floor behind him.

Left!

Another deafening roar pierced the air.

Adonis bolted up the hall and skidded to his knees at Arianna's cell door. He opened the narrow metal flap and pressed his face to the slop slot. "Ari!" He hissed. "Arianna!"

Nothing. He peered through the louver and blinked until the darkness yielded more than the scent of straw. A pair of abandoned, iron wrist-cuffs hung from their anchor like a pendulum out of steam.

The Inquisitor had come.

His stomach twisted and threatened to expel whatever contents might still have remained within. He had lost her. But was he too late? *Where are you, Arianna? Where did he take you? Where?*

He turned his gaze up the hall.

As if in answer, the Thing growled. Adonis turned and froze as the beast shouldered its smoldering form through the ruined doorframe. Its eyes narrowed upon Adonis. Yellow stumps of teeth glistened behind curled, quivering lips. Blood and a tatter of the decapitated guard's tabard clung to its chin.

Persistent creature.

Adonis moved.

A group of soldiers rounded the next corner.

"Run!" he shouted.

One of the guards raised a sword at Adonis. Then his gaze passed beyond, and the group disintegrated into a ball of fleeing chaos.

A scream and a crunch of metal and bone told of the monster's nearness. Adonis doubted multiple targets would long distract the Thing from proper revenge, but the more enemies he could put between himself and the creature, the better his chances of escape.

"To arms!" he cried. "To arms! The Thing is loose!"

Strings of curses filled the underground. A door slammed. Moments later, a cacophony of mismatched bells clanged throughout the corridor.

The gloom burst to life. Men poured from everywhere. Doors wrenched open, barrels overturned, and arrows whizzed by Adonis from points beyond his vision. No one batted an eye at him, as if a beaten, naked prisoner streaking through the hall were a mundane occurrence. Though compared to the burning monstrosity, it might be.

Adonis glanced behind. His moment of hope faded. The burning, arrow-ridden Thing smashed through a barricade of men in a fury of fists that did little to slow him.

He swallowed. As much as the prospect galled him, he needed desperately to find Arianna with the Inquisitor. He knew of nowhere else to look and had no hope of returning to the depths.

Funny how all the years of labor and sweat and tears he had invested in obtaining her freedom legally had combusted into this. He should have raised hell years ago.

A whisper of fresh air stirred. Adonis careened left at the next juncture. The floor sloped upward once more. A less-black darkness, the faint gray light of dawn, crept into the corridor. Slits of windows lined the walls of the side rooms. He had escaped the bowels.

The screams of battle faded. Almost there. He wondered if a weapon might prove more vital than a master key. He clenched his fists. They would have to do.

He burst through the next door on his right and stood, once more, in the interrogation room. At first glance, it appeared empty, but something stirred in the shadows.

"Ari!"

Adonis shut the door and dived to her side. His heart clenched at the sight of her. A wave of cold shock coursed through his limbs. Bloodstained ropes bound her torso to the chair he'd just left. Her forearms were lashed together at elbow and wrist and lay limp in her lap. Deep scores split them open like a boned fish. Blood soaked her thin shift, but the wounds had clotted and already begun to mend.

"Ari." He stroked her tangle of black hair. His hand trembled. "Ari, can you hear me?"

She blinked and looked up. Her eyes widened as recognition lit across her bruised face. "Adonis!"

"We have to move."

"What? Why are you here? You said …" Her gaze flicked across his body. "Look what they've done to you!"

"Nothing that isn't healing." He pulled at the ropes lashing her ankles and trunk to the chair, but they held tight.

"It's no use, Adonis. Please, *please* just run."

"Like hell."

"Adonis—"

He grabbed the chair and swung it, Arianna and all, over his shoulder. "Can you walk if I get you out of this?"

"I can fly if you get me out of this."

"That's my girl." He cracked the door. The cries of conflict still echoed from somewhere beyond the last turn, but for the moment, they were clear. He eased the door open with his foot and slid around the corner.

A figure exploded from a side room and crashed into him. His head cracked against the wall. Arianna yelped and tumbled from his grip.

"You!" The Inquisitor pressed his knees into Adonis' upper arms, pinning him to the floor. "You're far too clever for a blacksmith. And far too much trouble." He tore away the hair obscuring Adonis' brow. "And look at this." The Inquisitor poked at the scab above his left eye. "You've healed as swiftly as the girl. You two have miraculous regeneration, even for elves. How on earth did I get so lucky as to have two of the finest specimens …"

His eyes lit and he turned from Adonis to Arianna and back. A bark of laughter escaped. "You're not her lover." He leaned into Adonis' face. "You're related."

Adonis spat, this time with much better effect.

The Inquisitor wiped his face and laughed all the harder. "Dirty little elves. I've never met any as sturdy as the two of you." He turned his gaze back to Arianna. "Imagine the fortune I'll make in the pleasure market with such a resilient beauty."

He raked his eyes over Arianna and returned them to meet Adonis'. A fell mischief burned within. "You're right. Eighty gold is nothing.

And to think my pocketbook would have missed it all without you and your ... sister?"

Adonis bit his tongue.

A smile spread across the Inquisitor's face. "So, there's no grand plot here after all, just the devotion of dogs who should know when to quit."

Adonis swore through clenched teeth. "The only dogs here are the ones like you, waiting to be put down."

The Inquisitor clenched Adonis' face. "Feral male elves are the only thing that get put down here."

"Adonis ..." Arianna's voice trembled. Stone ground under the chair frame as she inched away.

"Forgive me, Ari."

"Poor sister. At least you'll get to die knowing she lived ... technically." The Inquisitor unsheathed a curved dagger. "Time to find out exactly how thick your filthy blood runs."

A stench of burning flesh gagged Adonis and the Inquisitor alike as two shining orbs blinked to life, full moons wreathed in flame. A putrid puff of air stirred the Inquisitor's hair. The warp of hate fell from his face, and his flesh paled.

In one swift movement, he released Adonis and twisted around to face the Thing. The dagger glinted in the creature's grisly glow.

"M-my pet—"

The Thing snapped the Inquisitor backward with a whack of its mammoth hand. His body cracked against the wall.

Adonis cowered, certain those monster hands would tear him in half. Hoping it would be over so fast. Hoping Ari would be spared. Hoping she'd forgive him for not coming sooner.

Deliver her.

A wet scream gurgled around Adonis, one that would forever infect his memory.

He opened his eyes. The Thing exacted its revenge. But not on him. Adonis lay frozen by the image of terror not six feet from his nose. The Inquisitor's eyes bulged. His breath huffed in terrified bursts.

The shout of men echoed in the back of Adonis' consciousness.

Run. Run now.

Adonis stumbled to his feet, petrified the Thing would lash out and drag him beside the half-dismembered pile of the Inquisitor. But even the Thing had priorities.

Adonis gasped and stumbled along the wall. He grabbed Arianna and swung her back in place. An arrow screamed past, but whether intended for him or the beast, he'd no idea. The Thing would hold their pursuers at bay for a few moments longer.

He ducked around the next corner and through an open door. The wide stone hearth of the Imperial Guards' brass and cherry-paneled lobby opened before him. Crimson velvet softened his footfalls.

A pair of broad, ebony double-doors heralded the final threshold between them and freedom.

Adonis glanced around the room, looking for some hidden ambush to keep them from their prize at the last moment, but they were alone.

He kicked the door to the dungeon under-vaults shut and set Arianna to the side. The ebony did little to stifle the screams.

He looked up. A coat of arms adorned the wall above the doorway. He climbed atop a leather-studded chair and wrenched the short swords free. Flimsy and unbalanced. Not worth calling a sword, but they would cut.

"Here." He jumped down and knelt at Arianna's side, slicing the cords from her legs and arms. He tipped her forward and cut the final bindings from her back. The bloodied chair toppled free, and she fell into his arms. If only this were a moment for peace.

"Take this." He straightened her and handed over the blade. "It's scrap, but you know how to use it."

She smiled. "Better than nothing, though you might need clothes more than I need the sword."

He looked to her soiled rags. "You too." Adonis scanned the room. A series of brass hooks lined the wall, several of which held long, black-and-grey military cloaks.

He ran to claim one of the wraps. He swung the cloak around his shoulders and raised the hood to cover his battered face. He cinched the chest tight and grabbed another for Arianna as he turned.

She stood and held her head high. Noble as a queen.

"There you are." He smiled and fastened the oversized cloak around her. "Ready, Ari?"

Tears brimmed in her eyes. "It's good to see you, Adonis."

His throat clenched. "It's good to see you too."

They turned to the door. Adonis hesitated. He rested his palm on the relief-carved surface. Images of the sword-wielding valor of heroes and legends past were carved deep into the ebony. Valor traded for villainy. But it wouldn't stand forever.

Nothing ever did.

He grasped Arianna's hand and they slipped out the doorway and into the gray whisper of dawn.

And the screaming died behind them.

Ruth Mills began her writing career in high school as a film critic, winning multiple college-level competitions in entertainment journalism through the University of Illinois ... but fantasy is her first love. Last year, her first fantasy short story, "The Renewal," was published in the *Bonté Review* alongside several other wonderful stories. She looks forward to many more years of writing and enjoying her family in her southern Illinois community.

Changeling

By Janet Sketchley

A FINGER OF SUNLIGHT touched the wheel dangling from the overturned wooden cart. Wind in the trees shifted light until it pointed silent accusation at a charred pile of rags among the wreckage: Tarq.

He'd dashed from the forest, a camo-colored blur, and vaulted into the enemy cart. The second he landed at my side, he detonated his personal explosive to salvage my failure. Because I, Aida Maria Solis, token female on the team, had been captured alive.

I couldn't even die decently. I'd been thrown clear.

My head throbbed fiercely enough to blur my mind. I lay on my side, one arm dead behind me. A stream chuckled in the distance. My mouth felt like an ash pit.

Time to move. I rolled onto my stomach, got my knees under me, and did a shaky, one-armed push-up. Pain in my left shoulder said my arm was caught on something.

My one duty now was to get out of here before they came looking for the cart … and its driver. Vague alarm slid through my mind and I scanned the area. The beast pulling the cart had vanished. If my enemy had gone for reinforcements, there wasn't much time.

Gritting my teeth, I turned to free my arm and found rumpled clothing instead of decaying deadfall. The driver hadn't gone far, and now I remembered why—the cursed strips of metal that had bound us together and neutralized my own explosive.

A neural inhibitor, he'd called it. I called it a thing of shame and defeat.

I balanced on my knees and reached with my good arm for his wrist. No pulse that my numb fingers could find. I pulled the camo hood away from his head and the sight drove the air from my lungs. Pale skin, wisps of close-trimmed drab-brown hair, a mouth I'd always thought too wide: *my face.*

Everything froze. A searing ripple emptied the contents of my stomach onto the forest carpet. Tremors seized me, and it was by luck more than choice that I landed on the corpse and not the splatter of sickness.

I flung myself off the body. Chest heaving, I wiped my mouth on my sleeve and blinked hard.

I wore my enemy's flesh.

My left arm hung numb, but with the other hand, I raised the metal-wrapped wrist. The release mechanism had to be on this end. If the wires had saved my consciousness when my body died, had they sent my captor into my now-dead body?

A tiny indent in the metal might be a key hole. I fumbled through his uniform's pockets until I found what I needed.

Would breaking the connection kill me? No matter. Death was part of the mission, we all knew that. Mine might just come in stages.

The clasp clicked open and I dropped it to the ground beside my former self. I stood on shaky legs and pulled in deep gulps of conifer-scented air.

Freedom. But for what?

The forest felt suddenly dank. Distant.

This war was my life. Fight, eat, sleep. Daily. Until we won. Without my teammates, I had nothing. *Was* nothing. And I couldn't return to base in an enemy's skin.

I kicked a fallen branch. It flew across the clearing and shattered against a tree. My new strength would take some getting used to. I glanced at the unfamiliar boot and my breath caught.

This heavy-duty soldier was my ticket into the enemy base. And my old body packed enough explosives to end this war.

***

The sun had nearly set when I staggered up to the compound. I solved any password dilemma by collapsing a few paces from the sentry. "No medic. Just a cold drink and a chair. I was ambushed. Been walking for hours."

Inside, the base was clean and orderly. Wall prints of unfamiliar plants and landscapes decorated the room where they led me. A small artificial waterfall trickled in one corner beside a potted fern. This didn't match what I knew of my enemies' cruelty.

After a cautious taste, I downed the flenx-berry juice in a series of gulps. The young soldier who'd brought it promised to find me another.

The base commandant arrived first, flanked by a white-garbed female medic who watched me non-stop. I focused on the commandant and fumbled through a report.

"Two of them blew up the cart. They're both dead." I tried to sound satisfied, but the image of my own dead face under the trees started my stomach roiling.

"No chance to use the neural override?"

Goosebumps slid along my spine. That thing had paralyzed me, blocked my own explosive device, and left me helpless as a baby bird. "They were too fast with their explosives."

"Next time, Elric." He stood and clasped my shoulder, then strode from the room.

The medic didn't move from her chair. Uncomfortable with her scrutiny, I got up and examined the wall prints, trying to massage some life into my dangling arm.

I sensed movement behind me and turned faster than a soldier in his own base should react. She smiled and reached for me. I stepped back. "It's been a hard day. The attacks …"

She nodded and tried to rub my shoulders. "Their deaths aren't your fault."

I had to make some distance between us. Except her fingers triggered a dull reaction in my lifeless arm. My attempted smile felt more like a grimace. "Can we try that with me lying down?"

Face into the couch, I'd be safe from any other ministrations she thought up.

**

I opened my eyes to what was clearly a hospital wing. Panic gripped me, then shook me like a limp rabbit. They'd changed my clothes for a robe. And fastened me down.

A door swished open and light footsteps approached. I steeled myself. The way the day was going, the duty medic would be Elric's love interest.

She moved into my sight range, hesitating at the foot of my bed. Her eyes closed briefly as if in prayer. She seemed paler than the first time I'd seen her, but I read determination in the set of her jaw.

What had she been to Elric? How would she take his death?

Our enemies' cruelty was legendary. Seeing a human side left me uncomfortable.

I frowned at her. No matter. They had stolen our greatest treasure. We would get it back, whatever it cost.

She took my hand. My left hand, and I felt her touch. Good. I'd need all my limbs functional. If I could talk my way off this table.

Her smile frayed. "How do you feel?"

I chose the offensive. "Why am I strapped down? What happened?"

"You weren't yourself. It seemed more than the grief over the latest suicides, so I played a hunch. You were wired."

She glanced at the table at the end of the room. "We got the detonator off you and defused it."

Defused. My mission was over, and with it, my chance to redeem myself. The only option was to finish dying before they started the interrogation.

I turned my face away from the ruined explosives.

She strode around the bed into my field of view. Her eyes shone dark in a death-white face. "You knew you were wired."

How could I not know? "We fought. I must have blanked out for a bit, and they set me up. Some kind of distance version of our neural override."

She pressed her lips together and breathed deeply through her nose, as if she couldn't trust herself to speak. She looked at the detonator pack, then back at me. "You're telling me you walked into this base fully aware you'd be forced to detonate that explosive—and kill us all—and you couldn't do anything more to warn us than act out of sync?"

It was no act, sister. "What do you want me to say? It's safe now, so how about letting me up?"

She rolled her eyes just like any of my own team would have done, then drilled me with a glare. "The guerrilla casualties—was that a lie?"

"No. Two dead." Their faces swam in my mind's eye, and my stomach clenched.

"*After* they wired you."

"Hardly before."

Her hand twitched, and her eyes tightened. She wanted to smack me. Instead, she shot another question. "When you … fought … did you capture one and hook up the neural device before the explosion?"

I studied the ceiling. "No." Let my shame stay hidden.

She waited until I looked back at her. "Elric was never any good at lying to me. You're worse."

My breath froze at her words, but she didn't leave them hanging. "I think there *was* a connection, and the explosion caused a transfer of some kind. *They* didn't wire you and send you back, *you* did it yourself."

Her finger jabbed my chest. "Tell me the truth. Is Elric dead, or a prisoner?"

"Be glad he's not a prisoner." The words slipped out before I could stop them. Our enemies had taught us well. If we had a prisoner, we'd find a way to make him talk.

Her eyes filled, but I had to make a futile effort to save the situation. "He's not a prisoner because he's right here. Stop playing games."

She didn't buy it, and I didn't blame her. She studied me through her tears. "Who are you?"

"Aida Maria Solis of Kaya Province, avenger of the wrongs your people have perpetrated against mine." The speech would have sounded better had I not been lying strapped to a table in a flimsy robe.

"Aida. Female." Her eyebrows quirked. "Quite the culture shock, I expect. My name is Kerti."

"If he hadn't trapped me with that infernal device—"

Behind me, the door swished again. "Enough!" Firm footsteps approached, and the commandant's face entered my sight. He clasped Kerti's shoulder and a long glance passed between them. Her lips quivered, but she gave him a crisp nod.

He turned an appraising look on me. No hatred, no bloodlust? *Toying with me. I'll feel their worst before long.*

"I'm Commandant Langton. Welcome to our compound, despite the … unusual nature of your visit." He turned to Kerti. "Let's make our guest a bit more comfortable."

She unfastened the restraints and helped me up. I quelled my instinct to run. They'd cut me down before I reached the door. Instead, I feigned weakness as she led me to a chair the commandant had pulled from a workstation. I placed my arms on the rests, but she didn't re-bind me.

Langton drew out a similar chair and sat facing me, palms resting lightly on his legs in a standard non-aggression pose. "This is awkward enough, but we can minimize the indignity."

My vision skimmed the light robe over my knees and flicked to his crisp uniform.

He studied me for a minute. "Why do your people choose suicide over capture?"

I stared back at him. Reminding me of my failure was a cheap shot. "You subject prisoners to experimentation and other atrocities."

One eyebrow twitched. "You're the first one we've caught."

Name after name from our group slipped through my mind, all in active service or dead by our own devices. I kept silent.

Langton slid a stylus from his pocket and rolled it between his fingers. "Your people show too much courage to fear capture, even if it did include torture. Again I ask, why the suicides?"

"It's understood. We must."

He waved the stylus and a monitor—how did I know what the little window was called?—flickered to life on the table.

Eight blocks of images appeared in array, then one expanded to fill the screen. My interrogator had decided to stop talking, so I studied the screen for clues. A girl, maybe ten years old, in a dimly-lit kitchen, stirring a pot on an old-style stove. My peripheral vision registered motion from the commandant's stylus, and the image zoomed in.

I studied her profile. Assessed her movements, the way she held herself. Listened to her quiet song.

In servitude, she possessed the courage to sing. I knew beyond certainty that this was she whom we sought. She we died to rescue. And heat blossomed in my chest.

"You recognize her." Langton spoke, but I couldn't look away.

"Have you seen her before?" His voice persisted like an annoying buzzwing. I twitched.

The screen blanked and I shot him a glare. The satisfaction in his face reminded me I was in the hands of my enemies. And the facade of gentility was about to drop.

Sweat prickled my hairline. I refused to lower my eyes from his. "My people will free her or die trying."

He shook his head, a tiredness to his expression. Aware of the hopelessness of his task? He slid the stylus back into his pocket.

"Did she look to be in distress?"

I strained forward in my seat as if the act would help me reach her. "She is my people's future, and you hold us all hostage with her." My need to detonate the base was gone. All that mattered was finding the girl.

He sighed. "That could have been any young girl. How are you so sure of her identity?"

For a second, I wondered, then opened my mouth to argue. He held up a hand. "Your reaction was strong and instantaneous. And while you won't admit it, I suspect it brought a sharp increase in the need to locate her instead of the standard wanton destruction."

He studied my face. "I don't know what this transfer will have done to your thinking, but the drugs in the neural bond should have had time to start before the swap."

"Drugs?" I fought to keep my expression neutral.

"The neural inhibitor … relaxes … the mind's motor control but also its … presuppositions. It leaves you open to see what really *is* instead of what you might expect. Any lethargy or heaviness in your bones?"

"I was thrown from an exploding cart, then hiked halfway across the continent before your medic kindly knocked me out. Of course I feel a bit tired."

"Mm-hmm."

I eyed the stylus tip, unguarded in his pocket. One grab might get it, but what then? I'd need time to study the thing, to see what it could tell me about that place it had shown. I was close, closer than any before me. Trembling filled me, and I clasped the chair arms to hide it.

Langton stood and circled the room. I refused to track his movements with my head. When he left visual range, I tensed for a blow to the skull.

Instead, he reappeared on my other side. "Dozens of your fellow combatants have fallen, and they are steadily replaced. Did you ever wonder from where? Or how?"

"Fresh troops come when we need them. One of us will be victorious." *It may be me.*

His pacing brought him to face me and he stood, staring me down. "Something is not as it seems. Pay attention to anything out of place, things you remember without knowing why. Something you recognize but you know you've never seen before—like the girl."

Our living treasure. Why had I expected jewels and ore? My lips tightened. This man would learn nothing from me. My mission was clear: locate and rescue.

The monitor flashed again and I hoped for more clues, but the display filled with a close-up of foliage. Image after image of plant life flashed on the screen.

Langton stood a few paces to the side. "Recognize any of these?"

Smaller versions of the pictures I'd seen coming into the base. They looked real, but I'd never seen anything like them. Yet—those tall leaves with the purple blossom—the word "iris" came to me. *Iris?*

It must be their drugs, messing with my thoughts. I glanced at the commandant, but his face gave nothing away. A new image appeared on the screen, comfortingly unfamiliar.

***

They confined me to a cramped, windowless room with a guard at the door. Saving the cell for later, I presumed. I filled the hours with simple exercises to maintain my strength and with reading.

Commandant Langton had given me a reader with access to a cross-section of basic files, from botany to medicine to literature. Nothing helpful like base schematics or the location of their prisoner, but she had to be somewhere in this facility. It was the only one our scout team had found.

I'd always had a way with gadgets, and my hands took to the reader like it wasn't new technology. A prototype, maybe, or a rich man's toy. Langton clearly thought he could lull my defenses before the torture began. Watch me find a way to escape, rescue the girl, and return to my own base a hero instead.

If I could convince my people to look past Elric and see Aida dwelling inside. My flesh prickled at what I might have to endure in the convincing, but I had to go back. The mission came above all.

The door slid open. I dropped the reader on the bed and sat up. "You could knock."

Commandant Langton raised an eyebrow. "I suppose."

He stepped into the room, and I stood to match his height. He carried a metal wristband in one hand. A single band, not a linked set like my first captor had used on me. The sight chilled me. My arms went behind my back without conscious thought.

He flashed a twisted smile. "I insist."

The burnished alloy caught the light. He held it toward me. "Let's do this the easy way. Please hold out one arm."

A thousand ice ants coursed over my wrists at the thought. I remembered the feel of Elric's cold band snapping around my flesh, the paralysis, the desperation to trigger my explosive. The impotence.

My glare should have seared Langton. He didn't react. "Aida. Please. I'd rather not use force."

At least one guard stood behind him. Force was a definite option. Why keep it in reserve?

Extending my left arm felt like lifting a tree limb. I stared over Langton's shoulder. Couldn't watch the trap spring around my wrist.

I felt it, though. Against my skin. In my mind.

I tried to step back. Nothing, like the last time.

Langton's eyes met mine. "You won't believe me, but I genuinely regret this. The inhibitor is keyed to my voice. You are free to talk, but your movement is limited to my spoken instructions. Now, please follow me."

Helpless, I obeyed, despite my fuming will and burning cheeks. *The humiliation begins.*

He led me into a small room in the hospital area. A body lay on a narrow bed, covered by a sheet. Kerti the medic scowled at me, then looked away. She raised the sheet.

My former body. The sight triggered another wave of vomit. The room spun.

Langton caught me before I fell and helped me into the next room. I sank into the nearest chair. Kerti brought a cup of yellowleaf tea to cleanse my mouth, and Langton told me to drink. I inhaled the steam appreciatively.

For a leader whose side had unprecedented access to an enemy corpse, Langton hid his triumph well. He held my gaze. "We'll run some quick tests and flash-freeze the body. As soon as it's released, I give my word it will receive a proper burial, for your sake as well as for Elric's."

Tests. I didn't challenge his euphemism.

I felt Kerti watching me as he left. I filled my mouth with hot tea, tasteless at first, and held it until the flavor rioted. It tingled all the way to my stomach, and I didn't try to repress a groan of contentment.

She sat opposite me, her face taut. "That's not native to this planet, but you remember how to drink it."

The gleam in her eyes rattled me. What if Elric's consciousness was buried in mine—and their drugs could raise it? I took another mouthful of yellowleaf for strength.

"What I *remember* is being ambushed by your precious Elric—captured and humiliated. This is his fault. You people are the aggressors here. You've invaded and betrayed, but you have *not* conquered. We will have justice. And our revenge."

Kerti bolted for the door but stopped before it opened. She kept her back to me, shoulders stiff, fists clenched. Radiating fury.

I'd spoken the truth. To a grieving woman in no position to hear it.

My heart ached as if I shared her loss. Foolishness. I had to get a grip. Her weakness was an exploitable opportunity.

"Kerti, I'm sorry I spoke about Elric as I did. I know you cared for him."

I counted to seventy before she turned. She took position behind her chair, fingers hooking into the upholstery. Not hiding the tears, the trembling lips.

Her throat worked a few times before she found her voice, and the sound came in a whisper. "You are not to blame. But someone—somewhere—is responsible for my fiancé's death. We *will* have justice. I swear it."

The intensity in her voice triggered a resonance. *My fiancé's death. I will have justice! I swear it!* The vow echoed in my memory, in my spirit.

Cold gripped me, a horror I'd never known. The tea slipped from my fingers and splashed against my legs.

I heard Kerti's cry from a distance, but another face swam in my vision. Young, male, full of life. Merrick.

The remembered words tore through my mind, shaped themselves into a scream. "I will have justice!"

Memories pounded my brain—sights, smells, sounds—sensations I'd sworn to remember, all tied to Merrick. Grief rocked me again like the first time, fresh and undimmed.

Grief and anger. Another man's face blocked Merrick's. Lean, mocking, self-satisfied. Responsible for my fiancé's death, condemning me to my own.

My throat closed. I was choking, dying. Couldn't die fast enough to end this torture.

My arm stung, then hands gripped my shoulders. Kerti stood over me, barely visible through the onslaught.

Her mouth moved, but no sound penetrated the roaring in my ears. Her features blurred, wavered, then grayed out, taking my life with them.

***

I woke in the examination room, restraints on my arms and legs. Déjà vu.

Langton stood at the foot of my bed, Kerti at his side. She'd been crying. They both looked on edge, watching as if I might have a second meltdown.

My head ached at the memory.

Memory.

I knew it all now.

Grieving for Merrick, I'd gone to the outpost mining operation where he died. To talk to his friends there, find out what happened. Gain closure.

Instead, I gained suspicions, made enemies. Discovered treason and got mind-altered out of my own identity into this guerrilla warfare farce.

I squinted at my interrogators. The insignia on their uniforms nagged at me. I'd seen it once, knew it from—the breath left my lungs. Coughing, I stared at the commandant. "You're Elite Force."

He nodded, face grim.

"And we've been trying to *kill* you." My life expectancy hit zero. Again.

"That does sum up the situation." He snagged a chair with his foot and dropped into it. "Do you know why?"

"Yes—no—it's something about that girl." My brain hurt, trying to string memories together and sort out the lies I'd believed. "When I saw her—I had to get to her and—"

The conditioning had been progressive: find a treasure, attack the garrison, rescue the girl. If I'd reached her, cold certainty whispered that my mission would have changed to kill her.

I licked dry lips. "If you're not going to execute me immediately, could I have a drink of water?"

At the commandant's nod, Kerti left the room. Langton configured my bed into sitting posture and snapped off the restraints. He didn't reattach the neural inhibitor.

I lifted my hand, glad of the freedom of motion. But I wasn't going anywhere without permission. Not now that I knew who I'd been fighting. Elite Force was feared and trusted throughout the galaxy, for both skill and integrity. Whatever was going on, I wanted to be on their side.

"Commandant, who is this girl you're guarding?"

He shook his head. "Who sent you?"

My mind flashed to that cold, unassailable face. Remembered those final moments as I fought the restraints and he threw the switch. My defiant vow: *I will have justice.* I swallowed bile. "Director Parris of

Axelon Mining Corporation."

Langton's face took a neutral cast. Behind it, he'd be assessing, correlating, assembling a strategy to follow Parris to the end of the chain. A tiny glow of hope lit my spirit. I would see justice done.

The doors swished open and Kerti returned with a tray. Langton accepted the offered cup, and I did the same. She took the third and sat in the spare chair.

The sweet scent, golden liquid: "More yellowleaf tea. I guess Elite Force has its privileges." Now that I remembered, this stuff was expensive.

I sipped gently. Last time I'd had yellowleaf tea—before the disastrous episode that put me in this bed—I'd shared it with Merrick. The week before he went away.

Langton watched me over the rim of his cup. "I assume Aida Maria is not your real name."

No, they'd stolen even that. "Sherida Terrin, from Elion. Axelon does outpost mining, with huge incentives for workers who'll take an isolated assignment with no outside communication. A five-year term would have given my fiancé a down payment on his own freighter. When he died—"

I pulled a slow breath and fought the grief. My listeners made no move to hurry me—nor to offer comfort. I appreciated their respect. Another drink of tea steadied me. I had a lifetime yet to grieve. *In a stranger's body.*

I met Langton's eyes. "Axelon agreed to let me finish Merrick's contract so I could keep his business plans alive. His friends said he'd transferred to some kind of experimental mining station on the far side of the planet. All top secret. I couldn't even visit the site where he'd died. The more questions I asked, the more suspicious I got.

"Director Parris finally hauled me into his office and said he'd do better than tell me what happened, he'd let me die the same way Merrick did. They did something to me and shipped me ... here, wherever this is."

Langton drained his cup and set it aside. "What they did was highly classified and illegally used—mental conditioning to insert operatives into deep cover situations. That's why so many things didn't make sense if you thought them through, like the endless supply of fighters. And why you couldn't focus on those inconsistencies without losing track."

Kerti nodded. "We have ways of reversing the conditioning, but we couldn't know what kind of safeguards our enemies had built in. Our best hope was that the inhibitor would help you remember on your own."

"That nearly killed me. I'm glad you didn't try to force it."

Langton tapped his fingertips together. "So. Axelon is our starting point. Parris will point us to the next link. Whoever's at the end is high up in the Sai Korion military."

He and Kerti pinned me with twin, speculative stares. Tiny hairs stood up all over my body as if I'd been washed in an electric current.

Langton leaned nearer. "Aida—Sherida—will you help us end this?"

I'd kill Parris bare-handed, but I didn't think that was on the table. Heavy wings flapped in my stomach. I swallowed hard. "Mental probe?"

He nodded. "A soft probe would capture enough evidence to warrant a full extraction from Parris and find our next target. Elite Force justice is swift. And permanent."

The granite in his tone sent shivers across my shoulders. My memories. Attacks. Deaths. By my hand if not my will. I wet my lips with more tea. Parris had to fall, with the ones behind this war. If I fell in the process, so be it.

I sucked a deep breath. "Do it."

***

Seventy-two hours later, Kerti led me to a room crammed with Elite Force soldiers. The air vibrated with energy. Commander Langton stood on a raised platform at one end, conferring with an aide.

Yesterday, a strike team at the Axelon outpost had pulled what they needed from Parris' brain. I smiled. My probe hadn't hurt. His ended with execution.

Mine also revealed how to break the conditioning without damaging the victims' memories. Langton's plan to capture the guerilla base had begun, timed to coincide with taking out the military official behind this war.

Langton stepped forward and surveyed his troops, his face grim. "The sleep gas will begin in five minutes. Enemy patrols or those still conscious in their compound are to be subdued with minimal harm. Get a neural inhibitor on each one and get them outside in case there's a physical destruct feature. I'm not losing these people after all we've been through."

I leaned nearer to Kerti. "Why didn't you do this in the first place?"

"They'd just have attacked from somewhere else. Plus, there's bound to be something in the conditioning that wipes the mind when it regains consciousness. We couldn't risk it."

And so they'd risked their own lives and lost some. Like Elric's. For people like me. And Merrick.

I remembered, Merrick. We have justice. My eyes misted. I shut them for a moment, breathed in. Let go.

***

Elric broke through a layer of cold, as if he'd been trapped under ice that was suddenly gone. Shivering, he gasped and looked around at his teammates. At his commandant. Into Kerti's puzzled eyes.

He flexed his hands, wiggled his toes. He was himself again, in full control. No longer a spectator in his own body.

He breathed deeply and took Kerti's hand. "I'm back."

 Janet Sketchley is a Canadian author who writes Christian suspense by day and reads speculative fiction in her free time. There's at least one science fiction novel steeping in her imagination, and she looks forward to discovering more about it. Janet is the author of the *Redemption's Edge* series, and she blogs about faith and books at janetsketchley.ca. She loves Jesus and her family and enjoys adventure stories, worship music, and tea. Best part of being included in this anthology? One of her sons has a story in it too.

The Nightmare is Real

By A.C. Williams

THE SKULL TORCH STABBED into the soggy loam of the jungle floor looks human. It's one of only six light sources guarding the gateway to Nightmare.

Whose idea was it to play this level anyway?

A hot breeze puffs out of the jungle beyond the gateway, as though the pale-skinned kapok trees with their towering, misshapen roots whisper my name.

"Yeah, that's not creepy at all."

What am I doing here?

Jabbing my staff into the moist soil, I reach into my pouch and pull out my quest scroll, unfurling it. The handwritten text on the cream-colored vellum shimmers in the flickering skull-light. *Onyx*, it reads up in the corner.

That's my name. I knew that. I just forgot in the ember-eyed stare of the skull torches.

"Deliver the Keystone?"

I lower the scroll and shove my hand back into my pouch again. My fingers brush the cold surface of something solid, and I remove it. The stone in my hand radiates its own light, faintly purple in color.

"You must be the Keystone." I turn the stone over in my hand. Strange that something glowing could feel so cold. "Weird."

Listening to the pained gasping of the malformed jungle on the other side of the gateway, I look at the Keystone, and then I look at the skull torches.

Had I really thought I was ready for this? I'm just a novice mage. I haven't got nearly the experience needed for a level like Nightmare. I drop the Keystone into my pouch.

I've got nothing to prove. Trying to tackle a level like this one could conceivably take months, and I don't want to start something I'm not ready to finish. Besides, without my timepiece, I don't even know how long I've been in the World this time.

"Screw this."

The scroll still glitters in the darkness, and I access the menu in the top right corner with a tap of my finger, selecting the log off option from the list.

I wait for the doorway to appear. But it doesn't.

I try again. Still no response.

"What the heck?"

Is the system locked up? There'd been rumors circulating that the World had been glitching recently—chugging on loading levels, graphic artifacing on the more detail-heavy levels. But that's just user error, n00bs who don't know system requirements or kids playing around with their parents' logins.

But the system is fine. The jungle is still breathing, the skulls are still flickering, and the World is still operating around me.

So why can't I get out?

I access the menu again. There should be an option to contact SysAdmin. It's for emergencies only, of course, but being stuck in Nightmare classifies.

There's no contact option on my scroll at all. Is it faulty?

I can see my inventory. Fine. I can see the log off feature. Useless, since it's not working. But no contacts. And no maps either.

"Perfect."

Well, if I can't contact SysAdmin, and I can't log out, there's only one thing I can do to get out of Nightmare. I have to finish the level.

If it takes longer than a week, someone from the office will miss me and come looking for me. If I'm lucky, someone will come and force me out of the World before I starve to death at my gaming rig.

I tuck the scroll safely into my pouch and grab my staff, gnarled wood rough against the palm of my hand. One step at a time, I move into the darkness beyond the flickering light from the skull torches. If they had eyes, they'd be watching me.

The path doesn't open up like it should.

Usually, in the dark levels, something beyond the gateway illuminates the path, but in this level, it stays black as ink. How am I supposed to find the end of the level if I can't even see my own feet?

The least the gamemaker could have done was provide a light source.

Oh, wait. He did. I glare at the burning skulls behind me, toothy grins full of fire, smirking at me like they know something I don't.

So I turn back and pause at one of the torches at the gateway. The wooden stakes the skulls burn upon tilt in the loose soil. They should come out easily.

I seize the base of a stake and pull on it, but the stake remains firmly planted in the fragrant dirt. I pull harder, but the stake doesn't budge.

What dumb programmer didn't include a command to let players pull stakes out of loose earth?

I yank on the stake again and growl. The stake shudders enough to shake the skull on top.

That might work. The skulls are actually what produces the light anyway. I grab the skull and hiss in pain as it sears through my skin.

The burning skull hits the moist dirt at my feet and sputters.

What was that? My hand throbs with pain.

Something is definitely wrong here. I should have felt it burn, yes, but it shouldn't have hurt. Not like that.

I check the underside of my forearm to verify my health level, but the meter just below my wrist is black. It should have been green. It should have shown I was at full health. But instead, it shows I have none.

"Something is very, very wrong here."

Has the World malfunctioned? Or is it just my gaming rig?

If I can't tell my health level, that's one problem, but if I can actually feel pain? That's something else. The World isn't designed that way.

The throbbing in my hand hasn't dulled. My fingers are curling up now. Am I actually hurt? That's not even possible.

This isn't supposed to happen. Not ever. The engineers and the SysAdmin have explained it over and over again since people started inhabiting the World. It's not real.

But somehow, Nightmare is. At least for me.

I shake myself.

"Get a grip." I rest my forehead against my staff. "Nothing's changed." I curl my lip at the skull torches that cackle at me. "I'm just as screwed as I was five minutes ago. Now I just know that if a wyvern impales me, I'm going to feel it."

The skulls keep laughing at me with their silent, fiery mouths. At least someone appreciates my humor.

I snatch a leaf the size of a dinner plate off the jungle floor and use it to grab one of the other burning skulls. Much better. The skull is warm, but the leaf protects my hands. I fasten it to the end of my staff and start off into the jungle again.

A little light makes a lot of difference. Now, the kapok trees look like they're reaching for me.

"Yeah, being able to see makes me feel loads better." I duck under a grasping branch. "Not."

The moist jungle floor squelches under my boots, and the air smells ancient and moldy. How many people have walked this path before me? How many other players have even attempted Nightmare with little more than a staff and a burning skull?

I should have loaded up on armor and health potions before stepping into this level, but I obviously wasn't thinking straight. Otherwise I wouldn't be here. I don't remember deciding to even come.

Maybe there's something wrong with my game visor. Could it have shorted out and stranded me here? That might even account for the memory loss, since the visor is the only interface people have to access the World.

Who knows how long I've been here? I can't remember logging in. My body could be on the verge of death right now.

It can't have been a week yet. Last month's rent is due at the end of this week, and my landlord has already threatened to knock down my door to collect it. At least I know my landlord will find me if no one else does.

My gait stutters as the harsh, cold truth registers in my brain. I'm on my own.

The ground beneath me rumbles, and a bloodroot vine snaps out of the loam, venomous fangs snapping at my heels. I spin to attack it with the end of my staff, but it jerks out of the way as I stab at it.

It whips around behind me and lunges again, and I can't get away fast enough.

Sharp fangs sink into my left calf, and blinding agony lances up my leg and into my spine. The muscles in my leg throb as the vine releases its poison and starts draining my blood.

Bloodroot vines can drain your health in seconds.

Nightmare wants my life? It can have it, but not without a fight.

I bend backward and shove the burning skull into the bloodroot vine. It squeals and hisses and releases my leg as it begins to shrivel in the heat.

To my surprise, the skull keeps burning and doesn't fall off the end of my staff. But now my leg is numb. I limp away from the writhing bloodroot vine and rest against the giant root of a kapok tree.

"Well, that was fun." I grip the wound with shaking fingers.

The warm trickling down the back of my left leg tells me I'm bleeding. I don't know how much health the vine took. I don't know how much venom it put in me.

I've got to get out of here. Even if I stop the bleeding, the venom can still kill me if I don't have enough health to sustain my life points.

I gaze back down the path. "I could just sit at the entry."

The skull on my torch sneers at me.

"No, that's a lame idea." I shake my head. "Somebody will find me eventually."

The skull's mocking expression doesn't change.

"Yeah, right." I shut my eyes. "Eventually can be a long time."

My chances are better if I just finish the level. Deliver the Keystone.

"I'll deliver the freakin' Keystone, all right. I'll deliver it up this stupid level's backside." I rest my staff and my skull torch against the tree. "Then I'll go out for a big bowl of ice cream."

I tear a strip off my tunic and wrap it around the bleeding wound in my leg. The pressure of the rough fabric against the torn skin stings, and the venom still in the wound throbs in my veins. I can feel my life points ticking away even if my health indicator doesn't work. If I don't get an antidote soon, I won't make it to the end of the level.

But I gather my grip on my staff and the torch and limp toward the main trail.

Nightmare is a festering boil of a level, the bane of every player's existence because no one can beat it. If you believe the message boards, the jungle is only the first part of it. What follows is miles and miles of ancient ruins overgrown by bloodroot and lined with crumbling obelisks that threaten to collapse and crush you.

Every hallway is littered with shadow beasts and soul-leeches, manned by half-formed skeleton guards armed to the hilt with shock sticks and sharpsteel. Every horrible thing you've ever dreamed about and then some.

"This level's designer is a sadist," I say to my skull.

I struggle around the roots of another kapok tree and freeze on the trail. The ruins lie before me, spread out on the jungle floor like a tower of tumbled children's blocks.

"I'm not going to make it." I whisper it, because if the jungle hears me admit defeat, it'll try harder to kill me.

My burned hand aches. My wounded leg is stiff as new leather.

"But maybe …" I gaze into the burning eyes of the skull on my torch. "If I die, maybe my visor will reset. Maybe that's the way out."

The flaming eyes stare back at me unflinchingly.

"I know. It'll hurt." I turn my gaze to the ruins. "But it's better than dying for real."

Death in Nightmare is inevitable. I can't get around it. But still, something in me resents the idea of sitting back and accepting it. I'd rather go down swinging.

I grin at the skull. "Thanks for listening."

The skull has nothing to say.

I start awkwardly toward the ruins, trying to balance with my one bad leg. The ground is uneven. The roots are taller than I am. The darkness closes around me like a shadow trying to strangle me.

The twang of a bowstring shakes the air, and a bone arrow stabs into the tree next to me.

"Skeleton guards?" Panic rises in my chest. "Already?"

Two man-shaped figures lunge at me out of the darkness. Head and shoulders taller than me, armored, one with a bow and the other with a broadsword. Skin hangs from their bones like moth-eaten curtains, and their eye sockets smolder with brimstone.

The guard with the sword reaches me first. The soggy air whistles around his broadsword as he swings for my head. I dive under his attack and thrust the end of my staff into his dusty ribcage. Bones shatter on impact, and the guard gurgles in pain.

He gasps in my face, his breath reeking of sulfur and dust.

I throw him to the jungle floor and swing the torch at him. The embers in my skull torch catch his loose, dry skin on fire, and he goes up in flames, squealing like a rusted hinge.

Two dull thuds strike my back in rapid sequence, and sharp pain tears down my spine. I glance down to where two bone arrowheads have pierced my chest.

The second skeleton guard rushes up behind me. I turn to strike him, but my arms aren't working. My legs seize up. My vision blurs.

He knocks me down to the ground and hovers over me, his fiery-eyed leer sapping what remains of my will to fight. My body throbs with the dull ache of hemorrhaging. My life bleeds out onto the jungle.

That was quicker than I expected. And it doesn't hurt as much as I feared.

Blood dribbles from the sides of my mouth.

Nightmare is over. I die here and wake up in my apartment, and the first thing I'll do is send a scathing email to the SysAdmin.

Tingling begins in my fingers and toes, like life seeping back into a numb limb. The sensation grows and grows, flooding across my whole body, unbearably painful like all my muscles coming to life at once after being too long dead.

Is this what death is like?

I open my eyes to sunshine.

I'm standing in an open field, green with new life and bright with scattered butterflies dancing on the sweet breeze.

"What?"

I have my staff, but my friend, the skull torch, is gone. I'm healed too. My left leg is fine, and my hand no longer burns.

"But I'm still in the World." The whisper leaves my lips as horror twists in my gut.

What level is this? And why didn't I log out? Why am I still here?

My pouch pulses against my hip. I reach for my scroll and open it. *Onyx, deliver the Keystone*, it says. Fearful, I reach into my pouch, but there's nothing else inside. No Keystone. Nothing.

I let the scroll fall to the grass. The sun shines happily overhead, and the level smells of flowers and fresh air. Mountains tower in the distance. Birds are singing somewhere.

Now I've lost the Keystone, and I don't even know what level I'm on. I'm healed, but it's only a matter of time until I get hurt again.

There's no way out. Not even death can save me.

And I thought I left Nightmare behind.

 A.C. Williams, a founder of Crosshair Press, started writing at age 11. With 40 completed novels and more underway, she'll never run out of stories to tell. When she isn't writing, she hangs out at her family's 100-year-old farm on the Kansas prairie. She loves sharing what Jesus is doing in her life and believes there's a *Doctor Who* quote for every life situation.

To Leave His Mother's Tent

By Grace Bridges

THE STRANGER RODE IN on a beetle and dressed like a tribesman, but he was not one of them. Nolefin crept close to the edge of the campfire's light and listened to the man's tales of the coastal settlements and beyond, to his home city under the sea.

"What is sea?" Delri asked from her place in the circle. Her parents shushed her, but the visitor only smiled and told of so much water you could not see the end of it, like the sand in the desert.

Then he pointed to the sky and said, "There is even more: people who live on Avenir station. It is up there, orbiting Eclectia. Surely you have seen it at the times of its Approaching. But we all came from Earth to begin with."

At this, the elders rose as one and rushed him out of camp to where his beetle slept in the sands. Nole exchanged a glance with Delri, the one promised to him, and inclined his head toward the east where the stranger was being hustled. Delri returned a sharp nod and then turned away quickly. They must not be seen to communicate.

Nole straightened his stature, trekked around the camp at a safe distance, and called to the one-not-from-here. "Friend traveller! I must beg pardon for the ways of my people."

"But not for yours." The man formed a stiff greeting sign, as if it was new to him. "I am Eron. How is it that you are so unlike the others?"

"I …" Nole struggled to overcome the affront he felt at the direct questioning. And a name was not something to give away lightly. Yet these were the old ways, and if he held to them, nothing would ever change. "I am Nole. I wish to hear about the world, and maybe go there someday."

"Sit with me, and I will tell you what I know."

Nole dropped into a cross-legged position, back straight, attention focused. "Tell me of Avenir."

"Ahhh, Avenir." Eron smiled sadly. "From her springs all human life in our sphere, and all evil as well."

"How so?"

"The Avenir is a vessel that began her life as a generational ship. Across the vast distances of space, Earth's scientists had discovered our habitable world, and it was decided to found a colony. On approach, the travellers learned more about the volcanic surface. There were riots. Some people were for pushing on anyway, while others insisted on disembarking at a less optimal planet not far from the route. Finally, Commander Aleksei brought peace by promising to turn the ship into an orbiting station, where some of the people could live, while others would descend to work the land."

"And that is what our ancestors did?" breathed Nole.

"Yes. The Avenir has been expanded to hold more residents, and at some point, the underwater cities were found to be a good alternative. There is plenty of room in the seas, and plenty of metal in the hills."

"You live under the sea."

"I do. It's reasonably comfortable, safe from earthquakes, and kept at a livable temperature by the water around it—heated by volcanic vents on the sea floor."

Nole closed his eyes and tried to imagine so much water that a tribe could live in a shell inside it, and failed. He fixed a stare on his visitor. "I must see this wonder for myself. But I must wait until I am married and have authority over my life."

"It is good that you want to uphold your people's traditions."

"When I am married …" Nole's gaze was far away. Images of Delri in a wedding robe swam before his mind's eye. This, he could more readily imagine. "I will bring my wife to the underwater city."

They sat talking until the Whale peered over the horizon and the new day announced itself. Eron stood at last. "I must go now. There is a professor in Christchurch who awaits my return. He will be glad to hear of you, Nole. To know that even one tribesman is open to the outside world."

"What is his name?" Nole knew now that such questions meant no offence to his new friend.

Eron swung himself onto his mount and gathered the rigging as the bug pranced a few steps this way and that. "Stapleton. He will be your ally if you need one—as will I." With that, he rode away into the dawn—leaving Nole's head awhirl and adaze as he stumbled back toward camp.

"Nole! Is that you, Nole?"

He snapped out of his stupor and to his horror, discovered one of the elders bearing down on him. He must show respect or be punished. "Yes—yes, Wise One. It is I." He covered his face with his right hand and bowed his head as he should.

The old man's regard lifted to the horizon, even as other elders began to gather. "I see beetle tracks, young one. Have you been fraternising with the outsider?"

Nole saw his mother emerge from the family tent. Farther away, Delri's sweet face peered out from behind a spider-wool door flap. The elders were entitled to ask such a thing and be answered directly. He moistened his lips. "Yes, Wise One."

A shocked silence fell for a moment. The first elder found his voice. "Apart you have acted, apart you shall be. Be therefore apart from this tribe for one Founding."

The bottom fell out of his stomach. Curiosity could never be worth this price. He cursed his inquisitive nature by fabled Avenir and the stars above. *If only I had obeyed ... What's wrong with me to risk so much?*

Another elder took up the judgement. "If you commit no further sacrilege, you may return in fifteen months and marry your betrothed."

A whole Founding. To leave his mother's tent like this, instead of properly by marrying. So many months apart from the family tent, apart from even stolen glances with Delri ... Nole's insides quivered and threatened to shatter, but worse things would befall him if he objected. At least they were letting him come back at all—for Delri's sake, he could endure it. He swung to face the open desert, imagining Eron's water stretching to the horizon like sand, and slouched away in the proper penitent stance.

I am a man of the desert. I live by her laws or perish. Nole huddled over his small fire of lavabush and tore at the baby scuttlebug with his teeth. He'd grown up with that old adage, but now he knew it to be true. He knew in which direction to dig his night shelter in the sand—he knew when to hibernate for the two-day winter, where to shelter from the hot summer stars, and he knew the beetles came out to graze in the springs that followed. Six winters past already since his banishment. He felt every one in his bones.

Another fourteen months, and he could go home. Wherever that was. The tribe had already moved camp once. He kept a discreet distance but remained close enough to track where they went. He had in mind to sneak closer and catch sight of some familiar faces. The screeching, lonely desert was beginning to steal his sanity.

The new camp bedded in a slight dip scattered with large rocks, which was good for shelter but also for espionage. Nole flitted from one to another until he could peek over and make out the different tents. They huddled in the morning light of the Whale Star like sleeping beetles. The one nearest to his position was not his mother's—but he knew its patterns almost as well. *Delri.*

He pulled back as a guard moved at the edge of his vision. Then the tent flap twitched—someone coming out of it. The figure proceeded to sit on a stool and began to work with her hands in a bowl. He thought it might be Delri, slightly slimmer than her mother although they wore the same veil.

Straining his neck up just a little more, he spotted a smaller rock some distance beyond the one that hid him. If he could get to that, he would see her for sure.

He dropped to the ground and shimmied toward the stone, hoping against hope that it would hide him. Yet even if Delri saw him, would she raise the alarm? She was a good girl, but not *that* good, he thought.

Nole reached the small rock and slowly raised his head to look over it. He grinned. It *was* her. She appeared to be stripping bug-meat out of shards of exoskeleton, no doubt the fruit of her father's hunt.

Then she flicked back her veil. Looked up. Straight at him. And smiled.

Nole's heart almost stopped. She wouldn't make things worse for him. Of course she wouldn't. She was his betrothed.

He gaped as she raised her hand and waved at him, fingers dripping with yellow bug blood. *That's some kind of spunk, lady. What if someone sees you?*

Then he knew what he had to do. He couldn't stand fourteen more months of sneaking around just for a smile, and no other human contact. He responded to Delri's wave by beckoning her over.

Surprise painted her features for a moment, and she laughed. She looked this way and that, then cocked her head and listened as she carefully set down the food she was working with. She stood. Nole gulped. If she was caught being so immoral, there was no telling what the elders might do to her.

But she hoisted up her skirts and sped across the sands to him. He couldn't tear his eyes away, although it was so improper to see a virgin's legs uncovered. In just a few seconds, she dropped down behind his rock, panting slightly, and turned to lean against it as she sank into the sand. He moved to sit beside her, both facing away from the camp, and, hopefully, out of its view.

"Delri," he said. He had spoken her name so rarely that it seemed a rare treasure on his lips. He blushed. "I—I want to go to the sea. To Christchurch, to the university, to a professor who will be my ally. And to Eron, the one who visited us." He wanted so badly to look at her. Was that so evil?

"You want to see the world," came her voice from beside him. So close.

He nodded and turned, looking her full in the face. They were in so much trouble anyway if they were caught that it likely made little difference.

The sight of her so near made his breath catch in his throat. Such deep, shining eyes, like pools of water. So gladsome the smile she gave him.

She spoke again. "Do it. I'll wait for you."

Nole was on his own now. That much was certain. Delri had returned to her tent and now sat merrily shelling lavabush seeds. He skirted the edges of the camp and located the herd of riding beetles as well as his mother's tent. He was about to do great wrong, but he hoped his family and the tribe would one day understand.

Dusk fell, and with it a chill in the howling winds. Summer's day was well past and this night would see the coming of midwinter. Nole lit no fire; he would be away from here soon enough.

When it was fully dark and the camp had long settled into silence, he made his way on silent feet to the tent he'd grown up in. Fat old Usesto and his lazy son Rasek were on guard duty tonight, but they would be hunkered down in the cold and likely fast asleep, too, though they would wake at any sound.

He knew exactly what he was looking for—the jewel pouch his father kept under his pillow. Hopefully, they had not met any traders recently so as to exchange their diamonds for sought-after items.

Nole's sisters slept entangled under thick spider-wool blankets in the girl-cot just inside the tent door. He passed them by and approached the marriage bed of his parents. The air reeked of heavy sleep as he knelt down by his father's head and stretched out his hand.

His fingers met the grub-suede of the pillow, and slowly, he slid them underneath. For a moment, he thought the pouch was not there; then he touched its intricately embroidered surface and slipped it out quicker than he intended.

His father moved in his sleep, but he settled in a new position without waking. Nole breathed again—until he heard his youngest sister cry out. His heart tore for her, but he could not risk discovery now.

He stepped to the tent's flap and peered out. Usesto appeared between the tents and approached. Yanni cried again, and both parents grew more restless in their slumber. Soon, they would wake. Nole's fingers became clammy and thumb-like as he hoped beyond hope that the fat man would go on by.

A third cry, and a grunt from his father. Usesto walked past and Nole allowed himself just one breath. He gripped the jewel pouch. "I shall return this and more," Nole promised silently, then looked around. Tonight, he would leave his mother's tent more permanently than before. He slipped out and hurried in the opposite direction as the guard had taken.

Outside, the sky glowed orange from a nearby eruption. Nole wrapped his bandanna tightly around his nose and mouth to keep the ash out.

Now to borrow a beetle.

The aspbug herd wheezed gently within the rocky hollow, the entrance blocked off with thorny lavabush branches. Their scent rose to meet him, cold-blooded and as familiar as his parents' tent, but wilder and free, evoking the hunt on the wide open sands. The volcanic glow from the eastern ridge glinted off their shiny backs and the frost that encrusted them as Nole moved from one to another, searching for one of his father's mounts. If it was not exactly stealing, he was not exactly permitted to take it without approval, either.

He approached one of the beasts and ran his hands over the carapace at the neckline. No, this wasn't one of the Efin asps. He inspected several more in this way before the pattern of bumps finally told him he had found his quarry. "Come on, Adne," he whispered, and the head-high beetle jolted awake and turned her head toward him, her eyes dark and malevolent in the night.

"Shhh." Gripping the leading edge of her glossy hull, he led her to the gate, then paused long enough to throw a rigging over her head. She crunched the bit in her mandibles and let out a huff, barely mobile in the winter chill.

Nole led her out and shut the gate carefully. He mounted up and had Adne circle stiffly as he took a last look at the slumbering camp in the lava light. No bag weighed him down; only the jewels exacted as tribute from the miners of the Five Rims and his spear for hunting food. It would suffice.

He turned the beetle southward and galloped her into the night.

Grace Bridges wears many hats: writer, artist, editor, translator, cat herder (yes, really!), and hybrid publisher, empowering excellent authors via the Splashdown Books seal of quality together with full creative control. Her short fiction and nonfiction is found in multiple international anthologies and literary journals, and she continues to work on novels and short stories in *The Vortex of Éire series*. Book 1, *Mariah's Dream*, is a 2015 nominee for the Sir Julius Vogel Awards for New Zealand speculative fiction. Find out more about her writing, art, and other adventures at www.gracebridges.kiwi; about her publishing at www.splashdownbooks.com; and about the multi-author space colony and volcanic world of Avenir Eclectia at www.avenireclectia.com. Nole's story is just the beginning…

Darkness

By Kat Heckenbach

BOOKS SAY THINGS LIKE *darkness blanketed the city*. But blankets are comforting, and there is nothing comforting about the darkness that fills the forest surrounding our village. That darkness walls us in, infinitely high, leaving only a gray ghost of sky above us. It skitters and slinks along the ground. It clings to the trees like tar-covered tentacles, entwining the branches. It saturates the air, thick and heavy.

Maybe it is like a blanket, but only if that blanket is being used to smother you.

I've been told that things were different at one time. There was light beyond our village, light from a source other than the lantern centered in our village. No one knows exactly what happened. The darkness crept in, bit by bit, until eventually, it surrounded us. Since then, no one who has left has ever returned.

Which is why I am shaking now, standing at the edge of the forest. Today, I will enter the darkness in search of a way out.

"You're just going to your death." My brother's voice comes from behind me. He has an uncanny ability to move quietly when he chooses. Spying. It is why he, and he alone, knows of my plan.

I keep my back to him. I don't want to see the coil of darkness that has wrapped itself around his arm. He is unaware of its presence. Like everyone else, he believes darkness hasn't touched him because he is so loyal to the lantern that our village is built around. We've all been loyal, though. Each in our own way. It hasn't been good enough. Darkness has attached itself to us all.

Even me. I can't see it, but I can feel it. A coldness on the back of my leg that never goes away. Fingers of ice brush my skin constantly, pressing deeper with each passing day. I want it off.

"Death is already here," I say.

"You're crazy."

His footsteps crunch on the dry grass as he walks away. He takes no care to be quiet now. He is probably going to get our parents, but I will be gone long before they return. He knows this, which is why he has waited until now—he is glad to see me leave.

"No," I say once he's out of earshot, "I'm the only one here who isn't crazy." What I don't say is that I'd rather be crazy than stuck in this place. With family who refuse to see what is all around, what is clinging to them, infecting them, changing them. Changing me.

I take in a deep breath, tug the straps of my backpack to tighten them, and pat my thigh to feel the knife strapped there. It will do no good against the darkness, but it seems foolish to leave without it.

Swallowing, heart pounding, I step forward.

Darkness engulfs me. It is so cold, and it swirls around me like a whirlpool. I shiver even as I fight the panic that seeps into my muscles, nearly freezing them. I am only a few steps in and I have no sense of direction. The darkness presses against me, tries to twist me around. Does it merely want me lost? It can't possibly want me to return to the village. No one has ever returned.

There is only one option.

I take a step. Close my eyes, take another.

The cold wraps tighter, but my shivering has ceased. There is no other sensation. I cannot feel the ground beneath my feet. Nor the air through my nostrils, although my lungs fill and empty. It is quiet in a way I never knew possible.

Nothing indicates my movement other than the flex and release of my muscles. I could be walking in place for all I know, but it doesn't matter because I'm out, away from the village and the lantern and the bits of darkness that have invaded.

Time is impossible to gauge, but at some point, I hear noise. Ghastly, screeching, soul-staining. I listen more carefully and realize the sounds are human agony. I cannot help but wonder if the cries belong to those who have left our village before. Could they be out here, alive but trapped?

Although my shivering has long since stopped, I find the cold nearly unbearable. Not knowing which way I am headed is maddening. My mind spins with the image of me lost and wandering forever, my voice joining the chorus that I am unable to block from my ears.

I stop moving, gripping the sides of my head, squeezing the muscles in my face and neck.

Frozen, frozen, frozen.

Not moving calms the pain, turns the cacophony into a lullaby, beautiful and haunting, that makes me want to lie down. My eyes are already closed—it would be so easy. I lower my arms and relax my strained muscles. Inch by inch, the cold encasing me becomes blessed numbness.

There is no way out.

My will has become as heavy as a boulder. The desire to find the other side of the darkness has dissolved. The earth beneath me pulls, coaxing me downward—

A single discordant note breaks through the music and rings in my ears. It is wrong.

No.

It is the only part of the song that is right.

The thought sends pain shooting through my skull, but I cannot deny it. That note means something. It doesn't belong here. It rings and rings and the pain shoots deeper and deeper.

Finally, I can take it no more and open my eyes.

The ringing note is still there, barely a whisper now, but it presses into my mind. The rest of the music battles for my attention, its beauty beckoning, tugging me, pulsing just below my skin. All around me, the darkness is absolute, but there are shades of black, shadow within shadow.

And a light.

It is no more than a pinprick in the distance, but I know it is the source of the note I still hear. I put my entire focus on it and will one foot forward. The darkness grabs at me with oily tendrils. I step again. Again. Again. The pinprick of light brightens as I move toward it.

The note is joined by more, creating a new song that overpowers the other. It is all I can hear as I continue on. All I ever want to hear.

It is like stepping through a curtain when I reach the edge of the darkness, black fabric static-clinging to me. I look down to pull it away and see that it is fear, anger, hatred, guilt … woven together like a spider web. I simply step forward and it tugs from my skin and clothes, unable to enter the light in front of me.

The ground ahead slopes up and I follow it. The grass that covers it is like fine clothing, an outfit a king would wear, rich and colorful and woven with gold. The air is pure and the sky clear. Everything around me—the trees, the flowers, the very hill I walk upon—sings the song that had called to me. I can feel its meaning, sense the words I cannot hear.

There is no more cold. The spot on the back of my leg is gone. My entire body breathes with warmth.

I reach the top of the hill, and from here, I can see why books call darkness a blanket, the way it spreads out, covering everything. Through it, I see our village. The light out here is not blinding—it only illuminates—so our lantern glows, pale and sickly.

There are others as well, lanterns of different shapes and sizes, peeking through the blanket of darkness. Each is surrounded by a village like my own.

Kat Heckenbach spent her childhood with pencil and sketchbook in hand, knowing she wanted to be an artist when she grew up—so naturally she graduated from college with a degree in biology, went on to teach math, and now homeschools her two children while writing. Her fiction ranges from light-hearted fantasy to dark and disturbing, with multiple stories published online and in print. Her YA fantasy series includes *Finding Angel* and *Seeing Unseen* and is available in print and ebook. Enter her world at www.katheckenbach.com.

Pony of the Fells

By Tracy Snyder

MIRIAM FELT HER CHEST tighten as the carpenter sank the bolt into the ornate picture frame. Her portrait was now part of this manor house. It would never come down from the wall, never be able to leave.

She tried to imagine what her descendants would say about her as they walked visitors through the gallery. *Here is the eighth baroness, from America. The baron married her because he was broke.*

She studied the painting, searching for imperfections. It certainly resembled her, but the waist was narrower than her own, the complexion flawless, and her unremarkable hair had been given golden highlights. Above all, the eyes in the portrait held a commanding presence, one she knew she did not possess.

She used to think her husband's ancestors were more than human, their idealized images lining the walls of the gallery. Now she knew the truth. They were ordinary, flawed people who could afford to pay the artists well.

Her marriage had seemed so right, the perfect step in fulfilling her destiny. Miriam rehearsed the words of a prophecy spoken by an old woman on the steps of the cathedral in Philadelphia while she was just a babe in her mother's arms.

Across the waters will you find your nobility,
And learn to rule in a kingdom of old.

She had been sure she would find her rightful place here in England. How had it gone so wrong?

The carpenters stepped back to observe their handiwork. "I thought the other portraits would step down off the wall in protest when hers went up," one of the men said.

"Naw." The other shook his head. "The third baroness was a French tart, so she's got good company."

Miriam blushed and turned to slip away, but was brought up short by an expanse of heavily starched, black material. She managed to stop with her nose an inch from the bosom of the housekeeper.

Miriam backed up a step, surrendering strategic command to her opponent. "Ah. Mrs. Culley. I didn't see you come in."

The housekeeper looked down her long, narrow nose at Miriam, pulling her jaw in close to her neck as if she was trying to accentuate her double chins. "May I help, your ladyship?"

"Yes. I, ah …" Miriam stammered to a pause. What was wrong with her? At home, she had been full of laughter, ordering the servants here and there. It was as if an ancient evil lived in the shadows of this manor, siphoning off her ability to make decisions, her desire to speak.

Miriam lifted her chin defiantly. "I'd like to go for a ride. Could you please have the groom saddle a horse for me?"

The housekeeper drew herself up to her full height. "Of course. I assume you will take the gray mare. It was generous of his lordship to purchase such a beautiful mount for you."

Of course he was generous. It was her money. And the horse was just like him, gorgeous, high spirited, and mean as a snake. She still had a bite mark on her arm from the last time she tried to ride the animal.

Miriam shook her head. "I'm in the mood for a nice, safe pony. I think I'll ride the black gelding."

Mrs. Culley's eyes burned with offense, and her mouth pulled into a deeper frown. "Very well, your ladyship. I'll have Crispin saddle Bartholomew."

Miriam nodded and walked away. She kept her gaze straight ahead as she went upstairs to change into a riding habit, not daring to check if Mrs. Culley was still watching.

Twenty minutes later, Miriam stopped in the doorway to the courtyard. She had chosen a riding habit in a vibrant blue wool and a matching hat set at a jaunty angle. She glanced down and ran her hand along the skirt. The expanse of sturdy fabric made her feel courageous. She stepped down onto the cobblestones, her resolve held together by a bolt of blue cloth.

A groom held the bridle of the black gelding. Bartholomew was large for a pony, with the seat of the saddle reaching just below her shoulder. He had been curried until his ebony coat shone, with a thick mane descending well below his neck and a tail trimmed an inch from the ground.

As Miriam approached, the pony swung his head to the side in an attempt to sniff her skirts. The groom pulled him up short.

"Crispin?" Miriam addressed the groom. "I've got your name right, haven't I?"

The short, white-haired man touched the brim of his cap but said nothing.

Miriam held the riding crop under her arm while she snugged the fingers of her gloves. "Thank you for getting Bartholomew ready for me," she persisted.

The groom leaned forward and spoke to her for the first time. "Beware this horse, your ladyship," he said in a dry, cracked voice.

Miriam frowned. "What do you mean? I've ridden him before. He's the safest horse in the stable."

"He's tame, all right, but I don't know about safe. He's an ancient breed, he is, one of the Fell ponies. He was born and bred on the high moorlands of Cumbria, where he ran with the ghosts of the ancient ones. He speaks to them still, when the boundary between worlds becomes thin." Crispin smiled and wheezed an odor of stale tobacco at her.

Miriam stared at the groom in complete bewilderment. "When the boundary between worlds—" she echoed.

"Becomes thin. Yes, your ladyship. At Midsummer's Eve and the Winter Solstice."

"But Midsummer's isn't today. It doesn't come until tomorrow."

"Close enough, your ladyship," Crispin nodded sagely. "The boundary is thin for several days on either side, you know."

Miriam noticed a stable hand at her side, waiting to help her mount. He had wisps of hay in his badly cut hair and a large streak of mud along his nose.

The boy bent over, making a stirrup of his hands. She stepped on his interlaced fingers, and he boosted her onto the pony. Miriam took her time adjusting to the bumps and hollows of the sidesaddle, setting her feet securely in the stirrups.

"So don't let Bartholomew take you to the northern woods," Crispin continued. "It's a place of ancient magic, it is. If this Fell pony took you there this close to Midsummer's, there's no telling what might happen."

Miriam paused. She didn't know these people well enough to tell whether they were teasing or being friendly. She decided to err on the side of graciousness.

"Thank you for the advice, Crispin. I'll ride south towards the village."

The stable boy snickered, clapping a muddy hand over his mouth.

The realization they had been making sport of her landed like a blow to the belly. She shot a wounded look at Crispin, lips held tight in a quivering line.

His mischievous grin melted away. When the stable hand laughed again, he cuffed the boy on the side of the head.

Miriam heard the laugh but didn't see the reprimand. She rode out of the courtyard at a purposeful walk, back straight and eyes brimming with tears.

Once outside the gates, she urged the pony to pick up the pace. Growing up in Pennsylvania, Miriam had ridden a tall bay with a stiff-legged trot that rattled her teeth in her skull. Bartholomew had a different gait. He moved at a low, swinging jog that was quite comfortable.

Thinking of her childhood let loose a flood of memories. Miriam remembered the smell of smoke billowing from her father's steel mill and the soot-streaked workers who tipped their caps and called her "missy." She thought of her friends at Miss Pruit's Finishing School for Young Ladies and the way they visited each other's houses and talked about boys. How she had bragged of her English baron. How jealous her friends had been.

She imagined her brothers and cousins all gathered at her parents' estate. In her mind, she saw them smile and hold out their arms as she came up the drive, laughing and running to meet her.

It would never happen. Last night, Miriam asked Robert when she could plan a trip to America. He shook his head.

"I don't plan on ever going back," he said. "And if I don't go, my wife doesn't go." He had laughed at the stricken look on her face.

Miriam rode until a copse of trees hid her from the manor house. Then she kicked her feet free of the stirrups, slid off the saddle, and burst into tears. Stepping off the road, she leaned against an ancient standing stone tilted on the verge.

Warmth radiated from the druid's monument, loosening the stubborn lump of homesickness in her chest. Miriam abandoned herself to grief. She sobbed, cried, and kicked the age-old pillar. Finally, she rested on it, the stone rough and gritty against her cheek. Tears darkened the weathered surface that had listened to the prayers of men for thousands of years.

"I hate this country, I hate these people, and I hate my husband most of all," she whispered into the rock. "I want to leave and never come back."

Bartholomew nuzzled the back of her shoulder. He gave a comforting *whuff* and blew a fine mist of snot over the side of her neck.

Miriam pulled out a handkerchief. She turned and leaned against the stone as she wiped her neck clean. "All right," she hiccuped. "I like you. But that's it. The rest of this country can take a flying leap."

The pony leaned his forehead against her, and she reciprocated by scratching between his ears. Her fingers traced the length of his face and ended at his muzzle, soft lips twitching at her touch.

Miriam sighed. "I wish I could escape this life. I'd like to go someplace where Robert could never find me." She tugged on the pony's forelock. "You don't know how I can do that, do you?"

Bartholomew regarded her intently with one brown eye, as if he were considering what she said. Then he flicked his ears forward and stared down the road. Miriam turned to see what he was looking at. She couldn't see anyone, but she could hear voices. Villagers were coming up the road, laughing as they walked.

Miriam mopped at her tears with the soiled handkerchief. She wiped her nose and patted her cheeks before giving up. Gathering skirts in one hand, she scrambled into the saddle. Before she had a chance to set the reins, Bartholomew turned and made his way down a side path. She let him go.

After a few minutes, she glanced over her shoulder. Three village goodwives stood motionless in the road, watching her ride away. When they saw her look back, they dropped their bundles on the ground and began making ancient warding signs directed at the ground, as if they were deflecting a curse. Then they covered themselves with multiple signs of the cross. Father, Son, and Holy Spirit, all drawn in the air as a barrier to protect them.

A prickle of apprehension ran down her spine, and Miriam urged the pony into a canter. The path rose up a small incline, veered sharply to the right, and disappeared into a remnant of ancient forest.

She pulled on the reins, and Bartholomew halted within the shade, huffing breath through flared nostrils. She peered down the path. It was no more than a game trail, winding through brush for a few feet before disappearing from sight.

Miriam glanced at the empty road behind her. She didn't care if the groom had warned her away from the woods. She wasn't going to go back and risk running into any more of the superstitious locals. She urged Bartholomew into the forest.

He stepped lightly, blue-black hooves making no sound. The air was perfectly still, dappled with cloudy sunlight that managed to slip between the leaves overhead. There were no flutters of wings, no tails whisking behind trunks. A solemn weight settled on Miriam, slowing her breath and bringing a peaceful calm.

After ten minutes, Bartholomew stopped. A pond spread out in front of them, surrounded by massive beech trees. Their gray trunks were pillars, leaves forming a partial roof overhead.

"It's beautiful," Miriam whispered. She slid to the ground. As she did so, a twig brushed against her hat, pulling it from her head. "No." Miriam jumped to reach the offending branch. "You can't have my favorite hat."

She held the rescued hat in one hand and used the hand holding the reins to pat her head in an attempt to find errant hairpins. Bartholomew jerked the bridle so he could reach a tempting mouthful of leaves. Miriam stumbled after him, dropping the pins on the ground. She bent over, searching the debris on the forest floor. Several strands of hair hung loose beside her face.

Bartholomew swung his head over to see what she was doing. He put his muzzle next to her cheek and let out a mist-filled *whuff*. Miriam pulled out her handkerchief once again and found it was wadded into a sticky ball.

"This is ridiculous," she said. "I'm going to sit by the pond and clean myself off." She tied Bartholomew's reins to a low branch and dug in the saddlebags, pulling out a lightweight cloak. It was sage green, with roses embroidered at the neck where it fastened.

Miriam laid her cloak on a level spot next to the pond. She sat down on it and soaked her handkerchief, then wiped her face. The cool water felt wonderful as it trickled down the sides of her neck. She leaned over to rinse out her handkerchief a second time and paused. The water was so clear she could see the rocks and branches lying on the bottom.

Miriam caught a glimpse of her own reflection and couldn't help but laugh. She took an ornamental comb out of her hair and began coaxing loose strands back into order. She combed and pinned, staring fixedly at her image. As she shoved the last pin in place, a glimmer caught her eye. She glanced at the other side of the pond.

There it was again. A soft light flickered on the surface of the water, joined by another and yet another. It was like starlight.

"That's odd." Miriam rolled over on her back, one hand trailing in the water. She could see sky through the branches overhead, but there were no stars. Two hours remained until dusk, and clouds obscured most of the blue.

She closed her eyes. Faintly, beyond the edge of hearing, she felt a vibration rise out of the earth. Something brushed her fingertips. She rolled over and looked in the pond, expecting to see a fish. Instead she saw a reflection looking back at her.

She beheld the image of a young man, with sun-darkened skin and a torc of twisted silver around his neck. The reflection reached out his hand, breaking the surface of the water. Torchlight flickered off drops of water falling from his fingers as the hand slid out of sight once more, leaving a widening circle of ripples.

Miriam scrambled to her feet. She backed away from the pond, dragging her cloak. She backed up until she ran into the pony. She leaned against his side while she caught her breath.

"Did you see that?" she squeaked. Bartholomew didn't answer. He was busy eating.

She patted the horse's side. The certainty of his warm bulk comforted her, and her heartbeat began to return to normal. But she had had enough. Miriam swung the cloak around her shoulders, fastening it tight at her throat.

She hesitated a moment when she noticed her hat by the side of the pond. She considered leaving it behind, then set her jaw and inched forward. As she bent down to retrieve the hat, a fold of her cloak slipped into the water.

Miriam tried to pull it out, but the fabric wouldn't come. The tension increased, pulling tight around her throat. Music seeped out of the ground beneath her feet, just loud enough to hear. It was distant and wild, full of melancholy.

Miriam clawed at the ribbons securing the garment to her neck, but the bow had tangled into an intractable knot. She dropped to her knees and plunged a hand into the water in the hope that she could free the material from an underwater root. Unseen fingers gripped her wrist, jerking her flat to the ground.

"Bartholomew!" Miriam screamed. Her free hand slipped in the mud, and she slid another inch towards the pond. Water touched the side of her head. A shock of fear raced through her, and she dug her fingernails deep into the soil. Another jerk sent a stab of pain through her shoulder. She lost her grip on the shore as her head and upper body disappeared underwater. She screamed once more, the sound captured in bubbles of air.

The hand holding her forearm yanked again, pulling her down until her head broke the surface of the water. She gasped in a breath of air and music, her mind swirling with confusion. Was she facing up or down?

Her knees banged against rocks and she scrabbled to find her footing, the young man holding her steady by one arm. The water-soaked cloak hung heavy down her back, pulling tight across her throat. She pulled at the ribbons with her free hand and, this time, they came easily undone. The cloak slipped off her shoulders and into the water.

As soon as Miriam was steady on her feet, she twisted her hand out of the man's grasp. "Let go of me." She braced herself for a fight. To her surprise, he backed towards the shore, eyes wary, hands held with palms facing her in a gesture of peace and supplication.

Half a dozen women stood at the edge of the pond, dressed in woven cloth and furs. The youngest was no more than a child, the eldest bent with age. They blew into pipes and beat on drums, creating the song that pulled at her soul.

Miriam stood dripping water into the knee-deep pond and tried to figure out where she was. They were in a meadow instead of a forest, with a star-filled sky of midnight spread out above them. Near the horizon hung the moon, her moon with the familiar shadows forming a face across its surface. But it was huge, almost twice the size of the orb that would rise this night in the England she knew. A breeze cut through the wet fabric of her dress and raised goose bumps on her skin.

Miriam turned and splashed back towards the spot where she had entered this world, heavy skirts pulling against her legs. Ten feet away, the surface of the pond was translucent, showing a glimpse of the cloudy sky she had left moments before.

Bartholomew stuck his head into view, his muzzle elongated by the water between them. It seemed as if he was on the bottom of the pond, looking up at her.

The horse nudged something by his feet and her hat fell up to land under the surface of the pond. It floated upside down, brim at the interface between water and air.

Miriam stumbled deeper into the pond until she reached the edge of the opening between worlds. Maybe she could still get back.

She crouched, preparing to dive into the portal. But then she hesitated. Get back to what?

The words she had spoken by the ancient standing stone came drifting back to her. *I want to leave and never come back.*

Shock gave way to absurdity. Miriam threw back her head and laughed. "I guess I should have specified the destination," she muttered to herself.

The music stopped, and Miriam glanced over her shoulder. The women on the bank studied her with unreadable eyes. The young man stretched out his arms, calling in a plaintive language she didn't understand.

She looked down at Bartholomew. They stared at each other through the wavering substance of time. A faint whicker drifted up through the portal, calm and encouraging.

"Across the waters." She whispered the opening words of the childhood prophecy and paused. Maybe this was the destiny the old woman had prepared her for. Maybe this is where she would learn to rule. Slowly, thoughtfully, she picked up her hat, wiping moisture from the brim.

Miriam watched as the pony shook his mane in farewell and disappeared from view. The light faded until all she could see in the surface of the pond was the reflected glory of the stars overhead.

The music started up again, wild and free. She settled the hat firmly on her head and ran both hands across the damp fabric of her skirt. She was going to need all the courage she could get.

Tracy Snyder lives in Oregon, the wife of one husband, mother of two sons, and servant of two cats. She is a certified lymphedema therapist, helping people recover from surgery and injuries. In her spare time, she paddles for a competitive dragon boat team called the Angry Unicorns. She received first place for non-fiction in the 2012 Kay Snow Awards with Willamette Writers and has completed a manuscript for a science fiction novel. You can follow her on Twitter @tracysnyder111.

Time for a Change

By Ben Wolf

PERSEPHONE'S KICK DIDN'T BREAK Malthus' guard, but her follow-up punch to his jaw knocked him down.

He grunted. "I won't let you take her."

Persephone rolled her eyes. "You say that every heist, but you always end up on the floor, and I always escape with my prize."

Malthus tried to get his knees under him, but she kicked his gut and he toppled onto his side. "Please, you—you can't—"

"I can, and I will, old man." Persephone swept a lock of dark hair back under her beret and trotted down the hall.

Exquisite works of art surrounded her. Most of them would fetch millions back in her time, but she blazed past them all. This time, her mission meant more than mere money.

She checked her Timepiece. The backlit LED displayed 20:31 in big blue numerals and 8/20/1911 in smaller orange digits underneath. Smaller still, a purple countdown timer ticked the minutes away. She had 3:47 left.

Persephone rounded the next corner and came face to face with the *Mona Lisa*. She smirked.

No bulletproof glass or fancy security systems in 1911. All she had to do was reach up and take it. And when she swooped back to the year 2174, it would disappear from the modern Louvre as well. After centuries, Leonardo da Vinci's masterpiece would finally return to Italy, to her people.

She reached for it.

"Who are you?"

Persephone whirled around. A man in a three-piece suit approached. His dark hair and handlebar mustache betrayed his Italian descent. Vincenzo Peruggia.

"What are you doing?" Vincenzo's words curled with an Italian accent, even though he spoke French.

Persephone squinted at him. Why was he here so late at night? The files she'd studied said he wasn't supposed to make his move until tomorrow, Monday morning.

"I'm doing what you will fail to do," she replied in Italian.

He tilted his head.

She grabbed his wrist and kissed his cheek. Vincenzo staggered out of her grasp, blinked once, and then his knees buckled and he slumped to the floor.

Persephone grinned. Her good looks and the nano-toxins in her lipstick had come through once again.

Her Timepiece read 20:33, and the countdown timer showed 1:28 remaining. Vincenzo would sleep for a solid hour, but she still had to hurry. She couldn't be late to her swoop site or she'd have to wait another 24 hours to get home.

No way.

Mona Lisa came off the four iron pegs that held her in place, and Persephone's heels clicked on the wood floor as she headed toward her swoop site. In the next hall, she found Malthus on his back, wheezing. "Come on, Mal. I didn't kick you that hard."

Malthus stared at her with those stark blue eyes of his, now streaming with tears that ran into his gray sideburns. He didn't say anything—just gawked at her in desperation.

"You old faker." Persephone tore past him. Another 20 seconds and she'd reach her swoop site.

"Please," he gasped. "Please—h-help me."

She stopped, her teeth gritted. A trick? A ploy to get her close so he could slap some ion cuffs on her? She couldn't risk it.

Persephone fixed her eyes on Mona Lisa's. She'd get the painting back to the Italian government, and it would buy her some much-needed exoneration.

Malthus clutched his chest and squeezed his eyes shut. A heart attack?

Premature aging and the physical deterioration that accompanied it—the result of too many years swooping through time.

Malthus opened his eyes and reached toward her. His trench coat shifted and she saw the glowing white badge on his chest. "Please, Seph. Please."

Her Timepiece flashed its one-minute warning and the countdown timer overtook the screen. 59 seconds left. 58. She had to go.

But … if Malthus was in real trouble, she couldn't just leave him. Sure, they'd taken different paths all those years ago, but she owed him.

50 seconds. 49. She had to get to her site. He'd be fine once Vincenzo woke up.

An hour from now, Malthus could be dead. Maybe sooner.

43.

She couldn't leave him to die, but she couldn't save him *and* bring back the *Mona Lisa*.

Persephone cursed.

She laid Mona Lisa face-up on the wood floor and darted back to him with 40 seconds left. She yanked him to his feet and they hobbled toward her swoop site.

Her Timepiece chirped the ten-second warning and a triangular blue aura materialized in the middle of the hallway in front of Michelangelo's marble *David*.

Five more steps. As many seconds.

They crossed into the aura and blinding white light flashed around them. It ended quickly, and when Persephone opened her eyes, she couldn't move her wrists. She looked down.

Two black cords outlined with a green glow ringed her wrists. Malthus's ion cuffs.

The dreary greys and blinking lights of her swoop-pad materialized around them, and she glared at Malthus. "You *were* faking it."

He grinned at her. "Even an 'old man' has his tricks."

"I didn't steal it, you know. Doesn't that count for anything?"

Malthus raised an eyebrow.

"Come on, Malthus. After all these years?" She gave him her best puppy-dog eyes.

He unstrapped her Timepiece from her wrist, dropped it to the floor, and stomped on it.

"What are you doing?" Persephone shrieked.

The lights on the Timepiece faded to black, and he disengaged the ion cuffs from her wrists. "I'll give you a ten-minute head start."

Persephone grinned. Malthus, despite that badge on his chest, had always been reasonable. "You know I only need five."

"I know. Before you go—"

"What?"

"Maybe there's time for a change."

Persephone flashed him a smile, then disappeared into the shadows.

Ben Wolf founded Splickety Publishing Group (SPG) to meet the needs of busy folks like him: people who appreciate great fiction but don't have much time to read. SPG offers three quarterly flash fiction magazines: Splickety Prime (multi-genre), Havok (speculative fiction), and Splickety Love (romance).

Ben has written six action/adventure novels and has multiple other projects in the works. His first novel, Blood for Blood, debuted on October 31st, 2014 and has been characterized as "bold … with nonstop tension" and "hard to put down" and asks, "What if a Vampire got Saved?"

You can follow him on Twitter or on Facebook.

Afterword

ON BEHALF OF BRIMSTONE Fiction, an imprint of Lighthouse Publishing of the Carolinas, and the nice folks at the Realm Makers Conference, we would like to thank you for supporting future writers of speculative fiction. Each story in this anthology has been donated, from which any author profits will go toward the Realm Makers Scholarship Fund. We encourage you to keep this collection for yourself and consider gifting copies, either in e-format or print, to others who enjoy this genre.

We would like to especially thank Jeff Gerke, mentor and founder of what Christian speculative fiction is today, and Ben Wolf, on faculty at the Realm Makers Conference, for their story contributions.

To learn more about the Realm Makers, visit http://www. realmmakers.com/

To find this and other great books, visit: www.brimstonefiction. com and http://lighthousepublishingofthecarolinas.com/

It has been our pleasure to work with such an amazing group of authors on this anthology. We look forward to the continued development of the Christian speculative fiction genre and to one day meeting you in our travels, around this world and beyond.

Bethany Kaczmarek, a 2015 ACFW Editor of the Year finalist, is a fan of gripping Story. She makes sure every thread is woven consistently throughout a manuscript—whatever the genre. She points out ways to deepen and enrich the layers so the theme is vivid. And she's great at helping to develop compelling subplots and secondary characters if sequels are on the horizon. As a card-carrying grammar nerd, Bethany believes an author's voice comes from knowing the rules well enough to break them with flair. Though she takes editing seriously, she believes a healthy dose of humor can make the revision process fun. A member of the Christian Editor Connection and the Christian PEN, her goal is to help hard-working writers sound like gifted writers. She's one of the Editor Sisters at A Little Red Ink. You can check out their blog at www.alittleredink.com

Rowena Kuo is the managing editor for Brimston Fiction and development executive producer for www.lpcmediagroup.com. She has served as a judge for the ACFW Genesis contest and has mentored screenwriters as a development executive for the 168 Write of Passage Short Screenplay Competition. With over 15 years of ministering to children, youth groups, young adults, and now women and family groups, Rowena advocates for writers to build God-centered support systems consisting of people, perseverance, practice, and most of all, prayer. She has written for Christian Devotions, Splickety's "Havok Magazine," Written World Communications, and the 168 Write of Passage. When not working on words or films, she is a full-time wife and mom with secret aspirations for spaceflight. Find out more at http://www.rowenakuo.com/

Enjoy an excerpt from another Brimstone Fiction book, *Whiskey Sunrise*, by John Turney.

WHISKEY
SUNRISE

By John Turney

Brimstone
Fiction

Prologue

Locked in a car trunk, wrists and ankles bound with duct tape, Juan had no doubt this would be his final ride. Gritting his teeth, he pulled against the tape. His arms shook, and his shoulders and upper back burned. Sweat beaded his forehead. The tape refused to budge. Releasing his breath, Juan gave up.

He had tried screaming for help, but the duct tape across his mouth only permitted an elongated throaty grunt. Juan squeezed his eyes shut. The bump on the back of his head pounded in rhythmic harmony with the velocity of his heart.

Bile churned in his gut, and he gagged. *Jesús y la Virgen Bendita, no.* He relaxed, forcing deep breaths until the moment passed.

Hope faded like old blue jeans. He tried to swallow, but without spit, it was like drinking sand.

A metal bar dug into his side. Tire iron? A possible weapon, but it might as well be in Maine for all the good it would do him.

The numbing drone of tires on pavement toyed with his apprehension. From the outside sounds, Juan assumed they had left Phoenix. Probably headed into the desert.

The trunk reeked of oil, exhaust fumes, and the lingering stench of death. Juan wished the stench belonged to furry creatures and not people, but he doubted it. His captors only hunted humans. His captors? Hired gunmen, both of them. He'd seen their handiwork, bloodied victims lying in Mexican streets.

Not good. Stay calm.

During the afternoon, the temperatures soared into the hundred-and-teens, but night brought chilled air. His sweat-soured clothes stuck to his body, robbing him of warmth. He shivered. His own body odor mixed with fear like a Coke and rum. His watch dinged the hour. Midnight?

Time inched. The brake lights lit up his prison, and Juan perceived the car slowing down. The movement of the vehicle rocked him back and forth. Just enough to make his stiff body scream in agony.

After a few seconds of hearing pebbles pinging in the wheel wells and against the undercarriage, Juan figured they now traveled a gravel road.

He had to warn Rye, but how? Then it occurred to him … the Sharpie marker in his shirt pocket. The one Rye made all his officers carry. If he could only reach it … He twisted, so his pocket brushed against the tire iron, then using its claws, forced the pen out of the pocket. It landed under him, so he rolled the other way, and his hands found it. After a brief struggle, he fumbled off the cap and wrote in between his fingers. Hands behind him, he could only hope for partial legibility.

By the jolting movements of the vehicle, Juan suspected his captors had turned onto a dirt trail. The car headed up a low grade and bounced like a three-legged horse. The brake lights came on, and the car slid to a stop.

Seconds later, two car doors opened, one after the other. Panic slithered into his psyche.

The doors slammed shut, sending vibrations through the car body. Footsteps approached on either side of the car.

Keys rattled and then were inserted into the lock of the truck.

The car trunk popped open. The desert night rushed in with the scent of creosote bush, cooling rocks, sand … and booze.

Two men stood like hulking silhouettes blocking part of the starry night. One wore a bandana, and the other's shaved head reflected starlight. No city lights glowed in the skies, and that meant his captors had taken him deep into the desert's heart.

"Juan, time to meet your Diablo," Bandana said, heavy Español-accented English.

Both reached down, one grabbing Juan by the legs and the other by his shoulders, and heaved him out of the trunk. His head banged against the lid, and they laughed. His vision spun in momentary vertigo. Blood trailed down his forehead. He wanted to hurl curses at the two, but only managed weak mumbles against the tape.

They dumped him onto a dirt track. He lay there while they cut the duct tape from his legs and ripped off his gag.

"Get up, dog."

"How?" Juan said, his voice a croak.

Bandana kicked him in the side. An excruciating torrent ripped through his ribs. His vision exploded as if he watched a super nova.

He struggled to get to his feet. Baldy grabbed him by the shoulders and picked him up.

"Get a move on," the man said with a sneer.

One of the men shoved him in the back. He managed small shuffling steps.

"Where're you taking me?"

"Shut up and walk."

He staggered up the dirt trail in silence. He expected to hear the click of a round being loaded into a handgun, followed by an explosion, and then the blackness of death. But no shot came. The moonlight revealed they headed up a washed-out canyon strewn with boulders and gloom. Further up, bleak stone walls cast a shadow across the path darker than the night sky. It would happen there.

Baldy grabbed Juan's shirtsleeve and tore it, revealing Juan's shoulder tattoo of a skull-pommeled dagger dripping blood. A banner across the hilt read *Semper Fi*. "When you're dead, I'll skin them tats off you. Make me a pouch to hold my bad seed."

As his captors taunted him, Juan shot rapid glances at the surrounding area. Icy silver moonlight bathed the open land. Even if he could take down his two captors with his hands bound, there was no place within a hundred yards to run to.

An owl sounded far up the canyon. He shivered. In the Navajo tradition, an owl represented a newly departed soul.

Just then, about a hundred feet up the canyon floor, car lights blazed on, blinding him. High beams. Juan turned his head sideways to avoid the glare. Car doors opened and shut.

"Here comes da man," Bandana said behind him.

Squinting, Juan watched several people approach—shapes distorted by the illumination of the car lights. Boots crunched on the ground. He recognized the tall shadow in front.

Santo polvo. Demonio.

"Amigo," said the Demonio shadow. "I hate to do what I'm about to do, but even more, I hate when an ... asset ... steals from me. In my line of business, the mere appearance of weakness is a ... drawback. I can't have people thinking I'm weak. *¿Comprende?*"

"But ... but ... I didn't take anything ... I promise. Not a thing. Nada."

"I see with my very eyes what you take. The Indian trinket is nothing. A pretty bauble, *si?*" Demonio held up a silver wristband, gleaming in the headlights. "For that you'd lose the tip of your pinky finger. But taking my packets of merchandise?" He shook his head with a downward glance. "Not good. And for this, you must pay. A bullet to the knee. Maybe you never walk again ... but you're alive."

A person in the group behind Demonio handed him something and said, "*Caro petridas es.*"

Latin? There's only one person I know who speaks Latin.

"Then my security hands me photos. Like this one of you watching my wife swim in the natural." He flicked the picture, and it hit Juan in the chest. "Or one with you talking to her while she's in the pool." He flicked another photo at Juan. "You like to watch other men's wives? What are you? A pervert?"

"Wait. I can explain."

"No. No explanations. They are only lies. But there is more, no? I assume you recognize this." Demonio shoved a cell phone under Juan's nose.

Juan blinked, suppressing a wave of nausea.

"I search your room. When guests stay at my home," Demonio shrugged, "I take precautions. A business thing, you understand. I can't be too safe. And I find this cell phone. But it's not the cell phone I provide my associates. So I wonder ... why does he need another cell phone? I supply him the best. So I check. Can you guess what my technician found on your phone?"

"The latest Lady Gaga ringtone?"

Demonio laughed, smashed the phone against Juan's forehead, and dropped it. "You are a funny man. No, I find many calls to a number in America. So I think, 'Who is he calling in the States?' I find this very special phone number. To the police chief in Whiskey,

Arizona." Demonio drove his boot heel into the phone, shattering it. "You're an undercover pig. You have betrayed me. Sold me out to the people who stole our homeland. Sold out my plans for the new Mexico. You steal so much from me. From my associates. From my employees. From our countrymen. So I will take back from you … slowly."

"Plans for the new Mexico?" Juan licked his dry lips. "Your business is nothing but a bunch of self-serving drug smugglers."

Demonio responded by drawing a knife from its sheath. Juan tried to pull back, but Bandana grabbed him by the forearms. Demonio approached, waving a black-bladed combat knife.

"You delude no one," Juan said, calm masking his fear. "Our … countrymen know what you are."

Juan glimpsed the arc of the blade, followed by a searing sting across his chest. A downward glance showed him a sliced shirt and a crimson line from nipple to nipple.

Bloody minutes passed like eons before Juan could take no more. He opened his mouth and screamed. He didn't stop for a long time.

www.ingramcontent.com/pod-product-compliance
Lightning Source LLC
Chambersburg PA
CBHW020109180626
46812CB00006B/2540